MERCENARY

David Gaughran is the author of *A Storm Hits Valparaiso* and the popular writers' books *Let's Get Digital* and *Let's Get Visible.* Born in Dublin, he currently lives in Prague, but spends most of his time traveling the world, collecting stories.

Praise for *Mercenary*:

"Highly recommended to readers of adventure fiction and history, as well as anyone interested in American adventurism and meddling in Latin America."—*Wall Street Journal* and *USA Today* bestselling author Michael Wallace.

"Lee Christmas led a roaring life on and off the battlefield. Gaughran's great, fast-paced read keeps you right alongside all his exploits."—Richard Sutton, author of *The Red Gate.*

Praise for *A Storm Hits Valparaiso:*

"An ambitious story of love and betrayal, victory and defeat. In characters drawn from real historical figures, the author delves into the politics of war and how battles turn on the smallest of details or the whims of a single man."—JW Manus, author of *The Devil His Due.*

"A work of sweeping historical fiction that captivates and entertains ... engaging and richly textured."—John D. Glass, author of *Legend of Zodiac.*

Praise for *Let's Get Digital: How To Self-Publish, And Why You Should:*

"Even with my background as an indie writer, I picked up several valuable tips… simply the best book about the e-book revolution I have read."—Michael Wallace, bestselling author of the *Righteous* series.

"Credible and comprehensive. I'd recommend it to any writer who is considering self-publishing or anyone interested in the current state of publishing."—*Big Al's Books and Pals.*

Praise for *Let's Get Visible: How To Get Noticed And Sell More Books:*

"Gaughran distills complex subject matter and explains it in a way that anybody can easily understand, and takes the guesswork out of promotion at Amazon. He removes the mysticism and gets you as close as anyone outside of Amazon will probably be to understanding how stuff works behind the curtain."—David Wright, bestselling author of *Yesterday's Gone.*

"If you are a self-publisher looking to improve your ability to get eyeballs on your books, I can't recommend this title highly enough. The book contains many ideas I've used successfully and several I'm now excited to try."—Cidney Swanson, bestselling author of *Saving Mars.*

MERCENARY

DAVID GAUGHRAN

MERCENARY

ISBN-13: 978-1500620080

ISBN-10: 1500620084

Editor: Karin Cox

Cover Design: Kate Gaughran

Print Formatting: Heather Adkins

Cover photos © 2014 Shutterstock.com

Published August 2014 by Arriba Arriba Books

This first paperback edition was printed by Createspace

DavidGaughran.com

For Mark Spellman,

whose adventures ended too soon.

1

Leon Winfield Christmas had a habit of tapping his leg right before he did something impulsive.

"Lock the door!" his mother would shout. "Lee's legs are trying to catch up with his mind again!"

When his legs did catch up, he was a sight to behold. Darting between the ruined outhouses that dotted the dead fields. Shooting Yankee invaders with a cedar branch. And taking General Grant's unconditional surrender at the bank of the Amite river—the natural border of his father's old cotton plantation, before the war took it all away.

Lee's family had been spared the worst of the fighting. A few months before he was born, a Yankee scouting party had torched his father's holdings, but at least the homestead had been spared. His mother, heavily pregnant and peering out the upstairs window at the men whooping and hollering, had counted her blessings. After Lee came into the world and grew in size, his parents fought to keep him close, fearful of what the woods contained. Twenty miles east, Union soldiers had set Baton Rouge ablaze, but not before emptying the jails. Prisoners had melted into the dense woodlands all along the Amite River, giving quarter to neither friend nor foe.

The war was eventually settled, and the South began the

slow process of rebuilding. By the time Lee was twelve, his father moved the family deeper into the swamps of Livingston Parish, hoping to find peace and prosperity in one of the sawmill towns springing up all over Louisiana. His new home wasn't on any map. It didn't even have a name—not at first. The woods were known as Benfield's Cut, and the mill workers began referring to home as Benfield, but no one knew its provenance, or cared, to be frank. There was enough to be getting on with. The settlement had started as a few rudimentary buildings—the sawmill itself, stables for the workhorses, shotgun houses for the young couples, dormitories for the unmarried men, a saloon, and the company store. But it soon grew as the lumber concern expanded to meet demand and more labor arrived. The first children born there necessitated the trappings of society: larger houses, a lawman, and a place of worship. There was even talk of a school. Mostly, though, the children were free to roam the woods by day, sharing tales of pirates and bandits when they gathered in the evening. And it was there, in the dirt clearing that formed the center of Benfield, away from the noise of the mill, that Lee Christmas first met Mamie Reid, the foreman's daughter.

It was a friendship born of necessity, at least on Mamie's part. Most of the other children in Benfield were either several years their junior or were old enough to have jobs themselves. Lee, on the other hand, was immediately besotted. He would sneak out of his parents' house at night, tiptoe carefully across the creaking porch, and hurry over to Mamie's place to slip love letters under her kitchen door.

At first, Mamie didn't respond to his affections. She

would see him the next morning and wave, and when they got to talking, she wouldn't mention anything about the letters. Lee wondered if she felt the same way or whether she was just shy, but he persisted nonetheless. Soon, it became clear that Mamie's mother, the indomitable Mrs. Reid, had clocked his intentions from the get-go. She had been intercepting his letters, fearful of the intentions of a rough kid with no prospects. It was only when Mamie had trouble sleeping one night and came to the kitchen to sate her thirst that she discovered a letter: its contents making clear both Lee's feelings and her mother's deception.

It all changed one summer morning as Lee sat on his porch, staying as still as possible in the breezeless humidity. His father had been up half the night, coughing. His mother wasn't saying much, but he could tell she was worried. He had followed his father to the mill that morning, watching him take a docket from Mr. Reid and head up to the company doctor, out near the stables. On the way home, his blood pumping with the determination to confront his mother about his father's illness, Lee ran into Mamie. Instead of her usual smile, her face was drawn, her eyes narrowed.

He stopped in his tracks when he saw the letter she gripped. He stammered a greeting as he wiped his brow. "Mamie, hi. I didn't … I wasn't…"

Her face scrunched even tighter. "You're an idiot, Lee Christmas. You know that?"

"Um, I, uh…"

"And my eyes are green." She stepped closer to him, nostrils flaring. "Not blue."

Lee's leg started tapping. With one swift movement, he

encircled Mamie with his left arm, put his hand on the small of her back, and leaned in. Then he kissed her.

A moment later, Mamie wriggled away. "Not here," she said, glancing around. "Meet me behind the sawmill in an hour. And don't let Pa see you. You know the spot?"

He knew the spot, all right.

Soon they were arranging secret rendezvous, and stealing kisses in the woods behind the mill where Mamie's father supervised and Lee's father toiled. For most of their courtship, however, Lee's father was unwell. He had to assume familial responsibility as his father's condition deteriorated, working the schooners of Lake Pontchartrain as a ship's cook.

The young couple saw less of each other. Mrs. Reid kept her daughter on a tight leash, and Lee manned the galleys of the *Cileste*, the *Surprise*, and the *Lillie Simms*, as they hauled charcoal across the lake to New Orleans. Separation only increased the young couple's strength of feeling. Mamie and Lee were promised to each other, and nothing would stand in their way—a vow put to the test when Lee turned sixteen and his father succumbed to the illness that had been stealing him from the world one day at a time. His mother decided they would move to McComb, Mississippi, to be closer to her family. He begged Mamie to wait for him, fearful that her head might be turned by another, someone with money, and pledged to return with enough cash to build her a house and show Mrs. Reid he could provide for her daughter.

Despite the bluster, Lee was fearful. He didn't know what awaited him in Mississippi, or whether he'd ever make anything of his life. He had no money, no connections, and no education, concerns that bounced around in his head as the

Mississippi train pulled out of New Orleans, until a billboard caught his eye. It was map of North America, crisscrossed with railway lines both existing and planned. Some routes even went all the way up to Canada and down into Mexico. The legend made his heart skip a beat: *Join The Railroad, And See The World.*

Lee Christmas had no idea how true that would be.

2

While she consoled her daughter on the loss of her beau, Mrs. Reid was secretly relieved. She had hopes for a much better match for Mamie. Someone with a future. Not some rough kid working as ship's cook. There was something wild about the boy, an untamed streak a mile wide. Mamie could do a lot better. Her mother hoped the distance would end her daughter's romantic notions, and that the boy would find a new butterfly to chase.

Her husband's time in the sticks was at an end, so the Reid family moved back into New Orleans, purchasing a new home on Chestnut Street—the more genteel end, past Napoleon Avenue and away from the roughness of the Irish Channel. But Mrs. Reid's newfound peace was shattered when the first letter arrived from Mississippi; she destroyed it before her daughter could set eyes on it. From that day on, she was ever watchful for the mailman's morning appearance.

For all his churlish ways, she thought, *that boy has one thing in his favor—he doesn't give up easy.*

As for Lee, that poster sold him. He joined the railroad in McComb before the family had even unpacked. His mother was beaming with pride when he told her. Even if it was just waiting tables in the station restaurant, it was a foot in the door. Once he turned eighteen, he trained as a brakeman until a coveted spot opened up as a fireman's apprentice, back when those big old locomotives were still burning wood. At twenty-one, his frame considerably filled out by hard labor, he became an engineer, before being promoted to baggage master. The new role meant moving to Vicksburg, away from his family, but a friend of his by the name of Boyd Cetti was already working the yard there and promised to introduce him to all of the boys.

All through this time of restless change, one thing remained constant: Lee's ardor for Mamie. He still wrote to her, even though it had been three years since he had received any reply. He was sure Mrs. Reid was intercepting his letters again, but the way he figured it, he was playing the long game, showing Mamie's parents he would never give up his pursuit, no matter what obstacles they put in his way. They were promised to each other—back from when they were kids, stealing kisses in the woods behind the sawmill—and nothing was going to change that.

3

On a crisp spring morning in March 1885, the kind that banished all memory of winter, Lee turned up for work a little early. He checked in at the roundhouse, where Boyd Cetti was already warming his hands with a cup of coffee. Boyd looked up as Lee entered, and then pointed to an envelope on the table, grinning. "It's from home."

Lee lunged for the letter, but his friend beat him to it.

Boyd leaned back, just out of reach, holding the envelope aloft. "Do you think it could be—?"

Lee snatched it from his hand. "I don't think anything." He glowered at Boyd. "I ain't read it yet." His hands shook as he examined the writing. It had been so long since he'd heard from Mamie, but he still recognized the broad strokes of her elegant cursive script, such a contrast to his own hastily scrawled attempts. He carefully peeled it open and looked up at Boyd, smiling. "It's Mamie, all right."

"What does it say?"

He only read the first couple of lines before slipping the letter back in the envelope. "I'm saving this for later."

"Oh, come on!"

Lee smiled, toying with him. "I've got a long ride today." He tapped his shirt pocket. "This should help break it up."

But Boyd could match him at these games. "I'm not so sure that's a good idea." His eyes narrowed. "I mean … what if it's bad news."

Lee's face darkened. "What do you mean 'bad news'?"

Boyd paused for effect, enjoying himself. "I mean, it's been a while. You said she was awful pretty. Maybe she's—"

"Don't say it—"

"Getting married!"

With that, he chased Boyd around the other side of the desk, grabbing him in a headlock. "You good for nothing louse. Why, I oughta—"

Boyd squirmed free, rubbing his face where Lee's uniform had chaffed him. "Come on, knucklehead. Read the darn letter."

He chuckled. "All right." He sat back down at the table, took the envelope from his shirt pocket with great ceremony, removed the letter, and slowly unfolded it. Every couple of lines, he looked up at Boyd with a mock-worried expression. But by the time Lee got to the end, he couldn't hold back any longer. A huge grin spread across his face.

Boyd looked at him hopefully. "She wants to see you?"

"Yup."

"When? What's the plan?"

Lee's right leg began tapping. He smiled, remembering his mother's frequent admonitions. "I'm taking the first train down to New Orleans, I'm walking right up to her door, and I'm asking her to marry me."

Boyd let out a howl. "Damn, you don't waste any time. I suppose that's a better idea than just replying to her. She might take another three years to respond!"

Lee swung a playful paw at him.

"All joking aside, get up to the station-master quick," Boyd said. "He'll leave you off today if he can get someone to replace you."

Lee stood. "I think I'll tell him Ma's sick."

"Don't," said Boyd. "He'll smell a rat. Tell him the truth. Show him the letter. He's an old romantic at heart. He won't stand in your way."

Lee grabbed the door handle. "I guess I'll be seeing you."

"Good luck in New Orleans."

"Luck's got nothing to do with it." He grinned. "I ain't taking no for an answer."

4

Lee had been figuring out what to say all the way from Vicksburg but only started to fret when he turned the corner from Napoleon onto Chestnut Street. It had taken all his reserve not to dive into a saloon outside the train station for some liquid courage; however, the last thing he needed was to stink of whiskey when Mrs. Reid answered the door. He paused a couple of doors down from Mamie's house and adjusted his tie.

"Your father wore this on his wedding day," his mother had told him when he first left McComb for Vicksburg. The tie had lain in a drawer ever since, Lee unsure if he'd ever have reason to wear it.

He took a handkerchief from his pocket and bent down to wipe a speck of mud from his shoe. The sudden movement triggered a fresh round of perspiration, so he stood for a moment and let the slow breeze roll over him. Mopping his brow with the other side of the handkerchief, he ran through his speech for the final time, and then he walked up to Mamie's door and knocked.

Lee had been so dreading the prospect of dealing with Mrs. Reid that he was taken aback when the door opened to reveal Mamie. She was four years older now, and he didn't recognize her for a moment. When Mamie saw who it was, her eyes widened. She stepped outside and closed the door softly behind her, grabbing his hand and dragging him up Chestnut Street, away from her house. She didn't say a word until they turned onto Bordeaux. Then she spun around, eyes flashing. "What the hell do you think you're doing? Why didn't you tell me you were—"

He interrupted her with a long, slow kiss.

When he pulled back, Mamie looked stunned, patting her lips with the tips of her fingers. "Well," she said, "I guess you can't put that in the mail."

Lee grinned. "I came as soon as I got your letter."

"You can't surprise me like this." She put a hand on her heart. "You'll put years on me with this carry-on."

"You got no idea," he said, still smiling.

"What do you mean? What are you up to?"

"You ready to get married?"

Mamie's hand went to her mouth. "You can't just … I mean…" She paused to consider his proposal.

His face fell. "You know it makes sense."

"I know. It's just…"

"We're meant to be together, Mamie."

She leaned forward and Lee closed his eyes, expecting a kiss, but instead she clasped her hands over his face. "What color are my eyes?"

He panicked. "What's all this about?"

"What color are my eyes? Simple question."

"Blue?"

"Darn it, Lee." She took her hands off his face. "Green!"

He squinted. "Look blue to me."

"You're useless." Mamie punched him on the shoulder.

"So what about it?" he asked, serious now. "Will you be my wife?"

She gulped. "I've got to talk to Ma and Pa first."

"Nonsense," said Lee, taking her hand and growing in confidence. "You're old enough to make your own decisions. I know what your mother would say anyway. 'Ship's cook, not good enough for my daughter.'"

"Lee…"

"But I'm doing good now, Mamie. I'll show her. I don't know how many of my letters you got—"

"My mother…"

"I know. She got to them before you even knew—"

"She's very—"

"I know well what she's like. But you're of an age to decide your own future." He paused, hoping to calm his heart. "I've a house fixed up in Vicksburg, waiting for us. Tomorrow afternoon, I'm taking you to Spanish Fort. Then we'll go down on the evening train and be married."

Mamie held her emotions in check. She looked at Lee. He was tall and good-looking, with a strong pair of shoulders, and he had always been kind to her, kinder than most anyone else. She felt an attachment to him she had never experienced with another. *What the hell*, she thought. "All right, then."

He beamed. "You mean it? You'll be my wife?"

She nodded.

Lee stepped forward to embrace her, but Mamie leaned back, placing a hand on his chest. "Get going before Ma gets suspicious. I'll see you tomorrow afternoon. Don't come by the house. Meet me at two, by the French Market." She blew him a kiss and hurried back toward Chestnut Street. Lee punched the air, and then made himself scarce.

The smell of fresh beignets wafted over from *Café du Monde* as Lee stepped out from the arch to check the clock once more. He had arrived half-an-hour early, feeling so jittery that he needed a shot of whiskey just to get his heart to stop from jiggling around so damn much. But now it was well after two. His leg tapped as the clock ticked ever onwards. By quarter to three, he was beginning to wonder if Mamie was going to show at all; then he spotted her in the distance, waving.

"Sorry I'm late," she said as she approached. "My mother was asking all sorts of questions."

"What did you tell her?"

"Nothing about us. Don't worry."

He let out a sigh of relief. "All right, well, I'm fit for a stroll if you are."

"Why, I don't mind if I do." Mamie offered her arm.

5

Mrs. Reid had been shadowing her daughter all the way from Chestnut Street. She had known something was up the moment Mamie answered the door the afternoon before. Mamie claimed it was a delivery boy with the wrong address, but Mrs. Reid's nose had started twitching as soon as she saw her daughter's flushed cheeks. She knew darn well that Mamie had no suitors in New Orleans—her daughter wouldn't give the time of day to even the finest prospects—which meant only one thing…

She followed Mamie at a distance, seeing right through her ruse of a sick friend. Her daughter was never a good liar, doubly so when that boy was in the frame. Mrs. Reid tailed her daughter all the way downtown; the girl was so away with the fairies that her mother didn't even have to be circumspect. When the French Market came into view, Mrs. Reid merged with the crowd opposite the Indians hawking wares. She watched, her suspicions confirmed when her only daughter embraced that scalawag, Leon Christmas.

As the couple walked arm-in-arm down Bourbon Street, Mrs. Reid followed twenty feet behind them, hunched over, clutching her purse to her chest, and wary of drunken revelers who were too shameless to wait for sundown. She almost made her presence known when the pair ducked into some dive on Royal, but when they re-emerged soon after, she was glad she hadn't. A crowd of drinkers gathered around Lee at the doorway, slapping him on the back, slipping cigars into his breast pocket.

Mrs. Reid's curiosity was piqued—enough that she followed the pair out to Spanish Fort, all the way up by Lake Pontchartrain. Enough to track them for the entire afternoon while they canoodled brazenly among the penny arcades. Enough to keep her mouth shut, even though she was burning with rage. Something was up, but she wanted to determine what it was before confronting them.

On the way back from Spanish Fort, Mrs. Reid was scheming about how to end Lee's interest in Mamie for good, perhaps by insisting on Mamie's marriage to one of the many suitable boys her daughter had summarily dismissed. But instead of turning left to Chestnut Street, the couple made their way downtown once more.

Mrs. Reid, her nerves frayed, was tiring of the pursuit, and she resolved to confront the couple if they entered another saloon. To her surprise, Lee and Mamie stopped short of the French Quarter and turned toward the station. She lurked as they approached the ticket counter, but she was too far away to eavesdrop on the transaction. Instead, she noted the number of the platform and accosted the nearest porter. She seethed in the station house until departure time, holding out hope that her daughter was simply conducting a drawn-out goodbye, rather than engaging in something more sinister. The couple walked hand-in-hand to the carriage and paused at the doorway. Then Lee held the door for Mamie while she clambered aboard.

Mrs. Reid sprang into action. Running out from the station house, she shrieked, "Stop that train. Help!" She scurried up and down the platform, screaming for the watchman. "Help, please, someone. Stop that train!"

The train was already pulling out, however. Mrs. Reid grabbed the rear handrail, desperate to halt it any way she could, even to the point of doing herself an injury. When she was dragged from her feet, the screams from folks on the platform finally saw the train halted.

Inside the carriage, Lee made for the door, but Mamie stayed his hand. "You'd best stay here."

She noticed his wounded look and was touched. "I'm coming back, silly," she said. "I just need to check she's all right." Mamie stepped down onto the platform. The police, attracted by the screams, were already attending to her mother, who was shaken up but unharmed.

Mrs. Reid brushed a strand of hair from her face. "You plan to marry this boy without permission? You mean to elope? Bring shame on this family? After everything we've—"

Mamie stepped back into the carriage and shut the door. She didn't feel like arguing in front of a bunch of rubbernecking strangers—not when her mother was this riled up and unlikely to listen to reason. With Lee's hand around her waist, she watched through the grimy window as her mother flew into a rage, accosting the policemen, insisting they place Mamie and Lee under arrest. But no charge could be made—Mamie had reached the age where she could decide such matters for herself; the train was allowed to depart, and the two young lovers sped north.

It was more than six months before Mr. & Mrs. Reid calmed enough to allow the newlyweds to visit. Impressed by Mamie's letters about the house Lee had built in Vicksburg, his promising career, and, not least, the young couple's impending child, the Reid family eventually welcomed Lee and Mamie back into their fold. Once Lee ensured he could keep his job, the newlyweds moved to New Orleans a month later, taking a house on Poydras, a few block from the station, just past Lafayette Square.

The one concession Lee had to make to familial bliss was hiding his prized possession: a framed copy of the *Daily Picayune* detailing their dramatic elopement, which the boys in the station yard had presented them as a wedding gift. The headline always made him chuckle. "*BOLD LOCHINVAR—Steals His Young Bride From Her Mother and Speeds Away To Vicksburg—An Unwilling Parent But A Merry Christmas Pair.*"

It was a small price to pay for peace, much as Lee was fond of it. He guessed his father would never have dreamed of seeing his son in the newspaper—even if it was for causing trouble.

6

Lee clocked off a couple of minutes early and made his way to the entrance of the station yard with Boyd Cetti, who had moved down from Vicksburg to be closer to his ailing mother. Boyd elbowed him in the ribs. "That's him."

Lee thanked his friend and made his way over to the ruddy Irishman. As they passed through the gate of the station yard, he put his hand on the fireman's shoulder. "Say, you O'Brien?"

The man stopped dead and squared up to him. "Who's asking?"

"I'm Lee Christmas." He put out his hand. "And I'd like to buy you a drink."

"Then lead on, my friend," said O'Brien. "This drink won't buy itself." He clapped Lee on the back. "Had me worried for a second. Thought you were … oh, it doesn't matter. Hey, why don't we head on down to Tom Cook's place?"

"Sounds good to me." Lee caught Boyd's eye as he passed, winking, then headed down Poydras with the Irishman in tow.

A couple of hours later, their table filled with empty glasses, Lee began pressing him for more details. "O'Brien—"

"I told you already," he said. "Name's Benny. Every time you say 'O'Brien' I think I'm in some kind of trouble.

Lee chuckled. "Fair enough. Anyway, as I was saying, I got two young kids now—"

"What are their names?"

"Ed and Hattie. But as I was—"

"I've got three myself."

"That's great, Benny, but you must understand my predicament. Salary only goes so far."

"You want to know about the drainage gig?"

"Well … yeah."

Benny O'Brien turned and shouted for two more whiskeys.

"So what is it you do exactly?" Lee asked.

"That's not important. It's a city job, that's all you need to know."

"Meaning?"

"Meaning all you gotta do to earn your pay is…" Benny raised his forefinger in apology as he drained his glass in one gulp. He smiled, his lips glistening with alcohol, and then belched. "All you gotta do is turn up and collect." He wiped his mouth with the back of his hand. "That and kick up a piece to your supervisor."

Lee could barely contain his excitement. Money for nothing? It sounded too good to be true. "So what do I got to do?"

"That's the tricky bit," said O'Brien. "The lads handing out these gigs aren't the charitable sort."

Lee was expecting him to say more, but the Irishman fondled his empty glass instead. He waved for another round of drinks.

The bartender delivered them with a grunt; O'Brien waited until he was out of earshot. "I think you're getting more than your money's worth, but you seem like a decent skin, so I'll fill you in."

He clinked glasses with the Irishman, and watched as O'Brien emptied his glass once more. Lee followed suit.

"God, this American whiskey is awful shite." He grimaced. "Politicians run the whole game in this city," O'Brien continued. "They get elected, then they hand out favors to their supporters—guys like me who knock on doors and hand out pamphlets and then spend all of Election Day dragging drunks from the Irish Channel up to vote."

Lee pondered this for a moment. "How do I get in on this game?"

"You gotta start doing favors for the right people."

"And how do I meet them?"

"Jesus, you're eager." O'Brien paused, scrutinizing Lee's face. "All right. Look down at the other end of the bar, over my shoulder." Lee glanced to the left. "See all those guys at the end, with their fancy hats and jimswingers?"

"They the politicians?" asked Lee, confused.

O'Brien laughed. "Hell, no. They're the lads doing favors. You got to get in with them first."

Lee was about to ask another question, but the Irishman waved him away and stood. "Nice to make your acquaintance, but if I don't toddle off, my wife will have my guts for garters."

Lee stood and shook his hand. "Say, you wouldn't be a pal and introduce me—"

O'Brien was already shaking his head. "This is as far as I go. And, if you want my advice, greasy overalls ain't gonna impress those guys much. Best get yourself a new jacket. Silk hat too."

He watched the Irishman stagger out of the joint, and then turned his attention to the tyros propping up the bar near the entrance. He noted their clothes and their exaggerated gestures, as well as the furious rate at which they were consuming booze. Lee figured it was about time he made a name for himself in the political circles of the Third Ward.

With that decided, what little money he was bringing home was spent on a fancy clothes and nocturnal escapades. To get in with the political crowd, Lee felt he had to act like them, which meant drinking all evening in Remy Klock's saloon around the corner from his house, or Tom Cook's place near the station, before whiling away the small hours in one of New Orleans' innumerable gambling dens. He soon discovered a prodigious appetite for liquor, in all its many forms. His family only survived by leaning heavily on Mamie's parents—especially important now that they had two young children. Lee spent more and more evenings out of the house, to the chagrin of his wife. Election season was his excuse. He had signed on to hustle for the saloon-keeper Remy Klock as Sheriff of Orleans Parish.

Mamie watched Lee taking off his boots at the door. "You look tired," she said, fanning herself with one hand. "Want to take a nap while I fix you something?"

Lee shook his head. "I'd love to, but I'm not stopping."

"You're going out again tonight?"

He nodded wearily. "Election will be over soon."

"But you just worked a double."

Lee shrugged his shoulders and made his way upstairs. Mamie followed him, entering the bedroom as he was pulling off his socks. He smiled as he unbuttoned his shirt. "If you want a show, you just have to ask."

Mamie blushed. "You're incorrigible, Lee Christmas."

He took out his suit and laid it on the bed.

"You better be washing up before you put that on."

He saluted. "Yes, ma'am."

"It certainly cost enough." She pouted.

"Aw, don't be sore. You know why I'm doing all this."

"I remember," said Mamie, pursing her lips. "I just wish you didn't have to go to *those* places."

"Remy Klock runs a straight joint. Don't listen to that nonsense put about by his opponents. They're trying to drag his name through the mud because we're licking 'em fair and square."

"I'm not worried about Remy's place. It's where you go after."

Lee spread his hands. "Some of these rich types … I dunno. They have funny ideas about how they want to spend their money."

"Father McGinty says there's loose women in those sporting establishments." Mamie curled her lip with the last words.

"They got gambling too, but you don't see me losing my shirt," Lee replied angrily. He paused for a moment, deciding to change tack, and stepped forward, closing the distance between them. "Besides," he said, putting an arm around his wife and searching out the small of her back. "I got all I could ever need right here."

Mamie allowed herself a brief smile before pushing him away. "If you think you're going to get *that* before you head out for a night's drinking…"

"You afraid of a little grease? Never stopped you before."

"Lee!" She slapped him playfully on the arm. "You'll wake the children."

"You mean *you'll* wake 'em, if last time was anything to go by."

A cry from the neighboring room interrupted him. "Daddy!"

She waggled a finger at him. "Do *not* go in there until you've cleaned yourself up. I don't want them clambering all over your dirty overalls. Get yourself washed, and I'll tell them you'll be there in a minute to say goodnight."

"Sure thing."

"You certain you don't want something to eat? I've some stew I can heat up. Will only take a minute."

"Really wish I could, Mamie, but I'm already late as it is."

His wife looked deflated.

"Look," he said. "I was saving this as a surprise, but I got the day off tomorrow. How's about we bring the kids out to Spanish Fort and show them our old stomping ground?"

"That would be swell." Mamie's face pinched all of a sudden. "Just one thing."

"What?"

"I promised my mother she could spend some time with

the children tomorrow. You know she's always complaining she doesn't see enough of them."

"Bring her along," he said.

Mamie raised an eyebrow. "You sure?"

"More the merrier."

She pecked him on the cheek. "Thank you. Now go wash up. Can't keep these rich types waiting."

7

Mamie rose at the crack of dawn, awakened by the cries of little Ed demanding to be fed. She eyed Lee's empty side of the bed with dismay. *Things are never simple with this one.*

Her husband spent all his time running around trying to impress people in the Third Ward, but Mamie knew whom he truly wanted to impress. She couldn't help suspecting that her mother would be happier if he just spent more time at home with his children.

She felt guilty immediately, berating herself for the thought as she nursed Ed and gazed down on his placid face. *Lee is a good man and a good husband*, she told herself, *even if he is a bit scatty*. After finally lulling Ed back to sleep, Mamie tiptoed from the room and went downstairs to make herself some coffee. *No point going back to bed now. Hattie will be up soon anyway.*

The water hadn't yet come to the boil when someone knocked on the door. Surprised, she checked the clock; it was barely past six. Before she got a chance to answer, a second, more urgent rasp of knuckles echoed through the house, loud enough to wake Hattie, who began calling for her mother. Mamie hollered up the stairs to console her daughter, and then opened the door, slowly at first until she saw it was just a messenger boy.

"Sorry to disturb you, ma'am. Engineer Christmas is needed at the depot."

"But it's his day off."

"All I know is he's needed by eight. Boss has a shipment of bananas spoiling in the yard."

Mamie sighed. "Well, he ain't here. You best get up the road to Remy Klock's and ask around. If he's not there, try Tom Cook's.

"And if he's not there either?"

She tried to keep her exasperation in check. "Then your guess is as good as mine."

"Thank you, ma'am. Sorry once again for disturbing you." The boy dashed off.

"Make sure he stops here first," Mamie shouted after him. "He's wearing his suit!" Then, embarrassed at letting the whole street know her business, she went back inside and called up to the mewling Hattie, "I'm coming!"

When Lee finally made it home, just shy of eight, Mamie's mother was ensconced at the kitchen table, sipping tea and drumming her fingers. She stared at the clock and tutted when he entered. Mamie could immediately see the condition he was in, and enlisted her mother to help stop him. Not that Mrs. Reid needed much prodding. "You're in no fit state, Lee. Look at yourself. You can barely stand."

He swayed in the doorway before leaning against the jamb. "I'll be fine, ma'am."

She shook her head. "You can't go. Listen to me. I had a dream last night that if you took out this engine, you'd never take out another."

"Nonsense," he growled, waving away his mother-in-law's objections with a meaty paw. "Some coffee and I'll be fine."

He didn't have time for coffee. He barely had time to divest himself of his finery and change into his overalls before Mamie raced him down to the station—where she had to help hoist him into the cab. When she returned home, her mother was preparing breakfast for the children.

"Your father just left with the coffee," her mother said. "That pot was strong enough to wake the dead."

"You sure he'll get there in time?"

Mrs. Reid shushed her. "I told him to head for the crossing, to be safe. Lee's train will be slow enough there for him to pass it aboard."

"I should have done more to stop him. He's in no condition. What if—"

Mamie's mother shot her a look as she covered Ed's ears. "We'll have none of that talk around you-know-who."

Mamie bit her lip.

"And if you're worried about that dream nonsense, I only made that up so Lee might change his mind."

"Really?"

She drew her lips into a bloodless smile. "And we both should know better at this point."

8

Lee gathered speed as he left the crossing, careful to secure the coffee pot at his feet. He tried looking at the manifest again, but his eyes were still swimming. Anyway, it was pretty simple. It was single line track through LaPlace, so he had to pull in to the siding at Kenner and wait until the southbound train rolled by. Then it was clear all the way to Memphis.

Lee knew he wasn't supposed to work in anything approaching this state. Then again, he wasn't supposed to be working at all. He'd been up for two days straight with little or no rest. Not that he minded too much. It only happened now and then, and the extra pay made it worthwhile. That's what happens, he always said, when you work this route. Men don't show up and the train can't wait, not with bananas spoiling in the back. He wondered what happened to the man he was covering. Probably laid up after a brawl on Bourbon Street, he guessed, or got jumped down Smoky Row. Or, he chuckled at the thought, fast asleep in the arms of a big-breasted whore on Basin Street.

He felt bad about the plans he'd made with Mamie, but he'd be home soon enough and would do something nice with her and the kids. They didn't usually hang around too long in

Memphis. The boss was always anxious to get them back home, so the train could fill up with another load fresh off the steamers. He could hear his boss's mantra: "Empty trains cost me money. Slow trains cost me money. Stopped trains cost me the most. I like full trains. I like *fast* trains."

Lee liked fast trains too. He liked moments like this, on his own up front, barreling down a lonely stretch of single-line rail. Somewhat dozy now, he stuck his head out the side-window, buffeted by the dewy morning air rushing past his face. He closed his eyes and yelled. Still drowsy. He took another swig from the coffee pot at his feet.

He yawned once more.

The coffee wasn't having the desired effect. His eyelids felt heavy, and he could feel his head drooping. Lee pinched himself; he had to stay awake. Another train was coming in his direction, so he had instructions to pull in at Kenner. Maybe he'd get a chance for a quick nap then.

Liking the sound of that, Lee went full throttle to buy himself a little more sleeping time. He picked up the coffee pot and drained what was left, straight from the spout. His guts clenched for a moment as the coffee went down, but his nausea dissipated before he could open the cab window.

He knew Mamie was right, and her damn mother. He was spreading himself too thin. Not spending enough time with Ed and Hattie. Sometimes he felt like every time he blinked they'd grown another few inches. But he would be twenty-nine in a few months, and he didn't want to be doing this for another ten years. If he could get hooked up with a city job—which was looking good if the tallymen were right and Remy Klock was a shoo-in for Sheriff—he could cut back on his hours on the road. Maybe even work the yard with Boyd.

He knew men like O'Brien weren't ambitious; they were happy for the extra coin, especially when they had to do nothing for it. But Lee reckoned there was a lot more to this game. He didn't want to fight this hard just for a seat at the table. He wanted the damn table. Lee saw what politicians did, and how they lived. He wanted a piece of *that* game. Then he could really treat Mamie like she deserved. Then he could show the Reid family that Lee Christmas was meant for something different. Something special.

As he surrendered to wild fantasies of wealth and power, with armies of men to do his bidding, Lee didn't even notice he'd run straight past the switch at Kenner. His eyelids drooped until the horizon became nothing more than a dot.

A dot that soon filled with the light of an oncoming train.

9

The first thing Lee remembered—in fact, the only thing he could recall since being hoisted into the cab back in New Orleans—was being pinned to the crossties underneath his engine, his face scalded by the steam pouring forth from his 2-6-0 Mogul. So powerful was the blast that it knocked his right eye clean out of its socket.

He didn't scream or holler, despite the intense pain; or, to be more accurate, the *presence* of pain. The actual sensation was something he was only tangentially aware of, something he thought he was supposed to feel, like when a doctor prods an injured limb to check for paralysis. He didn't move either. The pressure on his chest told him he was trapped, at least until someone had the wherewithal to check if he was still alive. Instead, Lee just lay there, drifting in and out of consciousness, listening to the cries of harried men attempting to clear the wreckage.

When his legs started to grow cold, Lee started to worry. It was as if he only then realized the seriousness of the situation. Between fevered lapses of consciousness, he berated himself for his predicament. He swore that if he made it out of this wreck, he'd give up his fancy notions of a political career and stick to the railroad, maybe even cut back on his hours and find a way to make do.

He heard a voice from above somewhere, and he was about to yell back a response when the pressure on his chest increased unbearably. He figured someone was climbing around in the ruins of his cab, unaware they were crushing him beneath. He wanted to scream a warning, but couldn't, his shame further compounded by the realization that the warmth spreading down his legs wasn't a sign his strength was returning; he'd pissed himself.

Again the creaking came from above, and the weight on his chest made him feel like he was going to burst right open. Straining his one good eye, Lee lifted his head to see what was trapping him, but he couldn't see shit. Instead, he twisted his hips, trying to relieve the pressure, sucked in as much air as he could, went to holler, and then passed out.

Everyone was sure that the battered engineer they finally pulled from the wreck was dead. Even after they discovered a pulse, popped his eyeball back into its socket, and rushed him to the hospital, nobody expected him to pull through.

10

That's two now, Pa, if you're keepin' score. Let's just pray I don't have to go to such lengths next time. Lee smiled and gave the reporter another quote, looking forward to tomorrow's newspaper. Although he was still more than a little woozy, the pace of Lee's recovery had stunned the nursing staff.

Mamie had been in to visit on most days of his two-week convalescence, usually without the children. Ed and Hattie were so delighted to see him the first time that they wriggled free from their mother as soon as they entered the room and mounted the hospital bed to embrace him. Mamie, noticing Lee's eyes watering with pain, had grabbed the kids and rushed them out the door, right as Lee turned the air blue enough to embarrass a fisherman's wife. Toward the end of his convalescence, he had even convinced her to smuggle in a mint toddie. He sat up to sip his drink, taking her hand in his. "If you're short of money, talk to Boyd."

"There's no need. He's already been 'round. You're on half pay until they determine the cause."

Lee chuckled. "I think the cause of the crash was two trains running into each other at top speed."

"Don't joke! You could have made a widow out of me."

"I'm sorry." He squeezed her hand and smiled. "And

anyway. You think you're getting rid of me that easy?"

Lee and Mamie arrived a few minutes before their appointment and were asked to take a seat by the receptionist—a humorless lady with no interest in small talk. Opposite them was a door with frosted glass: *Capt. Sharp—Division Superintendent.* Mamie had insisted on coming with Lee to Memphis to help him plead his case with the railroad company, and they sat in silence in the musty reception, occasionally looking at the clock, and at each other. After they had been there for close on forty minutes, Lee shuffled in his chair, attempting to catch the secretary's eye.

She turned to him with a forced smile. "Shouldn't be too much longer."

As if on cue, a silhouette appeared behind the glass. Laughter spilled out into the corridor as a rotund man, puffing on a cigar, backed out of the office. Lee could see Captain Sharp leaning against his desk with a broad smile, and he nudged Mamie with his elbow.

The secretary stood, indicating the open door. "Captain Sharp will see you now."

Lee held the door for Mamie and then followed his wife into the small office, thick with cigar smoke. Captain Sharp, his back to them, rummaged in one of the metal filing cabinets that lined one wall. Without turning, the superintendent acknowledged them with a wave of his hand. "Please, sit."

Mamie raised an eyebrow, and Lee followed her gaze. The small, windowless office was piled high with clutter. Files were stacked at the base of creaking cabinets. The walls were covered with old photographs of the great locomotives and with framed newspaper clippings trumpeting that famous day in Utah when Leland Stanford had driven in the Golden Spike.

"Ah, found it!"

They took their seats as Captain Sharp turned from the cabinet, clutching a file. "Christmas, Leon. Engineer."

"Yes, sir."

Captain Sharp was in his late fifties and was stocky, but not overweight, with graying skin to match what was left of his hair. Thanks to a luxurious mustache that gave him the appearance of an amiable walrus, it was hard to tell if he were smiling or grimacing. As the superintendent waddled toward his desk, Lee noticed the open box of cigars.

Captain Sharp slammed the box shut, and shook his head. "You're the man that got drunk and had that wreck, ain't you?"

"Yes," he said, sitting up straighter in his chair. "I'm the man."

"What do you figure on doing now?"

Lee was confused. "I want to keep on railroading."

"Well, all I got to say to you is that it's a pity they ever got you out from underneath that engine." He shook his head. "That's all I got to say to you." Captain Sharp looked at Mamie. "With all due apologies, ma'am."

The sharp tone returned to the superintendent's voice as he addressed Lee once more. "You couldn't get another engine on this railroad no matter what, and I don't want to see your sorry ass ever again." Captain Sharp walked to the door and held it open, ignoring Lee and nodding to his wife. "Ma'am."

Lee wasn't just fired. He was blacklisted.

11

Mamie seemed to take the news in her stride, even when Lee made sure she understood that his railroad days were over. She only started crying as they approached New Orleans. He put an arm around his wife and drew her close, whispering, "I'll have a new job in days. You'll see." He donned his hat and set it at a jaunty angle. "What with all my new connections."

"You better." Mamie forced a smile and dabbed at her eyes with Lee's proffered handkerchief. "Because I don't fancy eatin' that stupid silk hat."

But he soon found that loyalty only lasted as long as he could pick up the tab. Favor after favor was called in, all to no avail. He had plenty of promises of work, but the jobs seemed to evaporate when he showed up. Someone else had beaten him to it, or business had suddenly slowed, or the boss remembered he had promised the job to a cousin—there was always something. Despite innumerable disappointments, Lee never lost hope. He remained *convinced* his luck would turn.

"It's just a matter of time," he'd tell Mamie, when she read him the latest headlines despairing the surge in unemployment. "I'll get something."

One day, while killing time around Congo Square, Lee

spied two young Italian kids in high spirits. As the kids passed, one of two cops resting in the shade of their horse-drawn police wagon, called out, "Hey kid, who killa da chief?"

The other laughed, but the kids kept walking, ignoring them.

"Come back here, I wanna talk to you." One of the cops began following.

The older kid turned and cocked a finger, pulling an imaginary trigger. The cops started chasing them, but the kids were too quick, and they disappeared down an alleyway. As Lee passed them, one of the cops sneered, "Fucking dagoes, worse than niggers."

The city had been on edge all year. Feelings had been running strong against the Italians ever since the police-chief—an Irishman called Hennessey—had been gunned down on the steps of his home. As the trial had approached, witness after witness dropped out, refusing to testify. Those who were compelled to testify soon developed a very hazy recollection of events. The city had exploded with anger when the nineteen men indicted for the murder were found not guilty. The next day, a mob formed at Congo Square, right on Tremé Street at the entrance of the Parish Prison. They stormed the building and lynched eleven Italians. For a while, things were running so hot that some folks thought Italy was going to declare war.

Lee knew some of those guys too, the Matranga Family, or knew of them at least. They pretty much owned the waterfront, controlling fruit shipments into New Orleans. They seemed okay, but he sure never wanted to cross them. The lynchers, of course, were cleared of any crime, and anyway, the jails wouldn't have been big enough to hold everyone involved. It didn't take much to get people riled up. A few newspaper articles and a couple of speeches—pretty soon you had ten thousand people marching with pitchforks and torches.

What the newspapermen left out of their accounts was that Hennessey was a corrupt bastard himself, famous for putting the squeeze on brothels then turning a blind eye, and he had even killed one of his predecessors, shooting the incumbent during their election battle and successfully claiming self-defense. The Italians had a personal beef with him too. Ten years beforehand, he had bagged Giuseppe Esposito—a fugitive from Sicily who had fallen in with the Matranga family. Hennessy had him shipped to New York and extradited back home, where he faced eleven murder charges and the death penalty. The Italians never forgot it.

Lee shook his head. *Here I am*, he thought, *filling my head with nonsense again, when I should be worrying about myself.* He wasn't looking forward to going home—another day looking for work, with nothing to show for it but more empty promises. Mamie was going to hit the roof. He needed some kind of job—some laboring, anything—to tide him over until something better came along. He headed for Tom Cook's saloon. *One whiskey*, he thought, *then I'll go right home.*

12

Lee never did make it home that night. One drink in Tom Cook's bar turned into a fishing expedition down Royal—hunting for some Pole who was running a crew out in the New Basin Charcoal Yards. After retreating to Remy Klock's, another tip came in: some guy from Missouri exporting mules through the port. But it all made little difference to Mamie when he stumbled home at sunrise, jobless, haggard, and drunk as a fool.

She managed to put him to bed before the children saw him, a chill prickling her spine when he cracked a dumb joke about needing some coffee to help him sleep. Mamie fretted the entire time he was passed out, barely noticing when he stuck his head around the doorframe, a sheepish look on his face. "Got a couple of leads last night," he said. "Couldn't track the guys down, but there should be some work when I do."

Mamie sipped her coffee, trying to keep her temper in check. "I borrowed another twenty dollars off Ma," she said.

He paused for a moment, chewing his lip, and then took the chair opposite her. "Really, I'm *this close* to getting something. I can feel it in my bones."

Mamie snorted.

"I'll prove it too. Sure, I just turned down a job yesterday, which means—"

"You did *what*?" She set her cup down.

Lee waved a hand. "It was out of town. Don't worry about it."

"Where?"

"Out of state, in fact. Not worth considering."

"What was the job?"

The following Sunday, Lee walked to the station alone. He'd insisted on saying his goodbyes in the house, not wanting to confuse the kids, or have them screaming and crying in the station, truth be told. He was trying to keep a low profile as he slipped out of town. Some of the boys were still keeping their distance since the crash—it had been all over the papers—and he was sore at them for cutting him loose.

On the platform, he pulled his hat down over his eyes, his back to the concourse. He couldn't hide his big frame, though.

"Lee Christmas," a familiar voice yelled his name.

He turned to see Boyd Cetti waving his cap and walking his way.

Boyd's eyes went to Lee's suitcase; he raised an eyebrow. "She finally see sense and kick you out?"

Lee punched him in the arm. "I liked you more when you lived in Vicksburg."

An awkward pause followed. *Even Boyd acts differently around me now*, Lee thought.

Boyd's eyes went to the case again. "So you took the job in Alabama after all."

"Yup."

"You'll be back though, right? We didn't even get a drink together."

Lee looked up at the station clock. "I got time now."

"Mamie and the kids not with you?"

"They're back at the house." Lee was about to tell him how bad things had gotten, but he bit his lip. "Say, how about that drink?"

"Can't." Boyd fidgeted with his cap. "Don't clock off till five."

Another awkward pause.

"I'll be back by summer." Lee broke the silence. "For a visit, at least."

Boyd tipped his hat. "Don't be a stranger."

Twenty minutes later, the Alabama train pulled into the station. Lee watched couples say tearful goodbyes, and reunited lovers kiss with abandon; he was glad Mamie wasn't there to watch him slink out of New Orleans.

He spent the next three years drifting, only holding down a job long enough to fall out with someone, the kind of disagreement that usually ended with that someone looking for their teeth on a barroom floor. Mamie returned to her parents' house on Chestnut Street more than once; Lee's promised financial support not materializing as planned. When he'd return from a stint on the road, his face dark and his mood clouded, Mamie often left him to stew on his own in their family home in Poydras. Eventually, she kicked him out altogether.

Lee knew it was a shot across the bows, but he couldn't catch a break. The railroad was the only real job he'd known.

Apart from a youth spent on the schooners of Lake Pontchartrain, it was all he'd ever done. Waiting tables in McComb station after his father died, making enough to support Ma too. Working the rails as a brakesman once he turned eighteen. Fireman's apprentice. Baggage master at Vicksburg. Then, finally, an engineer at the throttle of his own locomotive.

Twelve years climbing the ladder, all for nothing. All wasted. And for what? As long as he was blacklisted, Lee knew his life would never change. He'd drift from job to job, drinking his life away.

13

Sheriff Remy Klock finally came through with his patronage, even if it was too late to save Lee from being kicked out of the family home. He didn't even mind that it was real labor, part of a gang cleaning the open sewers, which were invariably blocked by the flotsam and detritus of the good citizens of New Orleans. Being Remy's friend had ancillary benefits, too, so one October night in 1894 found Lee sleeping off a heavy night in the warden's office of the Orleans Parish Prison on Gravier Street, rather than in a cell.

He was still sprawled on the floor, putting off the inevitable piss while he struggled to clear his head, when a kid burst in the door.

Lee bolted upright, grabbing his pants. "Shit, boy, you done scared me good." He shook his head. "No one ever teach you to knock?"

"Are you Lee Christmas?"

"Last time I checked. Just let me get my britches on." Lee rubbed his eyes.

"You better hurry," said the kid. "Your wife's about to give birth."

Lee jumped up and pulled on his pants. "Find my boots. Quick!" He swore. "She wasn't due for another two weeks."

"She's in the hospital on—"

"I know where it is," he growled.

Twenty minutes later, Lee was remonstrating with a nurse. "Her name is Mamie Christmas. Brought in a few hours ago. She's gotta be here somewhere." He thought for a moment. "Check under Mary Christmas too. That's what's on her papers."

"Is this some kind of joke?"

"Goddammit," said Lee. "Where's my wife?"

His bellowing attracted the attention of a passing doctor, who tried to calm him by promising to help. To Lee's embarrassment, they eventually found his wife registered under her maiden name: Mamie Reid.

"East Wing," said the nurse, while he scarpered down the corridor. "Second left, first right."

He reached Mamie's bed just as the nurse handed over the newborn. Mamie's mouth tightened momentarily when she saw her estranged husband, before she allowed herself a smile. "Want to meet your new daughter?"

"A girl?" Lee beamed. "It's a girl!" He grabbed the nurse next to him and planted a sloppy kiss on her cheek. Wiping his eyes, he strode to Mamie's bedside and leaned in, cooing. "Almost as beautiful as her mother."

Mamie snorted and offered up the child to him. He took the blinking baby into his arms, adjusting the blanket under her tiny chin. "To be fair, you've had a few years head start."

His wife put a hand to her mouth in mock horror. "Did you just make a joke about my age?"

"No … I…"

She interrupted his stammering with a laugh. "I'm

kidding, Lee."

But he was already back gazing into his daughter's eyes and kissing her cheeks. He looked up at his wife. "What are we calling her?"

Mamie thought for a moment. Just as she was about to respond, Lee cut her off. "What about Mary, like her mother?"

She smiled. "That might suit her, actually." Mamie held out her arms and he placed young Mary in her care, as gently as he could.

Mamie looked down on her serene face. "Sometimes I wish they could stay like this forever."

Lee watched them for a moment. "I almost forgot." He snapped his fingers. "I've got some *big* news."

"Bigger than this?"

He chuckled. "Well, no. But I think you're gonna like it."

"We'll see about that," she said.

14

"What do they mean by amnesty?" Mamie squinted at him suspiciously then handed her newborn to the waiting nurse.

Lee waited until she had left the room before replying. "The slate's wiped clean. All sins forgotten. I start from scratch." He smiled. "What do you think?"

She squeezed his hand, her eyes watering over. "I think that's a swell idea."

He went straight from the hospital to the station, hoping to catch Mr. Baldwin, the night yardmaster of the Illinois Central. The evening before, Boyd had tipped Lee off that the freight business was picking up—to the point where blacklists were being ignored. As long as Lee was content putting in his time at a switch engine in the yards—and he kept his nose clean—he would be back at the throttle soon enough. Of course, Lee was prepared to do anything to get his old job back. His family too. There was just one hurdle: the railroads had brought in a medical test, and all new hires had to be certified. Luckily, the testing car from Chicago was in the yard, so Lee could be examined that afternoon.

As he stood in line to see the doctor, Lee had no real reason to feel nervous. He knew he drank too much, and he probably didn't eat right, especially during the past three years of tramping and roughhousing, but aside from that, he was in perfect health. Thirty-one years of age. Fit. Strong. This was his chance, no more moving from place to place, getting paid at the whim of the boss. No more lumber camps or cane fields, and no more sewer work. But as each man in front of him left the car, smiling and waving their slips, his unease grew.

It was his turn. He knocked then pushed open the door. A wiry man sat behind a desk. "Mr. Christmas?"

"Yes, sir."

"I'm Dr. Allport." He indicated to a stool. "Please, sit. I believe you are last."

"There was no one behind me."

"Very well. We're going to conduct a series of tests, but they're not invasive in any way. In other words," said the doctor, smiling, "you won't feel a thing."

These words failed to reassure Lee; his throat was dry, his palms clammy, and he had a sinking feeling he just couldn't shift, or explain.

"Ever had any problems with your vision?" asked the doctor.

"No, sir." A lump formed in his throat.

"No blurriness, tiredness of the eyes, unusual discharge, strange sensations, anything like that?"

He shook his head.

Dr. Allport scribbled on his pad and then opened a small box. He removed three tiny skeins of silk yarn, laying them out in front of Lee before swiveling the open box around. Inside were thirty or forty more woolen threads. "You can see the green, blue, and rose yarn in front of you there. What I need you to do is match the rest of the wool in the box to the colors on the table, or as close as you can."

Lee froze.

The doctor looked puzzled. "Let me show you. This greenish one here would go with—"

"Doc, I don't think I can do this."

"What's the matter?"

He picked up two of the samples. "I can't tell them apart."

Dr. Allport nodded, and then resumed taking notes.

"What's wrong with me?" demanded Lee.

The doctor fixed his glasses, and placed his hands back on the desk. "You're color-blind, Mr. Christmas."

"What do you mean?"

"I mean that you can't tell the difference between red and green. More importantly, for the company's purposes, you can't distinguish between a danger light and an all-clear." The doctor stood.

"What about the rest of the tests?"

"That won't be necessary." The doctor walked around the desk and held open the door. "You seem like a strong fellow," he said with a smile, "you'll find other work."

Lee pushed past the doctor. He stepped down out of the car, his legs a little shaky, glad there was no one around to see the state he was in. Taking a deep breath, he began walking with no particular direction in mind. He decided to avoid the saloons, at least until he calmed down a little. He was liable to knock someone's block off if they so much as glanced at him the wrong way.

Color-blind. What a stupid name.

It wasn't as if he saw the world in black and white, or gray for that matter. But he did have some trouble with colors. He could never tell when his steak was cooked, or whether a tomato was ripe, or, more importantly, the difference between a blue-eyed blonde and a green-eyed redhead. But what did it matter? So what if an orange was yellower than a banana or if spinach looked like cowshit, he still knew how to drive a damn train. It was a trick, he reckoned, feeling anger build inside him. Remembering the frosty exchange with Captain Sharp, he figured the railroad's amnesty mustn't have extended to Lee Christmas. He wandered over to the roundhouse to seek his friend's counsel.

Boyd watched him approach, all hunched over. "What's wrong, Lee? Ain't you coming to work for us?"

Lee frowned, his bushy eyebrows near meeting in the middle. "That doctor from Chicago says I got the color-blind."

"Aw, you don't believe all that nonsense. Ain't no such thing. Come inside. Let's talk." Boyd took him into the roundhouse and sat him down. "I'll be back in a minute," he said. "Wait right here." He headed to the testing car, reaching for the keys in his pocket. Once inside, Boyd fumbled around in the darkness until he located the testing kit. He grabbed a pile of the floss, and returned to the office.

"Let's put an end to this right here," Boyd said as he laid the wool out on the table and separated out a red and green skein. "Tell me straight. Do those colors look the same to you?"

Lee scrunched up his face. "Ain't they the same?"

"The same!" Boyd yelled. "Can't you see one of 'em's greener than the greenest grass and the other is redder than the reddest blood?"

Lee shook his head slowly. "Before God, Boyd, you ain't fooling me now, right?"

15

Lee sometimes liked to while away time down at the port, just before the bend in the river at Algiers, watching the steamers ferrying bananas in and people out.

"Join the railroad, and see the world," he boomed, drawing sharp looks from passersby. He took another swig from his hip flask, glowering at the rubberneckers. "Mind your own damn business," he slurred.

The slogan that had drawn him in now served as a bitter reminder of what his life could have been, if things had turned out different. In truth, even before the crash, the railroad had never taken him much further north than Memphis.

Memphis, he thought, *Mamie's on her way there right now.*

That he hadn't done right by her or the kids weighed heavily on his heart. They had sold the furniture in their rented New Orleans house for the princely sum of twelve dollars, and he had sent Mamie north with all of it. He wondered when he would see her again, and the kids: Ed, Hattie, and Sadie—the name Mary not sticking after all. But he knew it was the right thing to do. He couldn't put Mamie through any more pain. The boys said there was money to be made down in the Tropics—banana trains, no less. Although

Lee still wasn't sure it was the right move.

"Why go all the way to Memphis? It makes no sense," he had asked Mamie.

She had ignored him at first, continuing to empty drawers onto the bed. "Makes plenty of sense if you've half a brain."

"But we don't know anyone there."

She picked up a frame that had been knocked to the floor: a picture of their wedding day—the only picture. No one they knew had been in attendance. They only had a photograph at all because a reporter from the *Picayune* had telegrammed Memphis and got a stringer to the church, desperate to add a picture to the paper's juicy headline. She removed the photo and tossed it at him. "Frame's worth keeping anyways," she said, as she dumped it in her case.

"But Memphis?"

"Darn it, Lee, my mother's there. And she's been looking after us for three years now, while you…" She spread her hands.

"It's not my fault I got the color-blind."

His wife sighed. "Do you always have to see things in black and white?"

"That's not how it works," he said. "It's more like I can't see the little differences you can see."

Mamie had stepped toward him then, brushing his face with her hand. Tears welled in her eyes. "I know," she said.

Then she continued packing.

The memory of that conversation hit him hard; Lee cleared his throat, looking to the sky, blinking away tears. A storm rolled in off the Gulf, right up the Mississippi River.

The jostling crowd at the end of the pier caught his eye, passengers taking the place of bananas on a vessel to his left. Boyd told him all sorts were heading south now, trying their luck. Fare was next to nothing too, given that most steamers went back empty after dumping their crop in New Orleans. Lee strolled down to the boat, more curious than anything.

He paused at the gangplank, his right leg tapping.

He stepped aboard.

An hour later, Lee wiped a tear from his eye as the boat cut through the Gulf of Mexico. He took the last swig of whiskey from his hip flask and then balanced it on his palm, tracing his finger across the inscription: *To Lee & Mamie. Remember this day—Boyd.*

He cocked his arm back as far as he could, hurling the hip flask high and long. It hit the water in the distance, a wave rolling over it right away. As soon as the wave crashed, it bubbled up again, light bouncing off it for a moment before it sank beneath the surface, lost forever.

Lee blew his nose, hiding tears from his fellow passengers, and then made his way to the prow. Nothing but endless blue sea, the water clearer now they'd left the industrial ports of America behind. He closed his eyes and tilted his head back, letting the sun fall on his face. Pinpricks of heat spread across his cheeks. Sweat trickled down his back. In the distance, a seagull called. Lee kept his eyes squeezed shut, right until the purser tapped him on the shoulder and asked to see his ticket.

Rubbing his face, he turned and pulled all the money he had out of his pocket—two dollars and change. "This enough?"

"Where you headed?"

He smiled for the first time in days. "I was hoping you were gonna tell me."

16

Puerto Cortés was supposed to be the largest port in Honduras, but it didn't look like much. Lee couldn't believe he'd landed somewhere even more humid than New Orleans, and this was only October. He stepped off the steamer, not even knowing what time it was supposed to be, and cursed the heat sticking the shirt to his back.

The sleepy town he'd viewed from the boat sprang into life once they'd docked. Lee stood to the side. This part, at least, was somewhat familiar. A boat was just like a train, he reckoned. The longer passengers took to disembark, the longer them bananas went spoiling. Ripes weren't worth half the price of nice green bananas that would stay fresh for days. But the giant, oblong blocks of ice, steam rising from them as they were dumped right in on top of the boat's cargo, really caught his eye. *One way to keep 'em fresh*, he supposed. He waited by the steamer as the crew finished loading, and was still standing there as it puffed away into the distance, belching a trail of smoky breadcrumbs all the way back to America.

Lee turned to face the town, such as it was. It had only one street to speak of, which bent down to meet the wharf. A narrow-gauge railroad track ran right down the middle, curving away from the coast at the end of the street. *Dirt road,* he corrected himself. Nothing was paved, not as far as he could see. He hunkered down and patted the earth, saying a silent prayer, then began walking.

The line of tin-roofed, single-story buildings was punctuated by a sole structure, the Hotel Lefebvre; Lee figured that was as good a place to start as any. He managed to talk his way into a room on credit—thanks to the intervention of the manager, who knew a few words of broken English. The manager was curious about his lack of luggage, but Lee talked his way out of it. "Bags went ahead on the Wednesday steamer. Don't tell me they didn't arrive! I bet Mr. Bluth didn't pay for my room neither."

"No pay," the manager said.

"Damn it." Lee struck the counter. "I knew these guys were amateurs." He raised an eyebrow at the manager. "Say, you couldn't spot me a room till we get this straightened out?"

"You want room?"

"Yes," said Lee, slowing down. "Money … after."

"*No hay problema, ven por aquí.*"

Lee followed him down the hallway.

After a short nap, he washed up in the sink and dressed in the same clothes. Any notion of needing a fresh shirt was forgotten as soon as he stepped outside, sweating once more.

"Hell," he said to himself, "what's this place like in summer?"

Raucous laughter rolled down the street and Lee decided to find the source. He walked by a line of houses until he got to a set of buildings with *Cantina* or *Estanco* above the door; he walked into the loudest.

Locals hunched over the tables, deep in conversation

and gesticulating wildly. Their eyes went to him when he walked in, and then looked away.

Friendly bunch. Feeling like a fish out of water, he marched to the bar and ordered a whiskey in the most confident tone he could muster.

"*No hay*," was the immediate reply.

He shook his head at the strange bottle offered instead, scanning the shelf for something vaguely familiar. When the bartender offered something else, he thought it best to agree.

Lee grabbed a scrap of paper from the counter and pointed to it. The bartender looked confused, doubly so when he reached behind the bar and grabbed the pencil from the man's ear. He scrawled, "Lee Christmas, Engineer, Hotel Lefebvre, I.O.U. one drink."

The bartender read the note, nodding, pointing down the street in the direction Lee had gestured.

"Hotel Lefebvre," said Lee, before pointing to himself. "Me, Lee Christmas."

He looked at Lee; then he smiled, pointing to the last words on the page. "*Una bebida, no. Muchas bebidas, sí.*"

Lee laughed along with him, wondering what the hell he'd said. He turned to face the room and noticed a louder crew in one corner, a table crowded with sweating foreigners. Taking a big swig of his drink—which tasted something like rum, close enough anyway—Lee made his way over.

"I see you figured out the credit system." One member of the group rose to shake his hand.

He smiled. "Just gotta figure out some darn way to pay the tab."

"What's your name?"

"Lee," he said. "Lee Christmas." He raised his glass and drained it in one go. "Pleased to make your acquaintance." He almost yakked the last word. "Sorry, guys. Not used to the local hooch."

"You just get here?"

"Fresh off the boat," he said. "And I think I might be here for a while."

17

His new acquaintances set him up with a job right away, working for the Honduran National Railroad, ferrying ice down from the provincial capital, San Pedro Sula. Some sixty miles inland down a single line of narrow-gauge track, the city was home to the only ice factory in Central America. The train was an old wood-burner, about the only thing that pleased him about set-up. Three times a week, he would make the round trip, hauling bananas up to San Pedro Sula and carrying several two-hundred pound blocks of ice, along with empty banana cars, back to the plantations on the coast. Each time, Lee pushed that tiny train to the limit—full throttle, all the while furiously puffing away at a *puro* clenched between his teeth.

When he wasn't working, he propped up one of the many *cantinas* and *estancos* of Puerto Cortés, *aguardiente* never far from his lips. Despite its diminutive size, the town was never short of the kind of action Lee liked. It was enough to keep him thinking of home, right up until Boyd's letter arrived. It didn't say much, just supplied Mamie's new address, as requested, and wished him luck. He was hoping for more, but he remembered that Boyd was never one for flapping his gums.

In response, Lee spent hours trying to write Mamie a letter, burning through most of the stationery he'd cajoled off the hotel manager. In the final draft, he kept it to current events, leaving all mention of the past where it belonged—in the trash can. Apologizing to Mamie for his silence, he explained how he'd found himself on a steamer bound for Central America, and how long it had taken him to get her address. He promised the enclosed twenty dollars was just the beginning, and that he was back at the throttle in a place that didn't care if he mixed up his colors. He wrote at length about the opportunities in Honduras. The rapidly expanding banana plantations along the Caribbean coast. The coconut trees that lined the beach. And his little toy train, which hauled all that cargo to the steamers.

He got no reply, but he was never one to give up easily. He wrote a second letter, and then a third. Each tale grew a few inches in the telling. Each lucrative opportunity sounded more and more like a sure thing.

Between the letters, he kept hauling ice down from San Pedro, filling his train up with bananas, and loading American steamers with cargo until they were fit to burst. He sent home as much money as he could with each letter, his nightly carousing limiting what he could salt away.

But he couldn't take the silence. Less than a year after he first stepped onto that banana steamer, Lee was back in Louisiana, hauling cane in Burnside. He telegrammed Mamie, letting her know where he was, and she surprised him four days later by arriving with the three children.

"The job is only temporary," he was forced to explain. "I … I didn't think you would turn up immediately. There wasn't room in the telegram for all the details."

The light in her eyes was extinguished right away.

"I'll have something real soon, Mamie," Lee tried to explain. He even tried to convince her to move to Honduras with the kids, telling her all about the job he had waiting for him in Puerto Cortés.

Mamie nodded, mumbling something about the children, but he was too focused on her face to hear her words. She didn't believe him; it was plain as day. He had thought to argue the case, but even he saw the pointlessness. Instead, he insisted on escorting them back to the station.

He hung on in New Orleans for a few months, working a stretch at the New Basin Charcoal Yards. But after a month without any reply from his wife, other than a curt note reminding him of his financial obligations, he decided to return to the banana plantations of Puerto Cortés.

Lee got his job back with the Honduran National Railroad right away, and he spent even more time in the *cantinas*. He tried to save money to send home again, he truly did, but every time he sat down to write a letter back to Memphis to accompany it, the missive ended up curled in a ball on the hotel room floor. Scooping up the money instead, he would head out, trying to impress the regulars by ordering whiskey cocktails for everyone within earshot—now that he'd convinced the bartender to order in a shipment of his favorite tipple. Lee felt the pull of politicking once more as the bars filled with talk of customs duties and inspectors on the take, of Honduras's fate, sandwiched between the jealous lovers of Nicaragua and Guatemala, and of how things should change, and could change, with the right man at the helm.

This new excitement was broken by news from home: Mamie formally requesting what she had frequently threatened. A divorce.

Lee crumpled his latest letter and flew out of the hotel in a fit of rage. He walked into the nearest *cantina* and punched the daylights out of the first guy to look at him the wrong way. Then, he finally succumbed to the temptations of the *putas* working the *cantinas*, his reserve cracking when one of them bandaged his hand. Lee's lust rose as he gazed on her long, dark hair and lithe figure, his conscience numb with *aguardiente* and regret.

Time and again after that, he'd fall into the arms of a *puta*, drunk and cursing the name of his wife, blaming Mamie for the guilt he felt in failing to keep his promises, for abandoning his family, and for reneging on his commitments. In February 1897, Lee finally agreed to release Mamie from her matrimonial vows. He wrote offering to pay the costs of the divorce and pledging to support their children.

A new game was coming his way.

18

At dawn on April 14, 1897, a sentry watched the morning's first *cayuco*, piled high with fruit, exit the Chamelecón River into the bay of Puerto Cortés. The native paddled his way to the banana wharf, signaling his arrival with the customary cry. "*Plátanos.*"

The watching sentry licked his lips and turned toward the *cuartel* on the other side of the railway tracks, cupping his hands. "*Plátanos,*" he yelled. "*Vamos amigos.*"

Half the garrison poured out of the *cuartel* in various states of undress, bleary-eyed but smiling—some not even bothering with footwear. Their unofficial inspection regime always took the edge off the invariable hangover; their ever-rumbling stomachs rarely sated by government rations.

The soldiers dashed across the railroad track, chasing the sentry, who was already on the other side of the gardens and approaching the waterfront, beckoning the *cayuco* to draw alongside the banana wharf. The natives were so used to this informal taxation system that the soldiers didn't even have to bring their weaponry anymore; the uniform was enough to compel obedience. The sentry saw that the native looked worried, probably because his unusually large bounty of *plátanos* was about to be defiled by his ravenous colleagues, now arriving at the pier. As the first soldiers reached down, though, the mountain of fruit erupted and thirteen armed men—*banditos*—emerged from beneath the shelter of large banana leaves and ordered the stunned soldiers to kneel.

With half the garrison captive at the pier and under the care of two men, the other eleven raced toward the *cuartel* to surprise the remainder. The *comandante* surrendered in his hammock—consumption, rather than laziness, confining him so—and the rest of his men followed suit. In twenty short minutes, the *banditos* had captured Puerto Cortés. Their leader, José Manuel Durón, readily accepted the enlistment of half the government soldiers, pleased he now had an army for his twelve *generales* to command. Once he had taken stock of the armory—a Hotchkiss gun and two old muzzle-loading cannons, as well as rifles and munitions—General Durón sent a party of men out past the edge of town to block the trestle bridge; then he sat down to celebrate his victory. Meanwhile, after retrieving what fruit he could from the waters around him, the terrified native paddled back to the sanctity of the Chamelecón River, saving his commerce and his *plátanos* for another day.

Though their town had been captured by rebels, the civilian inhabitants of Puerto Cortés merely shrugged and got on with their business. Most had seen enough revolutions roll through to know how these things went. The *cantinas* filled up early, speculation centering on who had armed the rebels, with Guatemala the chief suspect. Puerto Barrios, just forty miles east along the Caribbean coast, was a notorious meeting point for mercenaries and soldiers of fortune. The townspeople continued to debate the revolution's chances until sundown—

all except for Lee Christmas.

Unaware of the drama unfolding in his adopted hometown, Lee was chugging along happily in his toy train. Smoking a *puro*. Making the return journey from San Pedro with his usual haul: a line of empty banana cars strung out behind him, with two boxcars of ice at the back.

Heading right into an ambush.

19

Lee pulled into the siding just shy of Puerto Cortés, eyeing a rough-looking pair standing on either side of the rail. That itself wasn't particularly unusual; locals often tried to hitch a ride in the empty cars, and everyone turned a blind eye. He eased up on the throttle, allowing the engine to coast a little before applying the brakes. As he came to a halt, six more men sprang from the bushes, rifles drawn and bayonets fixed, jabbering in Spanish.

"Shit," he said.

Lee emerged from the cab, his hands raised, noting with some amusement that he was a good foot taller than most of them. "*Tranquilo, amigos*," he said. "*Tranquilo*." He could only make out some of what they were saying, but he knew they would understand that.

One of the *banditos* approached, waving his rifle, the bayonet getting a little too close to Lee's neck for his liking. Another removed his only weapon, a knife at his belt. Their yammering got more intense.

"What do you want?" Lee addressed one of the men—he looked like the leader—in broken Spanish.

The leader ordered his men onto the flatcar.

He tried again. "Where do you want to go?"

The *bandito* raised his rifle, aiming at Lee's head. "Puerto Cortés."

He smiled, replying in English. "I was going there anyway." He got into the cab and the *bandito* squeezed in beside him, pressing the bayonet to his neck once more, making it quite plain that he was to try nothing. Lee fired up the engine, wondering what the hell he had gotten himself into now.

When they had made the short trip into Puerto Cortés proper, Lee noticed an eerie calm in the streets. There were no natives hawking the usual array of *plátanos* and papayas and cassavas; in fact, the only people wandering around the town's single thoroughfare were groups of armed men, some dressed in the uniform of government soldiers, others looking altogether more ragged—like the *banditos* who had commandeered his train.

He was marched through the town at gunpoint, toward the *cuartel*, looking for any familiar faces to explain what the hell was going on and what was about to happen to him. He spotted the American consul on the other side of the street in a heated discussion with one of the *banditos*, and called out to him.

The consul turned away.

Lee wasn't having that. "Allen! Where are these sons of bitches taking me? What's going on?"

The consul avoided his eyes.

"I'm an American citizen," he protested, before being jabbed in the back with the tip of a bayonet. "An American citizen!"

One of the *banditos* grabbed him around the neck,

standing on tiptoe to do so, and Lee had to stifle a chuckle.

"*Vamos, yanqui.*" He shoved Lee again.

Not wanting to feel another prick of that damn bayonet, Lee resumed his forced march, occasionally looking over his shoulder, trying to catch the consul's attention. Embarrassed by his own powerlessness, the consul soon disappeared into one of the *cantinas*.

When they reached the *cuartel*, Lee was pushed inside. Once his eyes adjusted to the darkness, he noticed a mustachioed man sitting at a table, a near-empty bottle of *aguardiente* in his hand. He took one more swig and stood, swaying. Lee noticed he must have drunk most of that bottle himself.

"I am General José Manuel Durón." He brushed his hands on his sweat-stained shirt while he sized up the *gringo* in front of him. "You must be the *yanqui* engineer."

Despite his slurred speech, the general spoke a little slower and was easier to understand. "Yes, sir," said Lee.

"News of my capture of Puerto Cortés is making its way to the capital. I must take San Pedro Sula before the government forces can come down from Tegucigalpa." The general paused for a moment before bearing his teeth. "At dawn, you will transport my men in your little train. Either that or…"

Lee raised an eyebrow. "Or what?"

The general thumped the table, upending the *aguardiente*. He swiped the bottle clear, dashing it against the wall, and fixed Lee with a steely gaze. "*Muerte.*"

Lee was of half a mind to smack him just for the hell of it, consequences be damned. Instead, he drew himself up to his full height. "If you are going to make me a target, General, then at least give me a gun so I may kill some sons of bitches."

The room fell silent. The general stared at him, his moustache twitching. Then he began to laugh. "This *gringo*, eh?" He looked at his men and was just about to speak when Lee interrupted him.

"General, sir, that train is a death trap, especially for anyone upfront in the cab—which is me, I suppose. But if I get shot, you have no one to drive the train. If any of your men could do it, I wouldn't even be here, right?"

The general nodded, seemingly intrigued.

"We have some time," he continued. "There's plenty of old scrap up at Laguna. If you give me some men, we can put a flatcar in front of the cab and armor it. You'll have some shooters at the front, in case we hit any trouble along the way."

The general considered the proposal for a moment before barking orders at his men. He turned back to Lee. "You have until dawn. And no tricks, or—"

He waved a hand. "I know, I know. I'll be shot."

Lee was up half the night, but he was happy with what he had rigged up—a little traveling fort in front of his cab. The Hotchkiss cannon captured at the *cuartel* was mounted at the head of the flatcar, and the sides were walled in with three-quarter-inch scrap iron fronted by a row of sandbags—enough protection for a line of marksmen on either side. He examined his handiwork. *An armored train*, he thought, chuckling, and turned in for what was left of the night.

Unbeknownst to Lee and the revolutionaries, the

comandante of the San Pedro Sula garrison had decided to put down their little rebellion before it got underway. Deciding not to wait for official orders from the capital, the *comandante* took a company of men and rode through the night, down toward the coast. The following morning, just as the rebels were readying to board, scouts brought word: the *federales* would be upon them shortly. The train was stationed at the far end of a large lake, and the likely point of attack was across the trestle bridge that bore the single line of narrow-gauge rail inland to San Pedro. General Durón, showing few signs of his night of carousing, sprang into action, ordering the mouth of the trestle barricaded with the only thing to hand: the gigantic 200-pound blocks of ice, slowly melting in the back of Lee's train.

Behind their icy fortifications, rebels took position. The armored flatcar afforded the sharpshooters both protection and a vantage point. And the *federales*—instead of waiting for the ice to melt in the sweltering tropical heat—forsook prudence and charged into battle across the trestle bridge, toward the revolutionaries. Lee sat in his cab, watching the spectacle unfold. The rebels had given him a rifle, but despite his bravado the night before, he had no intention of joining the battle. He was just hopeful that his "side" would be victorious—else he'd have some real explaining to do. A potshot ricocheted off the side of the cab, snapping him back to attention. Something stirred inside him. He grabbed his weapon and jumped down from the train.

When Lee looked back on this moment of his life, he could never quite explain it. His father had been a military man—a veteran of President Polk's Mexican campaign—who had stormed Chapultepec with General Scott. Maybe it was in his blood. Or maybe he was plain crazy. Whatever it was, Lee raced to the icy barricade and took position right beside Durón.

His first shot flew high and wild, his arms shivering involuntarily when they rested on the ice.

Durón turned to him and smiled. "*Frio, no*?"

As Durón resumed shooting, Lee took position again, letting the cold burn through his arms. He took aim. His first target hit the deck before he could even curl his finger around the trigger. Someone else must have beaten him to it.

Lee took a breath and carefully picked another. The *comandante*—Lee could see him now, urging his men forwards. "Just like shootin' rabbits," he said as he squeezed the trigger.

The *comandante* went down with a desperate cry, first to his knees, and then slumped forwards onto his face. The enemy charge faltered almost immediately. Some threw themselves to the crossties, others turned tail altogether, seeking out the sanctity of the other side.

The rebels cheered, firing the occasional shot as the government troops retreated, before fleeing altogether. Durón embraced Lee and promoted him to captain on the spot. He insisted on calling off their planned assault on San Pedro Sula, so their victory could be properly celebrated.

20

At the throttle of his toy train, Captain Lee Christmas took advantage of a curved section of track to gaze back at his unusual cargo—eight empty banana cars crowded with rebel soldiers. In front of him, a row of sandbags lined the rudimentary armor plating he'd knocked up a few days earlier. There were no shooters up front yet; they wouldn't take position until just outside San Pedro, Lee having convinced General Durón that the drag would slow their passage. He had the cab to himself, no bayonet at his neck. He looked down to the rifle at his feet and chuckled at what he'd signed up for. After his service at the Laguna Trestle skirmish, Durón made it clear he was a free agent. But he'd willingly taken that gun and pledged himself to the cause.

The other expatriates in town thought Lee was crazy. The evening before he had departed with the rebels, he held court in *cantina* after *cantina*, relishing each retelling of the battle. Several acquaintances took him aside and tried to impress on him the seriousness of the situation. The current president—Policarpo Bonilla—was nearing the end of his term, and the Constitution forbade him from contesting the upcoming election. His party's favored candidate was the current minister for war, Terencio Sierra: the very man who'd be heading up any effort to quash the revolution. He's smart, they had warned Lee, and ruthless too—unlikely to show mercy with an election looming.

Lee waved their concerns away. The way he figured it, he should have died in that train wreck. And it wasn't like he had much to live for now, with Mamie gone for good. He wasn't much for the finer details of politics, but he wasn't ignorant in the ways of the world. If he helped put his man into whatever the hell they called their White House, he was bound to land some plum role. He had his eye on Customs House in Puerto Cortés, reckoning it did pretty damn well from creaming off the top of all those bananas.

His fantasies were interrupted by a soldier banging on the side of the cab. They were approaching San Pedro; it was time to get ready for a shootin' match.

21

Lee never got his battle, but he didn't know whether to be disappointed or relieved. The government troops had abandoned the city to the rebels. Sympathizers told them the *federales* had fled over the mountains to Tegucigalpa. The *federale*s had too much head start on the ten-day march to the capital to be overtaken now—not when the only railway line in the country went the wrong way from San Pedro, down to the coast.

Thinking the *federales* cowed by his bold invasion, General Durón resumed his carousing. Lee suspected otherwise, remembering the admonitions of his friends. It seemed more likely the government sought to concentrate their forces before engaging the revolutionaries; the upcoming election demanded a quick end to the war. But Durón couldn't be convinced, not when he was already cattle-eyed on *aguardiente*.

Lee continued in his regular job, ferrying ice down to Puerto Cortés and hauling bananas from the plantations. Commercial exports were unimpeded, except that now the customs duties lined the rebels' coffers. Steamers still needed ice to cool their American-bound cargo, and he didn't mind increasing his workload—now that he was drawing a captain's pay on top of his regular engineer's wage.

A couple of weeks later, Lee pulled into Puerto Cortés as usual, ready to disgorge his cargo. Normally, the handlers would unload the ice he had hauled down the mountains in no time, nesting the giant blocks in the shade while he did a quick circuit of the coastal plantations, filling his cars with bananas. But the yard was empty.

Suspicious, he jumped down from his cab and headed to the seafront. Before he even got there, he was surrounded by kids screaming, "*Barco*, *barco*," and yanking him toward the shore. He freed himself from their attentions and turned to the *cuartel*. Two soldiers were blocking the entrance, attempting to extricate the old colonial muzzle-bearing cannon they'd captured along with the town.

"You guys finally taking this beauty for some air?" Lee asked, to quizzical looks.

"*Barco*." One of the harried soldiers pointed to the sea.

Lee turned to see what he meant, and finally saw it: a gunboat anchored in the bay, teeming with soldiers.

He gulped. "Say," he said to the soldiers, who had finally maneuvered the cannon out the door. "They wouldn't happen to be on our team, by any chance?"

"Nicaragua," was the reply.

Lee wasn't sure what that meant exactly, but by the look on the soldier's face, he figured it wasn't anything good.

He stooped and grabbed one end of the cannon, surprised at its weight. "I see why you were having so much trouble." He set the cannon back down and told the pair of soldiers to wait. There had to be an easier way. Heading back up to the yard, he scouted for something to help. The winch was fixed in place, so that was no use. Instead, he grabbed one of the sturdy pull-carts and a length of rope, the kids delighting in wheeling the device down to the *cuartel.* As they all rolled the hog-tied cannon toward the wharf, Lee wondered what the spotters on the gunboat made of it all, but all he really cared about was that the guns trained on Puerto Cortés remained silent.

With the weapon finally in place, he stood back to admire his handiwork. He stepped back even further when a soldier returned from the *cuartel,* bearing a sack of gunpowder. As he stuffed more and more into the cannon, Lee moved further and further back. He was soon glad for his caution; the rebel only succeeded in searing his eye. The noise must have woken General Durón from his slumber, for he appeared at the entrance of the *cuartel*, swearing loud enough to be heard all the way down at the pier. As the stricken soldier received treatment, Lee looked out to the gunboat once more. The troops on deck had barely moved.

He stepped away from the shambles to meet Durón's approach, but the general merely waved him up to the train, where the rest of the rebels had taken position. "San Pedro," the general ordered, "*Vamos ahora.*"

Lee didn't need to be told twice.

The rebels wound their way up through the mountains toward San Pedro Sula, the mood tense. It was a marked contrast to the jubilant raiding party of a fortnight ago. On arrival, they received more grim news. The minister of war, Terencio Sierra, was marching down from the capital at the head of two thousand *federales.* He'd maneuvered them into a trap, and he would be upon them in a matter of days.

Lee knew he was between a rock and a hard place, and he was becoming aware that Honduras faced the same predicament. Sandwiched between Nicaragua and Guatemala—who despised each other—Honduras held the balance of power in Central America. It was a poisoned chalice, however. If the Hondurans proposed legislation deemed favorable to the Guatemalans, the Nicaraguans would throw their support behind the opposition, who were always keen to reach for the rifles in those days.

The current Honduran government was allied to Nicaragua, which owned the impressive gunboat blockading Puerto Cortés. And which meant that the rebels—Lee Christmas among them, now that he had willingly taken up arms against his adopted homeland—had only one place to shelter, and that was back in Guatemala, where Lee soon realized their little revolution had been planned and financed.

And so the rebels fled, straight over the mountains, driving mules ahead of them.

22

Lee wrapped the blanket a little tighter around his shoulders, stomped his feet, then sat back down on the dirt. He wished they could light a fire. He grabbed the bottle of *aguardiente* as soon as it came his way and grinned at his new brothers-in-arms before swallowing as much as he could manage. It tasted like crap, but with Durón ordering no campfires, it was the only way to keep warm. He didn't understand much of what his *compadres* were saying, but it didn't matter. Tipsy now on the local firewater, he laughed as they struggled with his name: *Señor Crees-mas.*

The march was tough going. Durón didn't want to go anywhere near the coast until he was absolutely certain they were safely over the border in Guatemala, which meant hiking over endless hills and getting no relief on the other side when faced with yet more jungle. Each step was preceded by a slashing machete, as if they were carving the first human path through endless bush. Lee tried to remember how far the border was from San Pedro. His memory of the map in the railway office, where he'd first signed his work papers, was faded. Sometimes, when they reached a summit, the vegetation thinned and he could just about spy the coast in the distance. He wished he could plunge into the clean, blue depths and wash the past few weeks away. More often, they got no respite from the jungle hanging over them, surrounding them, closing in on them as they crept west.

The only moments of levity were provided by General Durón and his inexhaustible supply of *aguardiente*. Lee had silently questioned the decision to abandon munitions to make space for more hooch, but lost in the highlands of Honduras, Lee realized the general was more than a simple lush. The only enemy they faced the whole way to Guatemala was in their own damn heads, and he knew that booze was a man's soundest ally in that fight.

Five days' hike from San Pedro, Durón finally rescinded the order forbidding campfires. The men were energized by the command, using their ever-present machetes to hack free whatever dry wood they could find. Once they had fire to warm them, the general spent more time with his men, instead of skulking in the shadows. He joined the *aguardiente* circle with vigor, challenging Lee with his eyebrows each time he tilted the bottle and emptied a staggering quantity down his throat. After passing the hooch to his left, Durón would stand and describe once more the grand "battle" of Laguna Trestle.

Each night, the story grew legs; by the time they finally cut down toward the coast and entered the Guatemalan town of Puerto Barrios, Señor Crees-mas was a giant *gringo*, seven feet tall, with a *puro* clenched between his teeth and no care for his own safety, a man who single-handedly charged the *federales*, scattering them in his wake.

Lee didn't mind one bit.

23

Puerto Barrios was a lot smaller than Puerto Cortés, but there were still plenty of *cantinas* in which to waste the days. It wasn't quite as bustling either; it seemed the soil in these parts was less conducive to banana cultivation. But it had an edge to it that Puerto Cortés lacked. British-owned Belize was only two ports up the coast, which meant the bars were filled with all sorts: prospectors, adventurers, historians, mercenaries, geologists, and folks like Lee—who weren't sure how they ended up there or where they were going next.

He'd assumed the rebels would regroup and re-arm to mount an immediate incursion over the border. But not long after their arrival, General Durón and half of the rebels simply disappeared. When Lee did bump into one of his old comrades, he got few answers to his many questions, and the scraps he got didn't line up. Durón was in the capital, bending the ear of President Cabrera. Durón was in Mexico, retired from politics. Durón was over the border, arming natives for another uprising. He couldn't figure out whether people were just engaging in barroom speculation, or whether the rebels were throwing informers off the scent. Regardless, there was always someone willing to buy a drink in exchange for news.

One night as Lee left the *cantina*, hoping for an early

night for a change, he grew suspicious when a young kid collared him and insisted on bringing him to a meeting. The boy ushered him down to a darkened *estanco* at the end of street, which only opened its doors as they approached. His suspicions deepened once they got inside, as the curtains were drawn and the door was locked. He braced himself for an attack.

Instead, an unarmed stranger wearing a crisp linen suit stepped out from an adjoining room and smiled. "I apologize for the secrecy," he said, removing his hat. "Our friends in Guatemala City think you could be useful. Are you interested?"

Lee laughed. "Yeah, sure. Who?"

"That's not important," he said. "You want to go back home?"

"And finish the war? Of course."

"Good," he smiled, "but that's not what I meant. I'm talking about *home*. New Orleans. If we're going to win this war, we need weapons." He paused. "Are you in?"

24

May was always a special time of year in New Orleans, bright and warm, without the oppressive humidity of summer. But Lee found it surprisingly cool as he stepped off the steamer, tipping his hat to the waiting stevedores. He shouted for a porter, and one commandeered his grand traveling trunk before they'd even agreed a price. The Guatemalans had a local contact arrange a room on Basin Street, and as soon as Lee had dumped his luggage and changed his shirt, he headed straight for the capital of the Third Ward, Remy Klock's combination saloon and grocery store.

As he entered his old haunt, Lee caused quite a stir in his fancy suit hand-stitched by President Cabrera's very own tailor. He rapped his ivory-handled cane on the bar and called for a whiskey, offering to stand a drink for whoever would join him. Lee's newfound wealth became the subject of much speculation among the saloon's regulars, but he was circumspect about the source—at first. The temptation to appear a big deal was all too great, the narrative of the hometown boy done good just too compelling. With the money he'd been sent home with, Lee was supposed to be greasing wheels and making connections, quietly preparing the ground for a purchase of rifles and ammunition. Instead, he greased his own wheels and filled the cash registers of Tom Cook and Remy Klock, and those of any other saloonkeepers who would take his money.

The first time he saw his old friend Boyd Cetti, Lee almost crushed him with a bear hug. "How are you doing, partner?"

"Your suit," said Boyd, pushing him away and gesturing to his own greasy overalls. "You'll ruin it."

Lee enveloped him again. "Don't mind that. I got a whole box of 'em."

Boyd raised an eyebrow in response.

"He ain't sayin' much," said Tom Cook, wiping the counter. "But as long as he keeps paying the tab, I'm asking no questions."

Lee tilted his glass in the bartender's direction. "While you're not busy," he said with a growl. "Boyd, too, while you're at it." He gave his friend a wry grin. "As long as he's off duty, of course."

"Ya big galoot," said Boyd, punching him in the arm. When the drinks arrived, they clinked glasses and Boyd pulled him over to a table where they could speak privately. "Railroad must pay better there than here, huh?"

Lee smiled. "You know I always had my eye open for … business opportunities."

"What game are you in now anyways? Did you knock off a bank or something?"

"Close enough." He laughed. "Close enough." He waved for two more drinks as Boyd filled him in on all the latest news. When they were all caught up on local politics,

Boyd stood to go for a piss, eyeing Lee's meticulously tailored suit once more. "Damn, you finally got lucky."

By the time his friend returned, after getting sidetracked at the bar, Lee had already polished off another whiskey and was feeling pretty damn good.

"I want to hear all about Honduras," Boyd said. "What are the girls like?"

"Pretty." He grinned. "Prettier than you could imagine."

Boyd let out a howl. "I'll say. And is it hot?"

"Hotter than here, and summer lasts all year long." Lee paused. "You should visit sometime."

"I dunno," Boyd said. "My wife probably wouldn't like that too much."

The smile vanished from Lee's face.

"Sorry, I didn't…"

He waved a hand. "Don't matter none. You're probably gonna hear soon anyway. Waiting on the divorce papers. She might have sent 'em already, but I had to get out of Honduras in a hurry."

"Oh, yeah?"

"Actually, I'd really appreciate it if you could send her a note with my new address." He wrote down the number on Basin Street. "Should be there for a while. And if I write her myself…" Lee gazed off into the distance.

Boyd put a hand on his shoulder. "No problem. I understand."

Lee stared into his drink for a moment before draining the contents and approaching the bar. "You best leave the bottle this time, Tom. We got some catching up to do." He returned to the table, waving his trophy.

Lee woke the next morning stark naked on the floor of his Basin Street place, not having made it to the bed the night before. His pants were crumpled on the floor beside his head, but his shirt and blazer were nowhere to be seen. *Must have been a hell of a night.*

He washed his face in the sink, the pounding in his head refusing to quit. Rubbing his temples, he went over to the sash windows to air the room while he lit his last *puro*. Two drunks brawled in the middle of the street outside while a prostitute screamed at them to quit. He wondered why the Guatemalans had picked Basin Street, of all places, to set him up. A cop strolled down the sidewalk, and everyone scattered, all except the drunk who'd been losing the punch-up. He watched as the guy gave short shrift to the cop, claiming he'd been jumped from behind and didn't see his assailant. As the cop fruitlessly knocked on doors, Lee realized Basin Street was perfect. On a street full of brothels, no one was too friendly with the law nor too keen on strangers poking into their business.

The Guatemalans had impressed on him the importance of keeping a low profile, which made him all the more worried when he went into Tom Cook's for an eye-opener. When Lee refused food, Tom made some aside like, "You can't go revolutin' on an empty stomach."

Lee stopped himself just short of grabbing the saloonkeeper. "What you say?" he demanded.

"Don't get fresh with me. It's all everyone's talking about."

He put his head in his hands, trying to recall the night before. Then he remembered confiding with Boyd and swearing him to secrecy. Throwing down the whiskey, he stormed out of the bar, heading straight for the station yard. He spotted his friend outside the roundhouse and grabbed his neck from behind. "I need a word with you."

Boyd squirmed free, his face flushed. "What's your problem?"

"You swore you wouldn't say nuthin'."

"I didn't!"

"I sure didn't tell no one else."

Boyd raised an eyebrow. "How much do you actually remember from last night?"

Lee's heart sank.

It didn't take long for word to trickle back to Guatemala City that their new agent was being indiscreet.

25

Lee's intelligence career was over before it really began. He was jettisoned by the Guatemalans and cut off from his new funds, but he wasn't sore at them. He knew they had to distance themselves from the newspaper stories; the United States Government took a dim view of any revolution organized on their soil—unless sanctioned by the White House, he supposed. But he was angry with himself for screwing up yet another opportunity by acting like a damn fool.

He went back to scrabbling around for any kind of paying work, desperate to make good on his promise to support his children, especially after letting his newfound fortune slip through his fingers. He managed to get some laboring over in Chalmette Harbor, just east of downtown New Orleans. Instead of being frustrated, he took pride in having some tough manual work again, earning his keep by the sweat of his brow. But then a letter arrived from Memphis. Divorce papers from Mamie. Although Lee was heartbroken, he recognized his failure as a father and husband, and he assented.

Mamie was four hundred miles north, yet Lee was anxious to put even more distance between them. When he walked down Bourbon Street, listening to the brass bands play on every street corner, all he could think about was the day he and Mamie had eloped. Passing by the station on the way to Remy Klock's saloon, all he could think about was the wreck. And when he drowned his sorrows, all he could think about were the many chances he'd let slip through his fingers.

So when he received word that the Honduran government had put out an amnesty, Lee was keen to take advantage, despite remaining a little wary of their motives. Any lingering suspicions were put to rest when he heard that the Hondurans thought it best to keep prospective revolutionaries in plain sight, rather than having them enjoy the largesse of Guatemala and potentially being prodded into action from abroad.

The following week, Lee decided to abandon Louisiana for the Tropics once more, setting sail for Puerto Cortés. He was soon back at the throttle of his toy train, winding up the mountains to San Pedro's ice factory and hauling bananas from the ever-expanding plantations. In June, he sent Mamie the fifty dollars she needed to finalize the divorce, along with a heartfelt letter wishing her all the best for her future and promising anew to support their children and visit them when he could.

This time, he was determined to keep that promise.

26

Lee soon settled down in more ways than one. Within a year, he remarried—a local beauty from Puerto Cortés by the name of Magdalena Talbot—and was determined to make a go of it and divest himself of his bad habits. He still visited the *cantinas*, reveling in the telling and retelling of war stories. But he avoided the attentions of the *putas,* and he never let slip his previous entanglements with the Guatemalan intelligence service, figuring the amnesty would be a little less comprehensive if that got out.

His former reputation as a ladies' man was something of a sticking point, Magdalena never fond of the whispers that trailed them as they took the evening air. Lee was desperate to make things work, however, so he gave up his steady railroad job when a business opportunity cropped up in Choloma—a small town ten miles shy of San Pedro Sula. The owner of a general store was seeking to retire, so had put a share of the business on the market for a discount—on the condition that the new investor took on the day-to-day running of the place. Lee hemmed and hawed, unsure whether he wanted to leave the coast, but Magdalena insisted.

In Choloma, he slipped into a more sedate existence. He diligently built up the general store's business, making full use of the contacts he'd established through the railroad and the friends he'd made in the *cantinas*. Knowing his old train was often half empty, Lee was able to come to an arrangement with his replacement. Reduced freight costs allowed Lee to undercut the competition; soon, he was even peeling trade away from more-established stores in San Pedro Sula. Magdalena gave birth to two girls—Leah and Juanita—adding a bustling household to a thriving business concern. But no sooner was the picture of domestic bliss complete before it all fell apart.

In later days, Lee would realize he remarried too soon, that the love he thought he felt for Magdalena was mere infatuation, and that he wasn't ready for the quiet life. But at the time, all he knew was that his demons had gotten the better of him, and he was chasing tail once more. This time, a blonde caught his eye—an Italian down in Puerto Cortés, named Adelaide Caruso. Once their affair became public, Lee begged Magdalena for a divorce.

She refused to budge.

27

Choloma was a small town, and Lee wasn't hard to find. If you had a bone to pick with him, a quick tour of the *cantinas* would find him holding forth over whiskey cocktails, his booming voice filling the room. His prodigious appetite for liquor and women had won him many friends and admirers, but plenty of enemies too. At thirty-seven years of age, he had already survived two attempts on his life. At first, the bullet that grazed his cheek in the *cantina* was considered a stray—a fortuitous escape from some drunken fool discharging his weapon in the street. But when he was struck down with a mystery illness, Lee began to suspect something more sinister. Only the intervention of San Pedro's sole *gringo* doctor saved his life, the physician quickly identifying the poison coursing through Lee's veins and procuring the necessary antidote.

Lee promised the doctor he'd be more careful, since it was clear someone had his number, but it wasn't like he could hide away. He had a business to run, and the sole respite from his disintegrating marriage was the *cantina*. And anyway, he had simply crossed too many people to avoid them all—too many wronged lovers, too many cuckolded husbands. The only way he'd get a bead on who was trying to kill him was if he acted like normal and tried to flush them out.

He wasn't stupid, though. Before he began showing his face in public again, Lee finally accepted an offer from his old adversary Terencio Sierra, who was now ensconced in the Presidential Palace in Tegucigalpa. Sierra's henchmen didn't seem to want much, just an occasional report on the rabble-rousers of the plantations, eyes and ears on anyone trying to sow discontent or rekindle revolutionary sentiments. Seeing as the Guatemalans had dropped him like a hot potato, and no one was really up to anything, Lee figured it was harmless. A little extra money on the side, and maybe someone he could count on to have his back.

Some of the new business Lee helped build up came from a curious source. Lee's *gringo* doctor, he discovered, came from a settlement of former Confederate officers that had sprung up on the outskirts of San Pedro. Most of them had fled the South at the end of the Civil War. Fearing reprisals, they had instead brought their families to Honduras to start a new life.

A couple of months after the attempted poisoning, Lee was in his usual spot: propping up the bar of the *cantina*, cracking jokes, accosting newcomers, and flirting with every woman in the joint. The bartender caught his attention, telling him someone wanted to see him out back to talk privately. Lee assumed it was a mission from Sierra—orders were rarely written down, with intermediaries used to pass messages instead. He made his apologies and slipped out the side door.

He was immediately greeted by a shotgun blast.

Lee screamed and fell back, clutching his chest in agony. He tried to prop himself up on one elbow, desperate to gain purchase on the muddy ground so he could turn and flee, but he was already too weak. He slumped against the wall of the *cantina*, blood bubbling at his lips as he tried to call for help. The shooter stepped forward into the light, showing his face for the first time. He was just a kid, as frightened as Lee.

His hands trembled as he reloaded his weapon. Lee shook his head, silently pleading with his assailant. The gunman raised eyes wide with terror. He steadied himself. He took aim. And he pulled the trigger.

28

Dr. Sydenham Waller had established a decent practice tending to the increasing number of foreigners in San Pedro Sula, and his renown as a surgeon had spread. Late one night, a messenger bearing an urgent message rushed up to the doctor's house: a *gringo* had been shot. The boy told him the handcar was waiting to take the injured man up to Choloma. Dr. Waller grabbed his kit and hurried out the door.

When Dr. Waller saw the damage two shotgun blasts had wrought on Lee Christmas, he feared the patient was beyond even his restorative skills. The local doctor had done what he could—cutting away the patient's clothes, cleaning the wounds, and stemming the flow of blood—but he'd never treated a gunshot victim, and he didn't have Dr. Waller's battlefield experience. The doctor set his kit down on a bedside chair and grabbed his stethoscope. Bending over the bed, he listened carefully. Only the faintest of heartbeats was audible. Then Lee's heart stopped altogether. The doctor snapped into action, abandoning his stethoscope and reaching into his bag for a syringe that was already loaded with nitroglycerin.

After clearing air from the syringe with a quick squirt, Dr. Waller leaned down to his patient. "Listen to me, Lee."

He slapped his face. "Focus now, come on. Come back to us." He slapped him again, harder this time. "Listen to my voice. You're not dead yet. You hear me?"

Dr. Waller ignored the wailing behind him, focusing on his patient. "You gotta do what I say, okay?" He watched his patient until he thought he saw a slight nod of the head. "Your bit is easy," the doctor continued. "All you gotta do is clench your teeth." He felt out the spot on Lee's chest. "Clench your teeth. That's it. Good, you can hear me. We might save you yet, damn it. Now, clench your teeth and don't breathe. If you open your mouth now, you're dead!"

The doctor held the syringe high in both hands, centering it on the patient's sternum; then he jammed it down with all his strength, right into Lee's breast. He pressed down, forcing the nitroglycerin into that poor, failing heart. The syringe discarded, Dr. Waller wiped his brow, grabbed his stethoscope, and blessed himself. As he searched for a beat, he saw his patient's face grow redder and remembered his command. "All right, son. You can relax now. Breathe."

Dr. Waller wasn't sure if his words were registering, or whether the nitroglycerin had worked. But as he bent down to listen his patient's heart once more, Lee Christmas started to breathe.

29

Forgiving his indiscretions and the shame he had brought on their family, Magdalena nursed him through his long and difficult recovery. Before his convalescence was even fully underway, however, Lee somehow managed to accost his assailant. He hobbled to the jailhouse, bribed his way inside, and beat his would-be assassin close to death with nothing more than a rock.

As soon as Lee was well enough to wander around on his own, he sold his share of the general store and went back to the coast—straight into the arms of his Italian lover, Adelaide Caruso.

Lee was boldfaced enough to again ask Magdalena for a divorce; she was sturdy enough to resist. One thing was certain: she wasn't going to make it easy for him. Under Honduran law, both parties had to consent to the dissolution of the marriage—unless there was cause, that is, and Lee's wandering eye didn't qualify.

Meanwhile, he was back to his carousing best. Surviving a shotgun blast to the chest only added to his allure among his circles of hangers-on in Puerto Cortés. When Lee refused the offer of his old job in the railroad, yet still had money to splash around, rumors intensified. Some suspected he was working for Sierra. But since the episode in New Orleans, Lee had learned to keep his damn mouth shut.

The rumors did his reputation no harm. Lee had little to do for his government retainer other than file the occasional report on the old revolutionaries still kicking about in Puerto Cortés. Now and then, he made journeys to Guatemala, but they involved nothing more than passing messages by backdoor channels between emissaries of the respective governments. He was happy, of course, being largely free to do what he liked, which usually involved a day of heavy drinking before falling into the arms of one of the *putas* who plied their trade in that deceptively busy port town. Lee felt the matrimonial bond was no impediment to such romantic interludes; Magdalena's family, understandably, felt quite different. Everyone knew that one of her brothers was out for blood, hoping to restore the family honor by teaching the *gringo* a lesson.

One night, Lee joined some friends at one of the large round tables in the barroom of the Hotel Lefebvre. As soon as he hollered for a drink, Magdalena Talbot's brother entered and took the spare seat at the table. Lee pretended to pay him no mind, and kept on talking, but out of the corner of his eye he saw a pistol on Talbot's lap. He leaned in, on the pretense of sharing a lurid detail in his tale but actually readying himself to upturn the table should Talbot make a move. He watched his brother-in-law relax, waiting until his hand strayed from the gun. Lee then stood, still telling his story, acting out the parts, moving around the table.

All of a sudden, he lunged for Talbot.

Magdalena's brother started in surprise, but Lee shoved

him back in his chair and grabbed the pistol from his lap. Lee stood back and placed the gun on the table, keeping his eyes on his brother-in-law the whole time, then slid the weapon out of reach. Talbot slumped back in his chair.

"This is a family matter. We need to talk." Lee pointed out into the street. "In private."

Talbot nodded, and they both headed out the door and down the street in the direction of the wharf. Lee didn't say anything on the walk down to the waterfront. At the pier, he turned to Magdalena's brother, and quickly dropped his shoulder to punch Talbot in the gut. Talbot was doubled over, winded, before he even knew what was happening.

"That's for the shotgun," said Lee, grabbing him by the neck and forcing him to straighten up. "And don't say you had nothing to do with it." Lee checked his brother-in-law's pockets for further weapons. "I beat it out of him. Damn near killed him." He stared into Talbot's eyes. "Probably should have too."

Talbot went to speak, but Lee raised a hand. "If you were anyone else, you'd be dead already. But you're family." He let Talbot catch his breath. "I'm not going to beat you neither, though I've half a mind to."

Lee shook his head and dropped down to the pier, dangling his feet over the edge. "Now that's out of the way, let's sit down and talk this out."

Talbot looked surprised but nodded and sat down beside him.

"You got a right to be sore," said Lee. "If I was in your shoes, I'd be looking for blood too." He sighed, tossing a stone into the water. "And I feel bad for Magdalena. Never should have married her." He turned to Talbot. "But I want to make things right."

"How?" asked Talbot, speaking for the first time. "How will you do that? You've got two kids. You've shamed her. Ruined her life."

Lee hung his head. "I know, and if I could change things, I would. We never should have married. She knows that too. We'll never be happy together. It's better for both of us if we make a clean break and start over. That much I'm sure of." He turned to Talbot again. "What happens next is down to you … and the family. I want to set Magdalena up so she's got nothing to worry about. So the kids are provided for."

Talbot nodded.

"What will it take for the family to agree the divorce?"

Magdalena's brother spread his hands.

"All right," said Lee. "I don't enjoy this any more than you do, but let's get this over with. What's it gonna cost me?"

30

Lee didn't know whether to be excited or apprehensive when he was summoned to the capital for a meeting with his paymasters. Normally, if they had a mission for him to undertake, a messenger would suffice. A face-to-face meeting in Tegucigalpa meant something else. At first, he worried it was something to do with his amorous escapades: that his affair with Adelaide Caruso was causing a scandal, or that his loud insistence on a divorce from Magdalena was upsetting someone. He wasn't sure, but if they wanted shot of him, Lee figured they wouldn't call him to the Presidential Palace just to tell him to his face. He'd be on the next steamer north. Or worse, he supposed.

He wondered if it was something to do with the upcoming election. The *cantinas* of Puerto Cortés were full of talk of the rumored pact between the three leading figures of the Liberal Party—considered the main reason Honduras had been undergoing a period of relative stability. Policarpo Bonilla had given way to the presidency of Terencio Sierra, and the latter was slated to step aside for Manuel Bonilla—no relation of Policarpo.

What Lee wasn't expecting was a promotion. He was made a colonel in the army, and put on full pay, even though he wouldn't actually be serving. Instead, his time was to be spent undertaking another job: chief of police in Tegucigalpa. While he was nominally in charge of the local police chiefs in each municipality, Lee soon discovered it was a largely ceremonial role. Previous incumbents had been ready to put out to pasture. It was a distinguished, well-paid position that was normally a thank-you for a lifetime of service and offered no real power or duties—until Lee's real orders were handed down: whip the police force of Tegucigalpa into shape, and turn them into an elite fighting force.

Sierra had no intention of relinquishing the reins of power. He needed loyal retainers close to him, men whose bravery could stand the heat of battle. Lee soon realized his job was to build a private army, not bound to any creed or country but loyal to one man. Terencio Sierra.

Lee had his work cut out for him. The two hundred-odd police officers he was supposed to turn into a lean fighting unit were an ill-disciplined, poorly equipped mob whose duties rarely strayed from dragging drunks to the jailhouse to sleep off their tempers. The *gringo* colonel won them over straightaway, issuing them with smart new uniforms, shoes, and sidearms, and parading them around the streets of the capital.

Lee reported directly to the minister for war, Manuel Bonilla—expected to be the Liberal's candidate in the upcoming election. However, when Sierra put forward a patsy as the party's candidate, it was clear the president had no intention of honoring his bond and relinquishing power. Bonilla ran in the election as an independent, and, after a fierce campaign, emerged victorious. On entirely spurious grounds, Sierra declared the election null and void, and Lee realized his true role: protect the president at all costs.

However, he had struck up a friendship with Manuel Bonilla, recognizing in him a kind of kindred spirit. Bonilla had another trait, all too rare among politicians: he kept his word, inspiring fierce loyalty among his supporters. Lee could see which way the wind was blowing. There was going to be trouble, and Lee wanted to be on the right side when the shooting started.

On January 30, 1903, Lee stole out of Tegucigalpa. He had achieved what was asked of him: the capital's police force *was* loyal to one man … but that man was Leon Winfield Christmas.

His troops helped usher out deputies, officials, and businessmen loyal to the true victor of the election—Manuel Bonilla, who was safely holed up inside Tigre Island's fort, on the Pacific coast, surrounded by partisans. While Lee and his men were on the three-day trek toward the revolutionary forces, Sierra had his stooge declared president—a loyalist named Davíla, who in turn appointed Sierra commander-in-chief of the armed forces. Sierra had one mission. Wipe out the rebellion.

The first engagement didn't take place until the beginning of March, when Bonilla's troops routed the government forces, forcing Sierra back. Prior to the battle, Bonilla had sent four flying columns to surround Tegucigalpa. After this decisive victory, when Sierra refused to parlay, Bonilla ordered them to march on the capital.

31

Lee stared down at his throbbing feet and shook his head. His police-issue shoes had come apart two days beforehand, so one of the men had fashioned him a pair of *caites*—cowhide sandals the natives sported. They pinched his feet, and the blisters were killing him. His men took great joy in his discomfort, laughing at the *gringo* with the *caites*, and making jokes about the size of his feet. Seeing as he was a good deal taller than all of them, Lee reckoned they'd never seen feet his size either.

He was in a detachment hiking up from the Pacific along the San Antonio Valley, serving as second-in-command to General Saturnino Medal. As they raced toward the capital, each garrison they encountered had been abandoned, the *federales* having either pulled back or simply deserted their posts. Aside from Lee's chafing feet, the only thing slowing the rebels' march was the hostile terrain. They had one Krupp mountain gun borne by mules, but the inclines were so steep that the artillery often had to be unloaded and carried by hand—and sometimes the poor beasts of burden too. Their advance was only checked when they reached the brush-covered plain below Lamaní Hill.

General Medal called Lee over. "Bring the men to a

halt."

Lee called out the order and then removed his *caites*. His feet were swollen and blistered, which gave his troops unending merriment, but it felt good to get some air on his sores.

The general chuckled. "They take some getting used to."

"Ain't that the truth." Lee rubbed his feet as he looked up at the general. "But you aren't stopping for my benefit. Did you spot something?"

"*Federales*." Medal spat in disgust. "Two Gatling emplacements covering the valley. We cannot move until we silence them." He hunkered down beside Lee, pointing to the hill. "Look. Beneath the shadow of that rocky outcrop."

Lee scanned the area. "I see it."

"The second is thirty yards to the left … down a little."

"Got it."

"Excellent," said Medal. "Now, that *barranco* behind us crosses the plain and seems to continue all the way up to the hill." Lee peered down the gully as the general continued. "We'll hold position here to see if we can draw them out. Take a couple of men and see how close you can get to that hill without being shot. You might spot something."

Lee beamed. "With pleasure, sir."

He soon found that the gully didn't provide sufficient cover. Even if those old hand-cranked Gatling guns were no match for modern machine guns, he didn't want them raining down on him. Scouting around on his own, he found a vantage point overlooking the entire plain. The first thing he spotted were *federales*, creeping along that very same gully, right toward Medal and his men.

Wincing from the *caites* chafing his feet, he hurried back to the general and explained what he saw. "Let me take fifty men," he said. "We'll ambush the sons of bitches. Cut 'em to pieces."

General Medal thought for a moment. "*Bueno.*"

Lee barked the orders, and within a few minutes he had twenty-five troops on either side of the ravine, advancing slowly. When they reached sufficient cover, Lee raised his hand. The men stopped and took position, lying on their bellies, rifles pointed at the valley below. He'd ordered complete silence and warned the men to ensure their position was shielded. They were not to fire until he gave the order, no matter how close the enemy came.

Once he was satisfied his men had all angles covered, he positioned himself at the front of his group, careful he wasn't exposed in any way. After a couple of minutes, the first of the *federales* appeared; Lee instinctively tensed. It was all he could do to resist firing. He just hoped his men showed similar restraint. The first enemy soldier drew closer, but still Lee waited. He glanced across to his corresponding number on the other edge of the ravine and held his hand up. The soldier nodded. He took aim once more. *Wait*, he thought, *wait.*

The leading soldier walked beyond his position.

Lee took a breath. "*Fuego*!"

His men unleashed a volley of rifle fire, filling the ravine with lead.

"*Viva* Bonilla!" they shouted, as their withering assault engaged the enemy below. Only the odd shot was fired in response, and within a few minutes, the enemy fire quelled completely. Thirty *federales* had been slaughtered. Sixty more dropped their weapons and ran along the ravine, straight into the arms of General Medal's men, and surrendered. Only a handful escaped.

Lee raced back to make his report. The general ordered an immediate charge on Lamaní Hill. The *federales* had been expecting a victory of their own, so the confusion caused by the rebel advance meant the general's men faced little resistance and easily captured both Gatling guns.

Rather than holding the hill and taking stock, Medal ordered the men to march. Lee was on a high. It was his first real engagement as a commander, and he'd handled it resolutely. They headed south to join up with the other flying columns for a general advance on the capital. As they walked, Lee looked down at his *caites.* He hadn't noticed them cutting into his feet during the battle. *I could get used to this*, he thought. *The fighting, though, not these damn shoes.*

32

Once more their advance was halted short of the capital, another hilltop gun embankment preventing Colonel Christmas, General Medal, and the rest of the rebels from joining up with their *compadres* and seizing Tegucigalpa. This time, however, the challenge was more daunting than a pair of outdated Gatling guns. The *federales* were putting an Asbury mountain cannon to good use, shelling any suspected rebel position repeatedly. Lee was supervising his men as they hauled their Krupp cannon into place, when General Medal beckoned him. The general looked east. "Do you think you can take it out?"

Lee thought for a moment, scanning the hill. He'd never used an artillery piece before. "Sure," he said, and returned to his men. Once the Krupp was in place, he estimated the range and angle and then stood back, putting his fingers in his ears. "*Fuego*!"

The cannon roared into life, and the men watched in hope before their charge fell hopelessly short. Lee ordered the angle adjusted, but the next shot fell even further short. One more attempt, with the muzzle dipped slightly, landed inexplicably beyond the enemy position. The next time, however, he didn't adjust the angle. He fired again. It fell short, as feared. Lee grimaced. *Something must be wrong with the cannon*, he thought, examining it, *either that, or the ammo.*

The Krupp didn't use set ammunition like the Asbury; its individual projectiles were backed by cloth sacks that contained the black powder charge. Lee weighed two of the sacks in his hand. *They don't seem even.* He spread a blanket on the ground, while his men looked on, puzzled. Emptying the contents of the cloth sacks, Lee found his suspicions were correct. He grabbed his machete and hollowed out a gourd, using it to measure out equal charges before refilling the cloth sacks. Smiling, he handed them back to his gunners. "Let's try this again."

The fourth attempt was a direct hit, disabling the distant Asbury. The panicked *federales* attempted to flee but were soon swept up by General Medal's men.

Following another victory for the rebels, President Sierra panicked and fled over the border to El Salvador. Bonilla was with the main body of troops, pursuing him, but he couldn't cross the border without provoking an international incident. No matter. Sierra's men would melt away soon enough, eager to return to their homes and families, which left Tegucigalpa there for the taking.

The four flying columns took position on the heights surrounding the capital, where they waited for Bonilla to arrive with the rest of the army and lead in the victorious rebels. Surrenders were negotiated for the remaining *federales*, guaranteeing them safe passage to Nicaragua. During the victory march into Tegucigalpa, Bonilla's first act was to make Lee Christmas the chief of the federal police once more, and to promote him to general.

On May 12, 1903, Congress convened, ratified the stolen election, and declared Bonilla president.

33

Within months, Lee tired of his routine duties in the capital and longed to return to Puerto Cortés to resume his pursuit of Adelaide Caruso. Demented by desire for the blonde Italian, he plagued Bonilla for a transfer, but the president was unwilling to grant one. Despite the relative tranquility of his first few months back in office, President Bonilla was sure something was brewing, especially given his enmity with his namesake, Policarpo.

Lee probably would have resigned had it been anyone else in the Presidential Palace, but he trusted Bonilla, and, what's more, he liked him.

Besides, it doesn't hurt to have friends in high places, he thought.

Lee saw how businessmen like Sam Zemurray had been rewarded for financing the revolution: a permanent waiver on import duties, a reduction in banana taxes, huge land concessions, the right to build his own railroad, and the ability to draw half a million dollars in government-backed loans. Zemurray relied on this extensive backing to radically expand his operations along the Cuyamel River, eventually purchasing land abutting the biggest player—the United Fruit Company, a firm that dwarfed Zemurray's comparatively trifling concern.

Lee didn't think Bonilla was being paranoid; he could sense trouble himself. Policarpo was back in Congress, after grabbing the Copán seat, and was drawing the disaffected toward him, claiming Bonilla had abandoned the Liberals. If there was going to be another fight, Lee didn't want to miss it.

By the end of the year, Tegucigalpa was alive with rumors of revolution and invasion. Some were saying the coalition that had swept Manuel Bonilla into office on a wave of good feeling had evaporated. Others warned that Policarpo was just waiting for any kind of spurious pretext to launch a revolution. But everyone agreed that Nicaragua's President Zelaya was likely to be unhappy with a Honduran regime allied with Guatemala, and would be itching for trouble himself.

All the situation needed was a spark, but Bonilla was watching developments closely, snuffing out any trouble as it arose. One of the newspapers that had backed his original candidacy, *Diario de Honduras*—whose editor, José María Valladares, had fought alongside Bonilla to overturn the stolen election—suddenly turned against him. Bonilla summoned Valladares to the Presidential Palace in an attempt to explain the gravity of the situation. But instead of reaching an understanding, they quarreled. Valladares stormed out of Bonilla's office, pledging to run his paper as he saw fit.

Bonilla couldn't take any chances. On the final day of 1903, the president sent his *gringo* police chief to shut the newspaper down. Valladares was enraged, complaining of heavy-handed treatment at the hands of Lee and twenty of his officers, and fled to join Policarpo's disaffected mob. Then came the spark.

In the tobacco-growing region of western Honduras, the townsfolk of Santa Bárbara had gathered for a *fiesta*. A Liberal politician's daughter was getting married, which demanded a giant celebration. Even those without political inclinations turned up to pay their respects to the newlyweds; no one with any sense would turn down the opportunity to feast and drink at the expense of the region's biggest landowner.

With the band playing and the *aguardiente* flowing, the crowd was in high spirits, until a brawl ended the night early. One prominent Liberal had made a throwaway remark, quoting from an imported copy of Nietzsche, which he'd hoped would illustrate his educated but fatalistic outlook. Another local tyro, suspecting he'd merely scanned the text looking for something quotable, disagreed with his interpretation and refused to let it slide. The first stammered, surprised at the challenge to what he had thought was a clever quip. His interlocutor smiled, basking in the glow of his obscure knowledge, happy he'd given a metaphorical black eye to a rival, besting him in the arena of ideas.

Until his rival gave him a real black eye.

Both men were popular, with their own teams of supporters, and groups of revelers soon joined in on either side of the grievance. Such was the scale and ferocity of the brawl, the federal police had to be deployed to restore order. When the hotheads were detained and the debris cleared, two bodies were discovered—the pair at the genesis of the dispute. Both badly beaten. Both dead. Both also happened to be from Policarpo Bonilla's wing of the party. His speech in Congress the following week scandalized the nation. Policarpo bitterly alleged that both men had been assassinated on political grounds, charges that were seconded by his associate, Dr. Navarro. Soon, the accusations swept around Tegucigalpa.

Lee, infuriated by such baseless crap circulating as truth, encountered Dr. Navarro later that afternoon. He unloaded a foul-mouthed tirade, leaving Navarro in no doubt as to what he thought of the pair and what he would do if they made any such accusations in the future.

At the next sitting of Congress, Dr. Navarro rose and denounced "*el yanqui*, Lee Christmas," detailing the threats of physical violence that had been made against him—a Congressman, no less—by the president's chief henchman. Congress was in uproar, and voted to remain in permanent session until they got to the bottom of the matter. As soon as the vote was carried, however, something unprecedented occurred. The door to the chamber burst open, and in charged the subject of their outrage.

Lee Christmas, with a group of armed policemen at his heels, pointed to Policarpo and eight of his cronies, and had them hauled from their seats. Policarpo stood firm, calling him a "*yanqui* dog."

They were fighting words, and only the intervention of a bystander prevented Lee from shooting Policarpo on the spot. Instead, he lunged toward him and struck him several times. The nine politicians were sent to jail in shackles.

Policarpo had his just cause. Revolution was only a matter of time.

34

It wasn't just a display of hotheadedness on Lee's part. Bonilla had been gathering evidence against Policarpo for months, and it had been agreed they shouldn't let the president's opposition get up a head of steam and flout Bonilla's authority; doing so would only increase the numbers flocking to Policarpo's banner. A show of strength was needed, and planned; Policarpo's provocations merely accelerated matters. Details of the plot to overthrow Manuel Bonilla's government were announced by the federal police, and the disaffected Liberal was charged with sedition and treason.

Bonilla was determined to stop the revolution in its tracks; after all, power had been snatched from him once before. He suspended the Constitution. Dissolved Congress. He even declared martial law, which allowed him to try Policarpo and his gang of plotters before a military tribunal instead of in a civil court.

They received ten years apiece. While his cronies were pardoned within months, after spilling details about Nicaragua's backing, Policarpo remained behind bars and suffered the seizure of his estates. Meanwhile, a convention of technocrats rewrote the Constitution. The term of the presidency increased from four years to six, with Bonilla's new six-year term as president to commence from that date, greatly extending the period before an election. He needed time to strengthen his position.

On February 25, 1904, Lee arrived at the Presidential Palace to farewell Manuel Bonilla. Feeling secure at last, Bonilla had finally acceded to his *gringo* general's request and appointed him *comandante* of Puerto Cortés.

"You know what day it is today?" the President said, as he greeted Lee warmly in his private chambers.

"Sure," said Lee.

Bonilla raised an eyebrow.

"The day I finally head off to the woman I've been dreaming of all this time."

Bonilla smiled. "This day is special for another reason." He clapped his hands, and a servant appeared, bearing a gold-handed sword. "Two years ago today," Manuel continued, "you showed extreme ingenuity in taking out the Asbury mountain cannon that blocked our path to Tegucigalpa."

"I remember it well."

Bonilla held the sheathed sword aloft before handing it to Lee. "A remembrance of that day."

Lee took the sword and drew it from the sheath. He squinted down the point, admiring its fine craftsmanship.

"It comforts me greatly knowing that I can call on your sword in times of need." Bonilla placed a hand on his shoulder.

"You're damn right," said Lee. He was about to say his goodbyes, when he remembered something. "Hey, what's all this about a territorial dispute with Nicaragua?"

"Policarpo was only a tool." Bonilla's face clouded over. "There'll be others, especially now we know for sure that Nicaragua is plotting against me. But if I can get President Zelaya to strike before he's ready, we'll have the advantage."

"How do you plan to do that?"

"The territory under dispute … Zelaya acted too fast. He's already parceled up the land and granted numerous concessions. The Americans don't want war between us. They'll arbitrate, and our lawyers are sure they will find in our favor. Zelaya will suffer greatly when the land is returned. Politically and personally."

Lee frowned. "And what if he's ready for a fight before the Americans get involved?"

Lee packed his possessions onto a pair of mules and mounted his great white mare. Once the newspapermen had their quotes, and the photographers finally pronounced themselves satisfied, he kicked his mount into action and began driving his one-man convoy across the mountains to San Pedro Sula. Bonilla had tried to insist on an honor guard, but Lee wouldn't hear of it.

"They'll only slow me down," Lee had said. Truth was, he wanted some time alone to decide how he was going to approach the situation with Adelaide Caruso. He had been a free man since the Talbot family had consented to the divorce, but Adelaide had parents of her own.

And a mind of her own, too, he reminded himself. She was truly a free spirit, unbound by the expectations or conventions of society. It had been many months since they had spent any real time together. After so long, the impression he made had to be a good one.

Prodding the mule in front of him onwards, he reached back and grabbed the halter of the other, pulling the beast alongside his mare. He checked the straps on the saddlebags, ensuring they were tight; he didn't want that box from Paris wriggling loose.

With his mind at rest, he considered the position that awaited him. Power and money were within his grasp. Adelaide could finally be his too—if he played his cards right. Yet he couldn't shake the nagging feeling that this trouble with Nicaragua was just the beginning. That feeling shadowed him for the weeklong journey to San Pedro. He arrived saddle sore but happy, glad he wasn't loafing it this time in those damn *caites*. His journey down to the coast was less arduous; Lee took a childlike glee in watching the world whizz by from his vantage point—an empty boxcar in a banana train on its way to the ocean.

Lee entered the *cuartel* of Puerto Cortés, changed out of his dusty traveling clothes, and washed. He carefully unpacked the parcel from Paris, admiring the ostentatious gold-braided dress uniform he'd ordered. It fit perfectly. With his new sword of honor on his side, General Lee Christmas strode along the railroad track in his new custom-made leather boots, down Calle de Linea, by the Hotel Lefevbre, and right to the door of Adelaide Caruso, the blonde Italian who'd captured his heart.

35

Lee had faced many impediments in his pursuit of Adelaide. But after finally obtaining a divorce and a transfer back to the coast—dealing with the small matter of a revolution in the meantime—he could have been forgiven for thinking the path to consummating the relationship was now clear. Of course, he hadn't reckoned on the determined opposition of the Caruso family. All the trappings of success—wealth, power, prestige—did little to dissuade them. They pointed to his spotty record of honoring the marital vows, his renown as a playboy, and his two previous marriages, both of which had only lasted long enough to produce offspring before Lee was off chasing someone new.

He was on his best behavior, courting the family as much as Adelaide, making sure any rendezvous with his beloved was chaste, public, and chaperoned. There were several handcars at the *cuartel*—strictly for military use—but Lee requisitioned them for something a little more personal. They must have made a curious sight: the happy couple up front being propelled by the sweat of dutiful soldiers at the hand-pump, and the army band squashed onto a trailing car to serenade the *gringo* general and the target of his affections.

It took some time before Lee realized he'd never win

over Adelaide's folks. The only road open to him was to take matters into his own hands—to elope, as he had with Mamie, and to present their nuptials to Adelaide's parents as a *fait d'accompli*. It took some time to convince her this was the correct course, but she eventually assented. Stealing Adelaide away from her watchful, wary parents was no easy task, even for a man of Lee's means and ingenuity. So once again, a train was employed to spirit away his betrothed.

The following Sunday, with the help of an engineer, Lee rigged up a silencer on the stack of his old toy train. Together, they slipped out of the siding at Laguna Trestle and headed toward Puerto Cortés. The track bearing the pair ran straight down the Calle de Linea, right past the Caruso house. He nodded to the engineer, who eased up on the throttle as they approached. Waving his glowing *puro*—a pre-agreed signal with his betrothed—he spotted her at the window. Adelaide slipped outside and was hoisted aboard, and the toy train trundled away from her house, down to the banana wharf where Lee Christmas had first arrived some ten years before.

A little sailboat packed with provisions awaited them. The two clambered aboard, greeting the captain and his crew of two, and then settled down under a blanket, gazing out at the starless night. "You still want to do this?" Lee asked, his eyes dancing.

"Well—"

"Because it's too late now!" He nodded, and the captain pushed off. Their sail caught a strong offshore breeze and powered away from the coast, buffeted north by a swirling gust.

When the couple woke the next morning, their hands

still interlocked under the blanket, the sea hadn't calmed one bit. Sails snapped as the wind assaulted the boat from alternating directions.

Adelaide eyed the structure with concern. "How long did you say this might take?"

"Belize is maybe … two days, give or take."

Her eyes narrowed, and Lee put an arm around her. "Don't worry so much," he soothed. "She's perfectly seaworthy."

"What about that?" She pointed at dark clouds gathering to the northeast.

"We're fine." Lee's eyes darted to the captain, who shook his head and surreptitiously pointed east, where the Guatemalan coast had fallen out of view. "But if it gets too close," Lee continued, "We'll just pull in somewhere until it rolls over."

She raised an eyebrow.

"No big deal," he said.

Thirty minutes later, they beached at speed at Punta Gorda, the bump eliciting a yelp from Adelaide.

"That's normal," said Lee, squeezing her hand. "Don't worry."

Adelaide peered down at the waves lapping the side of the vessel. Seeing her trepidation, Lee stood, his sudden movements rocking the deck. When it had steadied somewhat, he clambered over the rail and dropped himself into the drink. It was only shin-deep.

She laughed as he beckoned her into the water. "But what about my dress?"

"At your service, ma'am."

As she climbed over the side and into Lee's waiting arms, the heavens opened—big, fat drops of rain that seemed to leap upward from the ocean. She let out a yelp.

"Quick," he said. "Sit down on the edge of the deck and I'll grab you." Once she was in position, he picked her up and flipped her over his back like a sack of potatoes, wading through the water until he reached the beach.

"Put me down, *idiota*."

"I dunno," he said. "I kind of like this. Less chance of you running off on me."

She punched him playfully in the back, and then Lee set her down gently on the sand, waiting as she fixed her dress. He pointed at the tree line. "Take shelter," he said. "But don't go too far."

"What about all our things?"

"Don't you worry. Just get yourself out of the rain before you get soaked." He waded back out to the boat, where the captain and his crew were securing the main sail. "Throw me that tarpaulin," he said. "Some rope too."

After finding a relatively sheltered spot, he began hacking away at the undergrowth with his machete, clearing space so he could erect a makeshift tent.

"Anything I can do?" called Adelaide.

He looked back over his shoulder. "Should be a bottle of something in one of the boxes the captain dropped off. Open her up!"

"Sure thing," she laughed.

Through the driving rain, he fashioned a shelter of sorts from the boat's tarpaulin; their little group waiting for the storm to ease. It took the bones of a day, but eventually the sea calmed enough for them to set sail once more. The crew reloaded the boat while Adelaide and Lee walked hand in hand along the beach, admiring the setting sun.

"You ready?" asked Adelaide, when the captain called over to the pair.

Lee pulled her close to him, planting a kiss on her lips. He pulled back, still holding her face and brushed a stray grain of sand from her check. "Now I'm ready," he said.

He waded through the water, Adelaide in his arms, and then set her down on the boat. Lee awkwardly clambered on deck and saluted the captain. "To Belize, my good man."

Blessed with calmer seas all the way north, they reached the city of Belize the following night, Adelaide delighting in how a single fiery dot in the distance gradually unraveled into a blanket of twinkling lights that rivaled the stars above. The next day, in front of a British magistrate, they were married.

Lee and Adelaide returned to Puerto Cortés after a month-long honeymoon. The Caruso family was furious, disowning their daughter and only relenting the following year, 1906, when Lee Christmas Junior was born.

36

As soon as Lee entered the *cantina*, the buzzing chatter ceased. Heads slowly turned in his direction before conversation resumed at a lower level. He understood their frustration; war was on everyone's lips. Catching the bartender's eye, he ordered a whiskey cocktail—a large shot of whiskey topped up with champagne and a slice of lime—and left a hefty tip. He turned and scanned the room, sipping his drink.

"They're worried," said the bartender. "Should they be?"

Lee turned to face him. "Peace conference is in Costa Rica next week. We hope to amicably resolve all outstanding issues."

"That the party line?"

"Yup." He took another swig. "But they're gonna pull out. It's their only move. Now that the court of arbitration has decided in our favor, Zelaya's bound to declare war." He drained his glass. "Bonilla's backed him into a corner."

"But they got Policarpo?"

Lee nodded. "He's back in jail." He signaled for another drink. "Never should have let him out in the first place, if you ask me."

"Why did they?"

He waved a paw. "Politics. I'll never understand it. El Salvador said they'd keep an eye on him." He shrugged. "Guess we can't say too much on that front, not after the Valladares mess."

"Have you heard anything about that?"

Lee spread his hands. "Nobody knows what happened."

The bartender raised an eyebrow.

"I'm serious." Lee pointed at the cabinet. "Hand me a couple of them glasses." He arranged them on the counter before pointing to his own drink. "This here is Valladares and that damn rebel army he raised right under our noses."

He placed a napkin a few inches to the left, putting a glass on either side. "Now here's the Honduran–Guatemalan border, with an army on either side."

Lee waggled the third glass, his drink. "Now, our spy has just shopped Policarpo, but before he gets scooped up by the Salvadorans again, he gets word out to Valladares that they've been rumbled." He moved his glass closer to the napkin. "So Valladares races to the Nicaraguan border, now that the army coming from El Salvador isn't rebels looking to combine forces but a hostile army—allied to us—with our guys hot on their tails too. And they run into two trigger-happy armies just waiting for…"

He looked up to find that the bartender's eyes had glazed over. "You following?"

"Not really." The bartender laughed.

Exasperated, Lee pulled the pistol from his belt and laid it on the counter. "Let me put it another way. Pretend it's the end of the night, you're here alone, cleaning up, and I stroll in and pull a gun on you, demanding your takings. But then I get distracted by a noise in the street, and you draw your own piece from under the bar and we have a stand-off."

The bartender nodded.

"Let's say this goes on for a while. Both men watching each other. Both getting jittery. And neither backing down. It's tense as hell. Both of 'em afraid to blink in case the other guy squeezes the trigger. Got it? Now imagine a third guy—a stranger to both—runs in the side door with his own weapon drawn. Who shoots first?"

"Everyone," said the bartender.

Lee grimaced. "Exactly."

37

As feared, President Zelaya ordered a nationwide conscription program. Within a few months, Nicaragua had twelve thousand troops within striking distance of the Honduran border. The following month, Zelaya gave the command to invade.

Bonilla sent two armies into the field. General Ordóñez was sent east to check the Nicaraguan advance, and Bonilla's minister of war, General Barahona, was sent south with the newly graduated cadets to form a reserve in front of Tegucigalpa. Nothing was needed to defend the Caribbean coast, as the US Navy had stationed bluejackets in Puerto Cortés, La Ceiba, and Trujillo on the pretext of defending the large foreign populations there. Lee Christmas was telegrammed and ordered to delegate his *comandancia*, come to the position south of Tegucigalpa, and join General Barahona as his right-hand man.

The Honduran army under General Ordóñez was defeated in its very first battle, and the Nicaraguan invaders captured the town of San Marco, along with two hundred rifles, ten thousand rounds of ammunition, and a Krupp gun. Bonilla decided to don his old military uniform and take to the field himself. In mid-March his fifteen hundred-strong force joined up with three thousand troops arriving over the border from El Salvador and together they pressed on to engage the invaders at Namasigüe—a town that would become synonymous with one of the bloodiest battles in human history.

With the fall of the northern ports, Zelaya threw every possible reserve toward Namasigüe, hoping to shatter Bonilla's army in one fell swoop. His troops didn't simply outnumber their counterparts; they were also armed with the Krupp cannons and Hotchkiss guns, as well as the latest in rapid-firing armaments—the deadly Maxim machine gun making its first appearance in Central American warfare. Unlike the old Gatling guns, the Maxim didn't have to be hand-cranked and could unleash a vicious, continual burst with the trigger depressed. And those bullets could cut right through an eighteen-inch tree trunk.

Bonilla's men were encamped in the hills overlooking Namasigüe. From mid-afternoon on March 17, Zelaya's army began a relentless barrage of their position. The shelling continued until midnight, resuming again at first light. Knowing they couldn't remain in the hills to be picked off by the enemy's superior artillery, Bonilla's army attacked the Nicaraguans head-on, charging straight into a hail of machine-gun fire that crisscrossed the plain in front of the town. Thousands of Bonilla's men were butchered on the spot, mercilessly cut to pieces by the continuous spray of intersecting bullets from the deadly Maxim guns. Almost his entire army was slaughtered over the next three days. Never in human history had such a high proportion of an army been destroyed in a single battle.

A fever spared Bonilla's life; the president had been left behind in a native's hut to recover, missing the entire debacle. This stroke of good fortune allowed him to escape to Tigre Island, where he gathered five hundred surviving supporters. Soon, though, this fortress came under siege. Keen to prevent another slaughter, Bonilla agreed to surrender, on the condition that he lay down his arms to a Honduran general rather than the despised Nicaraguans. President Zelaya agreed and dispatched Bonilla's old enemy, Terencio Sierra, to oversee Bonilla's disgrace. As part of the peace deal, Bonilla boarded the USS *Chicago* to Guatemala, where he was permitted to travel overland and take sanctuary in the British colony of Belize.

38

When he received President Bonilla's telegram, Lee packed Adelaide and Lee Junior aboard a steamer. With his family safely on the way to Puerto Barrios, over the Guatemalan border, he took his old toy train up to San Pedro Sula. There, he switched to horseback and raced across the country, all the way to Maraita, just south of the capital. His orders were simple. The men under General Barahona—Bonilla's minster for war and the *de facto* head of the armed forces—were the last line of defense before the seat of government at Tegucigalpa. Lee's job was to inform them that reinforcements were en route from El Salvador, and that Barahona must hold his ground.

By the time Lee arrived, the invaders had captured the heights of the Los Coyotes mountain range. Barahona had entrenched, and his position was easily defendable. For three days, a stalemate ensued. "I haven't been able to draw them out," Barahona told him.

Lee pursed his lips. "Sounds like they're waiting for something," he said. "Probably the same thing we're waiting for."

"Let's just pray our reinforcements arrive first, because there's no way we can retreat now, not in any orderly way."

Barahona's prayers went unanswered; the following day, scouts brought news of approaching Nicaraguans. Barahona soon realized his position was hopeless. Without experienced reinforcements, all he had at his disposal were cadets fresh out of the academy, most of them between the ages of fourteen and sixteen. One decisive charge from the enemy would likely end the matter; Barahona suspected most of the boys would bolt. He convened his officers to discuss the possibility of surrender.

Before the meeting, Lee went to speak to Fred Mills, a fellow American who had abandoned his mining concern days beforehand, bringing twenty of his native workers along for the adventure.

"Fred, this game ain't for you. We're in a tight spot."

"Aw, I'll be all right, Lee."

"I'm serious." He put a hand on Fred's shoulder. "This could get bad."

"You know what?" Fred grinned. "I was so bored up at that mine, I used to pray someone would take a shot at me."

Lee shook his head. "Don't say I didn't warn you." He looked over at the command tent where the other officers were beginning to gather. "Come on, Fred."

They entered the tent together, smiling, in contrast to the grim-faced Hondurans. General Barahona nodded at them and began. "*Amigos*, it looks like the reinforcements aren't coming. Our line of retreat to Tegucigalpa has been cut off. The enemy surrounds us on all sides. In short, our position is hopeless. I suggest we try to negotiate the best surrender we can, but I'm open to ideas." Barahona spread his hands.

"Please speak freely."

There was a moment of silence before Lee stepped forward, his right leg tapping. All eyes were on the *yanqui* general as he spoke. "I don't know about the rest of you." He smiled. "But I know what will happen if those bastards get their hands on me. After all, I arrested that damn Policarpo, right there in Congress. Slugged him too."

The men laughed as he continued. "And that general, Valladares, I closed down his print shop. That cost him a pretty penny. They ain't going to do nothing but shoot me for a lesson." He paused, looking at each of his fellow officers in turn. "And if I'm going to be shot, I want to take some of those sons of bitches with me."

Barahona turned to him. "You mean to break through their lines?"

"You're damn right," he said. "And you would be wise to come with me, too. Weren't you part of the court that sentenced Policarpo? That bastard won't have forgotten."

"A scattered charge might just work." Barahona rubbed his chin. "Some of us could get through. It's a roll of the dice."

"I've got eight bullets but the last is for me—in case they catch me. I'll never let anyone drag me out in front of a mob and make a show out of it."

Barahona pulled his shoulders back. "I'll ride with you."

"And I!" Colonel Reyes, Barahona's third in command, stepped forward.

"Well," Fred Mills put his hand in the air. "If you're all going, I'm coming too."

Lee shook his head. "Not you, Fred."

"Like hell!" said Fred. "Try and stop me, you big oaf." Laughter filled the tent.

The plan was set. At dawn, the four men would face an entire army. The rest of Bonilla's men were to wait in reserve, and Barahona made it clear to them that they were to decide their own fate. They could choose to surrender, they could melt into the surrounding countryside, or they could defend their position from attack.

He reminded them that living to fight another day was just as patriotic as a brave and glorious death.

39

Just as the sky began to brighten, Lee mounted his gray horse. He grimaced when he saw Barahona and Reyes had chosen a pair of mules; then he watched as a troupe of Indians helped Fred into the saddle of his white mare. Fred shrugged. "They insist on coming with me."

Lee shook his head and drew his Luger from his belt, checking the magazine. *Seven bullets and one in the chamber.* He looked to his friend. "Last chance, Fred."

"You kidding?" Fred smiled. "I wouldn't miss this for the world."

Lee gathered his reins in his left hand. "Good luck, boys. See you on the other side." He wheeled his mount around while Barahona kicked his heels in and charged ahead, his *tiente* Reyes in his wake. Lee snorted at the comical sight of two officers on mule-back attempting to outrun an army, before winking at Fred and racing after them.

The Luger was gripped tight in his right hand as he galloped, one eye on the distant, telltale puffs of smoke—rifles firing in his direction. Bullets whizzed all around him. The enemy charged down toward them, filling the slope. He checked his pace a touch, keen not to overtake the two Honduran officers in front of him, and then looked back over his shoulder. Fred was some distance off. Lee clenched his jaw. It appeared Fred didn't want to outpace his Indian companions. *That'll get him killed*, he thought.

Lee watched Reyes, now in the lead, hit the ground—both he and his mount shot dead. After letting off a couple of rounds, Lee looked back to see Fred's horse go down, its rider thrown clear. When Barahona went down next, Lee jerked on his reins, banking sharply, looking back to see if the general had been struck or whether his mount had taken the bullet. The general's chest was crimson with blood.

Still got three bullets. He'd been counting carefully, desperate to save one for himself and die by his own hand rather than face capture. Adelaide and Lee Junior would be spared the indignity of him being executed like a common criminal on some trumped-up charges. He kicked on, letting his mount out into a full gallop, only to feel something slam into his left calf. His horse whinnied and reared before collapsing in a heap on top of him, pinning his one remaining good leg.

Trapped, hopelessly contorted, and screaming in pain, Lee could do little as the enemy sped toward him. His eyes watering, he wriggled into a firing position and took aim at the leading charger, shooting him from the saddle. Then the next. But there was simply too many. As the pack drew closer, whooping and hollering, Lee said a silent goodbye to Adelaide and Lee Junior, and to Magdalena and their two daughters, Leah and Juanita, and then lastly to his first love, Mamie, and their three offspring—Ed, Hattie, and Sadie—cursing himself for not fulfilling his promise to do right by them. Lee raised the Luger to his temple, its muzzle still hot. With his eyes closed, his finger curled around the trigger.

He squeezed.

Nothing happened.

Lee examined his gun, staring in shock at the open magazine. In all the excitement, he must have counted wrong. *Damn it.*

He winced from the pain of his shattered leg as the enemy swarmed around him. A soldier lunged, bayonet fixed, but in his inexperience chose Lee's head as the target rather than his body. Instinctively, Lee rolled to the side, and the blade merely grazed him.

"Not the head, *puta*!" A bayonet thrust to the head would prolong Lee's agony, not end it. A fatal blow must aim for the breast, like that shotgun volley Dr. Waller had saved him from ten years beforehand. But before the second thrust could be delivered, a Nicaraguan officer appeared and stayed his subordinate's hand.

"*Bastardos!*" Lee was apoplectic. "Chickenshit sons of bitches. *Hijo de putas.* Finish me off. Shoot me!" He hoped to provoke them; Lee knew a soldier with a cooler head might seek his capture. A general was worth a lot more alive. "Shoot me, goddamn you!"

"Oh, you will be shot, General, *sin duda.*" The officer smiled. "But it will be a formal execution."

"Shoot me now, if you have the guts. But do me one favor." Lee paused. "Don't bury me."

The officer raised an eyebrow. "Don't bury you?"

A small crowd had gathered around the stricken *gringo* general. "No," Lee continued. "Don't bury me, you sons of bitches!"

"Why not?"

This was what he'd been waiting for. He glared at the enemy officer. "Because I want the buzzards to eat me, fly over you afterwards, and shit on your goddamn faces." Lee shut his eyes, bracing himself for the mortal blow.

The officer laughed. "You're a brave man. Maybe we won't execute you after all."

Lee blinked his eyes open in confusion, then grinned. The enemy soldiers smiled back. They removed Lee's fallen horse and tended to his wounds. To his surprise, he found Barahona wasn't dead after all—although badly wounded. The two generals were carried to a hut, and Lee's shattered leg was bound in a splint.

Barahona didn't make it through the night, but Lee was carried in a litter as the invaders marched on the capital.

40

Lee sat up in bed, mustering enough strength to tuck into a plate of oranges. He ripped the flesh from the skin and popped a piece in his mouth, not bothering to wipe the orange drool that dripped from his chin onto the bedsheets. His appetite was back, and the oranges were a hell of a lot better than the soup he'd been on. His leg had healed pretty well, too, considering. He would have a nasty scar, but he was going to walk just fine once he built his strength back up. A knock sounded on the door. Dr. Waller entered just as Lee wiped the juice from his chin and gathered the scattered rinds.

The doctor waved a hand. "Don't mind that. It's good to see you sitting up." He took the bowl from Lee's lap and set it down on the bedside table, dropped into a chair, and sighed. "I have some news."

"Fred?"

Dr. Waller nodded. "He's dead, Lee. I'm sorry. He didn't get away as you'd hoped." The doctor paused. "But there's more—"

"How did he die?"

"What I was going to tell you was—"

"How did Fred die, doc?"

"All right." Dr. Waller took a breath. "Way I heard was

Fred got thrown clear during the charge. I don't know if his horse bucked, hit a rock, or was shot. But he was thrown clear. The Nicaraguans caught up to him."

Lee punched the pillow. "Told him not to come, but he wouldn't listen."

"Seems like all he had to do was surrender," said the doctor. "Put his hands in the air, or just stay there on the ground. But he got excited and made a run for it."

"Goddamn it, Fred."

"Some Honduran rebel—"

"Who?" demanded Lee.

Dr. Waller shushed him. "I'll get to that. Anyway, this officer cocked his pistol and was about to shoot when Fred tripped." He paused before continuing. "Then he walked up and shot him right between the eyes."

Lee threw off the blanket and swung his legs over the other side of the bed. "I need a name, doc."

Dr. Waller didn't make a move, watching Lee sweat and curse as he struggled to put any weight on his leg.

Lee slumped back onto the mattress. "I still need that name."

"Rosa," said the doctor. "But you're too late."

"Huh?"

Dr. Waller tucked the blanket back over Lee's legs. "*Comandante* Rosa might have thought the matter settled when he put that bullet in Fred Mills, but his Indian companions were watching from the trees. Rosa returned to his general store in Tegucigalpa. I guess business was booming, given all those furloughed troops knocking around the capital."

"I'd never seen it so busy," said Lee.

"Anyway," he said, scratching his nose. "One day, some Indian came in looking for a weapon." He looked at Lee. "A thirty-eight caliber revolver, to be exact. The Indian asked permission to examine the gun, and Rosa took it out of the glass case and slid it across the counter to him, safe in the knowledge that it wasn't loaded. Pretending to examine the pistol, the Indian waited until Rosa was distracted by another customer, someone asking about a bulk order, and then slipped a bullet into the chamber. When Rosa returned, he raised the gun and shot him square in the chest." The doctor smiled. "Then melted away."

Lee looked down at his hands.

"It's not your fault," said Dr. Waller. "Fred made his own decisions. And his death has been avenged."

"I know."

"You should count yourself lucky the American consul intervened and got you safe passage out of here."

Lee sighed. "I know."

The doctor waited for a moment. "Remember the first time I treated you?"

"The poisoning?"

Dr. Waller laughed. "All right. The second time."

"Shit," said Lee. "That was a close one."

"I was scared. Thought you wouldn't make it."

"You were scared?"

"I saw a lot of men die in the war."

"Back home?"

The doctor nodded. "Most didn't have wounds as bad as yours." He gestured to Lee's leg. "You were lucky this time too."

"Don't I know it." He remembered the panicked recruit trying to bayonet him in the face. "I'm just looking forward to getting back on the road. Not that I'm ungrateful…" He chuckled at the doctor's mock offense.

"I'm sure you're anxious to get back to Adelaide and Lee Junior. Where are they now?"

"Guatemala City. Shipped them out as soon as this all started."

"Wise."

"Soon as I'm able, I'll head down to Puerto Cortés and take the first steamer north."

"That should be in a few days, the rate you're recuperating." Dr. Waller noticed his patient's eyelids growing heavy. "You're tired." He stood. "I should let you rest."

Lee began to speak, but the doctor waved away his protests. "One last thing, because I've a house call to make, and it'll be late when I get back." He smiled at Lee. "You're gonna like this. Give me a minute." He excused himself from the room but returned a moment later brandishing a newspaper, and a huge grin. "Picked this up in San Pedro this morning." He handed Lee a copy of the *New York Times.*

"I didn't know they got this in San Pedro."

"Depends what's in the news," said the doctor, eyes twinkling.

Lee began paging through the paper, but Dr. Waller grabbed it off him and flipped it back to the front page. "Read the damn headline!"

He focused on the block capitals at the top of the page. "*Christmas Slain In Battle: Daredevil American Cut to Pieces by Nicaraguan Soldiers.*" Lee chuckled, and handed it back. "Keep that for me, would you?"

41

Adelaide became pregnant again not long after the family reunited in Guatemala City. In January 1910, she gave birth to another boy, this one christened Winfield, for Lee's late father. She was nursing Winfield in the kitchen when Lee surprised her by coming home early. "I have some news," he boomed, as he entered the room. "Remember those new Shea locomotives I was talking about?"

Adelaide rolled her eyes. "How could I forget?"

"Yeah." Lee smiled. "I did go on a little. But here's the thing. The government went ahead with the purchase."

"Okay."

"Means more routes to those coffee plantations."

She gazed at him with a blank expression.

"Which means they'll need more engineers." He paused. "Better money, is what I'm saying."

"Well, that's something."

"And I won't have to work the passenger service anymore."

"You certain you'll get it?"

"That's the other news," said Lee with a smile. "New connection will make sure of it."

"I don't understand."

"Remember the … *other* job I told you about? The one I had the last time I was here?"

"Oh, yes. The reports for—"

"Yeah, those guys. They want me back."

Her brow furrowed. "Will it be dangerous?"

Lee chuckled. "Shouldn't be."

Adelaide's brow creased with worry.

"It'll involve a little travel."

"Oh?" She shifted Winfield's position and wiped some sick from his mouth.

"Just to Honduras and Nicaragua, far as I know."

"Nicaragua?"

"Only meeting contacts. Nothing to worry about."

She arched an eyebrow. "And this isn't dangerous?"

"I swear," he said. "No more dangerous than being at the throttle of a locomotive."

"You've already crashed one of those."

Lee's new role came at a crucial time. Discord was spreading in Nicaragua and Honduras, one faction seeking to overthrow another, and Guatemala's President wanted to make sure friendly regimes won the day in both countries. Manuel Bonilla was still exiled in Belize, but he corresponded regularly with his *gringo* general. When a fresh revolution broke out in Honduras, he stayed Lee's hand, arguing that any such revolt was doomed to fail without financial backing.

By the time Winfield was born, Bonilla had found his backer.

42

Sam Zemurray came from poor Jewish farming stock on the banks of the Dnieper River, in what used to be called Bessarabia back when he was known as Schmuel Zmurri. He came to America with his aunt at the age of fifteen, just two years before Lee Christmas fell asleep at the throttle and ran straight into an oncoming train. His uncle was already there, running a general store in Selma, Alabama, and enterprising young Sam worked every job he could get. Within three years he had saved enough to send for the rest of his family.

Wandering around Selma one day, Sam had stumbled across a man making a tidy profit from selling bananas to a grocer. Following the man's tip, he headed down to the docks at Mobile and spent all the money he had on ripes—one-hundred-and-fifty dollars' worth—from one of the United Fruit Company's steamers. Lacking his own fare, Sam bedded down with the cargo on the night express to Selma. Ripes were much cheaper than green bananas, but they had to be sold quickly before they spoiled. Sam fretted the entire journey, worrying the bananas would rot before they could be sold, leaving him substantially out of pocket.

Shortly after five in the morning, the train pulled in at Meridian and Sam woke to see he was still one hundred miles shy of his destination. After what seemed an inordinate delay, he complained to the yardmaster about his rapidly spoiling fruit.

The yardmaster sympathized. "If only you had some way of notifying the grocers in towns ahead." He let out a low whistle. "They'd likely buy the bananas right off the car."

Sam stood. "Is there a Western Union here?"

"Sure, right over—"

Sam cut him off by shoving a bunch of bananas into his arms. "Don't let this train leave without me." He ran to the office and wired every telegraph operator along the line to Selma, promising a free bunch to any who spread the word: fresh bananas were coming. By the time he sold his last bunch in Selma, Sam had five hundred dollars in his pocket—more than tripling his investment.

Sam plunged headlong into the banana trade, first hawking ripes all along the line from Selma down to the Gulf Coast, before tirelessly expanding into more distant territories. By 1898, not long after Lee Christmas had abandoned New Orleans for Puerto Cortés, Sam had salted away one hundred thousand dollars. All before his twenty-first birthday.

In 1905, Sam decided to head to Puerto Cortés to see what kind of operation would be required to grow his own bananas—just like the United Fruit Company. It took five more years before his business was stable enough to make such a huge investment. Sam borrowed two hundred thousand dollars and purchased five thousand acres along the banks of the Cuyamel River, twenty miles upstream from Puerto Cortés and just shy of the Guatemalan border.

Sam had gone from running a small but profitable

business to owning a huge concern that left him heavily in debt. He quickly realized that to compete with the other banana growers he would need similar concessions from the government: tax breaks, land subsidies, exemptions from customs duties on the equipment he would need to import, and, crucially, the right to build a railroad to ferry his bananas from the plantation to the wharf.

Disastrously, help was not forthcoming. The Honduran government—now led by Miguel Dávila after the ousting of Manuel Bonilla—was hostage to its creditors: European bankers who owned most of the country's debt. Dávila was attempting to refinance and was fishing for an American loan. JP Morgan was keen on taking that bet, but only on the condition their agents could take over the operation of Honduran customs houses and veto any government-supported commercial development.

Zemurray knew that meant his business would flourish or whither depending on the goodwill of JP Morgan—whose help he couldn't count on. Plus, it would likely cost him more than it was worth. He needed a friend in the Presidential Palace, someone opposed to the treaty, someone more favorable to foreign business.

Someone like Manuel Bonilla.

43

Lee Christmas watched the world go by from the window of the Puerto Barrio express. His last conversation with Adelaide hadn't gone well. She had been unhappy about Lee's frequent trips to Puerto Cortés over the past six months, but his hands were tied. His American citizenship made him the only one of Bonilla's men who could travel back-and-forth freely, and someone had to make sure that drunk Marín kept his part of the bargain. If Lee screwed up, without an armed force on the ground ready to join their coup at a moment's notice, the planned assault on Puerto Cortés was doomed.

Adelaide had really lost her cool when he told her he was heading down to Puerto Barrios and didn't know when he'd return. She didn't calm down when he explained that Bonilla now had his backer and had to move quickly. Instead, she seethed for a week, her anger not even dissipating enough to wish him a proper goodbye.

He replayed the conversation in his head, over and over, trying to figure out where it went off the rails. What could he have said differently? He moped all the way to Puerto Barrios, his mood so foul on arrival that he didn't feel any pull from his old haunts, instead hiding away in his hotel room, brooding. A couple of days after Lee arrived, he got the green light from Bonilla—a letter borne by a ship's captain who was to ferry him north to Belize, past Sapodilla Caye, and deliver him to the revolutionary headquarters at Glover's Reef.

He was preoccupied throughout the voyage, answering the captain's few attempts at small talk with a series of grunts. His mood only brightened when the captain woke him from his snoozing, pointing at Glover's Reef in the distance. Finally, Lee saw the full import of Zemurray's backing. He counted half a dozen boats at anchor, bobbing in the bay, filled to the brim with what he guessed was guns and ammo.

Most impressive was the *Emma*, an oyster lugger by the looks of it. The faded paint on the hull revealed she was out of Gulfport, Mississippi, which made Lee chuckle for no reason in particular. And from the modern-looking machine gun he spied on the deck, he figured she'd come in very handy indeed.

Manuel Bonilla was waiting to greet them when they finally hit dry land. He embraced Lee, planting a kiss on each cheek.

"Steady on," said Lee. "I haven't even had a drink yet."

"There'll be time for that," Bonilla said, "but not too much." He thanked the captain, who got the hint and disappeared toward the camp. Once the captain was out of earshot, Bonilla leaned in to Lee. "Date is set. July twenty-first."

"Good." Lee turned to take in the revolutionary flotilla once more. "So, Zemurray came through, then?"

"You can inspect everything tomorrow. But we got two of those new machine guns you requested."

He took in the view until Bonilla laid a hand on his

shoulder. "Can you win me back my country, General?"

Lee turned to face him, but before he could speak, Bonilla extended his hand. "Or, should I say, commander-in-chief."

Lee shook Bonilla's hand vigorously, but then stopped all of a sudden. "Wait. You said the twenty-first, right?"

Bonilla nodded.

"And what date is it today?"

"The nineteenth."

Lee glared at Bonilla. "Hell, why don't we just go tomorrow, while we're at it?"

The deposed Honduran leader raised a finger. "Because we're waiting for one more to join us. He is steaming toward Glover's Reef as we speak." His eyes twinkled. "And I think you'll find him useful."

44

A curious side effect of the outbreak of the Second Boer War was a huge increase in the demand for Missouri's mules, and Guy Molony was inexplicably fascinated with them. Only sixteen and already six-foot-six, his crouching gait and gangly limbs made him look as if he slept folded up in a box. Guy enjoyed making his way from the house of his Irish immigrant parents down to the docks of New Orleans, where he watched ship after ship fill with the recalcitrant beasts. *If I'm not careful,* he thought, *those damn mules will see more of the world than I will.*

Without informing his family, he obtained a job as caretaker to the beasts, tending to them during the long voyage across the Atlantic Ocean, all the way to war-torn South Africa. When the mules were unloaded at Port Elizabeth, Guy followed the last pair off. He had no real plan in mind, short of knowing that leaving the boat meant abandoning his pay and his ticket home. He didn't care. He was keen to see more of the country, now that he had come all this way. Soon, his lack of funds led him to the local recruiting office of the British Army, where he signed on to fight the Boer.

At the end of the war, he returned to New Orleans for

just long enough to see his family and enlist as a cavalryman in the US Army. When war broke out in the Philippines, Sergeant Molony was shipped out and learned how to operate the latest machine guns. By the time that war was done, the young sergeant could strip a machine gun down in the dark and put it back together without missing a beat, earning him the nickname "Machine Gun" Molony—a title he would truly earn in Central America.

He returned home from the Philippines by way of Tokyo, where he met a future brother-in-arms, Sam Dreben. Barely had Molony reacquainted himself with his family before his head was turned by Dreben's promise of action in Guatemala. Once Zelaya was ousted, Dreben had another gig lined up.

"There'll be a big show in Honduras next month," he said. "A kid like you who knows machine guns could go a long way."

"Who would we be working for?"

"Some hotshot called Lee Christmas—a Louisiana man. They're getting ready to knock off this Dávila. Want in?"

"Sure."

Dreben scribbled a message on a small piece of card and instructed Molony to take it to Greytown, a small port on the Caribbean coast of Nicaragua, about sixty miles south of Bluefields. When he reached the address and presented the card, Guy was given two hundred and fifty dollars worth of gold. He also received another card, this time with instructions to travel to an address in New Orleans. He recognized the place: Café Maspero on Decatur, in the French Quarter.

The mystery of it all amused him, and he was happy to

comply. At Café Maspero, which was frequented by the veterans of ten different wars, the regulars eyed him so much he thought there was going to be trouble. When the man he spoke to disappeared into the back, Guy was on guard, in case he was fetching a weapon. Instead, he received another hundred and fifty dollars in gold and a steamer ticket for Belize, with strict instructions that if anyone enquired, he was drumming hardware.

He met Manuel Bonilla the night he arrived in Belize. Despite his adventures in the Philippines and Nicaragua, the only phrases Guy had picked up were the inventive curses Spanish speakers were so fond of. The Honduran appeared to be asking him something about machine guns, so Guy took a chance. "*Sí*," he said, which seemed to satisfy Bonilla, whose only instructions were to keep quiet and not get drunk.

A week later, Guy was put aboard a sailboat. After sailing through the night, the crew stopped at a remote cay to collect conches for a lunchtime stew before continuing on to Glover's Reef. Guy was transferred to another vessel in the Zemurray-financed flotilla—a sloop called *Centinella*—and immediately bedded down for the night.

The following morning, as he shared a pineapple with a crewman, a tall, blond figure appeared at the side of the boat. *This must be Christmas*, he thought.

The man spoke in a low growl. "So you're the machine gun expert."

Guy nodded.

"We got two of 'em, brand new, and one of 'em won't work. Let's see what you can do."

The machine guns were the new, high-speed kind,

supposedly able to fire four hundred and fifty rounds a minute, but they must have been damaged during shipment. Molony spent the next few hours on the deck of the *Centinella*, stripping the gun down to its many components. Christmas checked his progress now and then, but Guy never even looked up. Eventually, he pieced the gun back together and set it up over the starboard rail for a test burst.

When he heard the noise, Christmas came running. "You got it working?" He slapped Guy on the back. "I'll be damned."

Guy allowed himself a smile. "She's down to about three hundred and fifty rounds per minute, but she's working."

"Good work, son."

Later that evening, July 20, Manuel Bonilla joined his little army and instantly ordered a hundred rifles and ten thousand rounds transferred to a little *goleta* and shipped to a detachment secreted in the bush outside Tela. When the wind picked up, the rest of the revolutionary flotilla cast anchor and headed south.

To Honduras.

45

The fleet reached Puerto Cortés two hours past midnight. Aboard the *Centenilla*, Bonilla ordered a messenger dispatched. Lee watched as he rowed toward the shore. "Now we wait," said Bonilla, joining him at the rail.

"I still think we should attack right away."

Bonilla sighed. "Then what was the point of all those trips to Puerto Cortés?"

"Pah," said Lee. "Marín and his boys would know to come running as soon as the shooting started."

"Lee, I trust your judgment but Marín has two hundred men under his command, and all of them should be armed now after that last shipment of rifles. This has taken months to organize. Months."

"As soon as the sun comes up, we've lost the best thing going for us." Lee looked straight at Bonilla. "The element of surprise."

"*Claro*," he said. "But while they're looking out at us, Marín will cut them to pieces from the rear."

"You hope."

Bonilla put a hand on his shoulder. "*We* hope. Now how about a game of cards? I need something to take my mind off this wait."

Lee wasn't done arguing, though. When Lee raised it the third time, Bonilla threw down his cards and walked to the prow. After a few minutes, he turned back and hollered. "*Vamos!*"

Lee raced to the front of the boat and peered out to where Bonilla was pointing. Sure enough, it was a *cayuco* bearing their messenger.

The messenger tossed up a rope and then climbed aboard. He saluted Bonilla as he unloaded an excited stream of Spanish, too fast for Lee to follow.

"Woah, there," said Lee. "What's going on?"

Bonilla's eyes flicked to Lee, his face drawn. "Marín was captured."

"What? How in God's name—"

He was quieted by Bonilla, who indicated for the messenger to continue. When he was done, Bonilla turned to Lee. "It seems Marín decided to start the revolution himself."

Lee cursed. "And the two hundred recruits?"

"No," said Bonilla. "I wasn't clear. Marín decided to start the revolution *solo*."

"Probably moon-eyed on *aguardiente*."

"He's already been executed."

"Shit."

"The papers," said Bonilla, rubbing his face. "Goddamn it! He had everything. Plans. Names. Dates."

The messenger burst in with another torrent of Spanish.

"He wasn't the only one executed," translated Bonilla. "Don't know how many, but they had all the names. We have to assume they're all dead."

Lee struggled to contain himself. "So let's attack now,

for God's sake."

"Don't you get it?" demanded Bonilla. "The whole plan is blown. The *cuartel* is on high alert. Soldiers have already been drafted in from San Pedro."

Lee cursed and strode off to the other end of the boat before he said something he might regret. He continued to cool his heels until Bonilla transferred over to the *Emma*.

The next morning, he saw how suicidal an attack on Puerto Cortés would now be. His binoculars revealed a town brimming with soldiers. Snipers on every rooftop. And streets barricaded, manned by what looked like machine gunners.

Lee was dismayed. It should have been so different. How had such a carefully calibrated plan fallen into such disarray? From Puerto Cortés, he'd intended to secure the northern coast, town by town, increasing his stores of men and ammunition with each conquest. With the lucrative customs houses under his control, he figured it would be only a matter of time before enough Bonilla supporters flocked to his standard that the whole country would fall. But none of that mattered if he couldn't take damn Puerto Cortés!

There is only one thing for it, Lee thought. *We need a new plan.*

46

As the wind picked up, the revolutionary fleet separated. The plan was to rendezvous the following night off the coast of Tela, twenty-five miles east of their target. Marín may have foolishly jumped the gun, but his bush army had more sense. Bonilla hoped they were still out of sight and awaiting orders. With their hidden reinforcements, they could still surprise the defenders of Puerto Cortés by storming the town from the interior, around the back of the defenses.

Lee watched the *Emma* and the *Britannic* slip out of view. His ship's captain was a bit slower to get going, only having a skeleton crew of one: his blind son. Lack of vision was no hindrance to the boy, who seemed to have memorized every square inch of the boat, moving around it so efficiently that the men had first doubted his sight was impaired. But no sooner had the sails filled than the wind dropped dead. The other boats had already disappeared over the horizon, and no help would be forthcoming. Most worryingly of all, dawn was approaching and the gentle tide was bringing them ever closer to the shore. If they had to beach the boat here, they were as good as dead. In desperation, the captain sent his boy out to the prow to whistle for wind.

As the sun began to peek over the horizon, all eyes were

trained on the coastline. Molony gazed through his binoculars, spying a trail of smoke in the distance. "There's a ship coming."

"A banana boat?" Lee growled. "Or have we got company?"

Molony played with the focus. "I can't tell."

Lee grabbed the binoculars off his subordinate and pointed them at the harbor. "Everybody below." He turned to face his men. "Now!"

"We got the entire Honduran Navy heading for us," he explained. Seeing the worried look on Molony's face, he grinned, adding, "It's only one vessel, but it's a gunboat, and we're a sitting duck."

"Armed?"

"And armored," said Lee. "She's steel, with two 42-millimeter guns."

Molony gulped. "I reckon we swim."

Lee laughed and slapped him on the back. "Let's save that plan for when we *really* need it." A telltale puff of smoke belched from the forward turret.

"Incoming!"

Molony went to take cover, and Lee chuckled once more. He leaned in to whisper. "There's no way he'll hit us from there. Don't you worry."

They couldn't even see where the shell landed and watched the unwieldy gunboat go through the laborious process of repositioning. With any kind of half-gust, they could outrun it. Another shell fell harmlessly short; the gunboat began chugging toward them once more.

Molony looked worried. "General, it's only a matter of

time before—"

"You don't know these guys. I bet he fires off a few more rounds and then quits."

Molony smiled. "What's the wager?"

He considered his answer for a moment. "A new hat," he said. "When we take the capital. This thing ain't done yet."

A call came out from below deck, and Lee realized that while his men could hear the gunboat discharging its guns and the shells whistling through the air, they had no idea how close they were landing. He decided to have a little fun.

"Shit, that one was close," he called down. "Just passed over our sail." But before Lee could continue his torture, the gunboat gave up and headed back to the harbor. He turned to Molony. "Too chicken to try and board. I knew it." He rubbed his palms together. "And you owe me a new hat."

"Only if we get to Tegus!"

Lee narrowed his eyes. "Oh, we're getting there all right."

They spent most of the day sitting there in a dead calm, inching toward the coast, until the *Emma* appeared—powered by gasoline and no slave to the wind—to tow them out to sea.

Bonilla had some more bad news, however. Their bush army had been surprised and scattered, no doubt tipped off by the papers found on Marín. Bonilla suggested returning to Glover's Reef to see if any of their plans could be salvaged.

As night fell, the now-terrified captain lost his bearings. When dawn arrived, the *Centenilla* was back where it started—right off the coast of Puerto Cortés. Lee turned the air blue.

Molony waited until Christmas had got it all out of his system before asking, "What now?"

Lee drew himself up to his full height. "We're going to get something to eat." He smiled. "And there's only one thing on the menu."

Utila was the smallest of the three Bay Islands—just enough room for a boatman's village guarded by six soldiers and a solitary officer. Lee had visited the islands when *comandante* of Puerto Cortés, so he knew the locals spoke English and were no friends of the Spanish-descended Hondurans. The Bay Islands had originally been part of a British colony, and the slave-descended locals were an independent bunch. He explained to Molony that they'd side with anyone deposing the hated garrison.

Night had fallen when the *Centenilla* reached Utila's small harbor. Lee squeezed as many of his thirty men below deck as he could manage and ordered the rest to lie flat. Satisfied they were out of view, he turned to the ship's captain. "Drop anchor, and don't be shy about rattling those chains. Make sure they hear you."

The loud crash alerted the garrison, and the entire complement of six soldiers and a *tiente* rowed out toward them. As the officer's head came alongside, Molony grabbed him and wrestled him onto the deck of their boat.

Lee took the dagger from his belt and kneeled down beside him. "Tell your men they're taken prisoner." He leaned in and pressed the tip against the lieutenant's throat. "I'm Lee Christmas, and Utila is mine now."

The garrison on this sedate island paradise had no interest in getting in a firefight. The men surrendered immediately before ferrying the rebels to shore in turn. A rudimentary watch was left on the boat, and the rest of the men sallied forth to enjoy the island's pleasures: fresh fish, lobster, and crab—all washed down with coconut rum served by exquisite women who greeted the men like heroes, kindly offering them a bed for the night. When the men returned to the *Centinella* the next morning, they found further tribute. The deck was piled high with provisions: coconuts, papayas, melons, and oranges—more than the men could hope to eat. But their joy was cut short when a kid rowed out with a message for Lee. He balled the message, tossed it over his shoulder, and began pacing the deck, muttering increasingly inventive expletives.

He stopped pacing only when he noticed the concern on his men's faces. "Boys, I'm afraid the vacation is over. It seems we left a bit of a mess behind in Glover's Reef. The Brits stumbled across our little hideout. All the ammunition boxes lying around on the beach…" He spread his hands. "They put two and two together."

The men groaned as he continued. "That's right. As far as they're concerned, we've launched an assault on a friendly nation from their soil—violating their neutrality. The long and the short of it is that warrants are out on all of us."

As the news sunk in, Lee kicked a loose coconut. "Goddamn it!"

Molony stepped forward. "What do you want us to do?"

"Well," he said, straightening up. "First things first. We have to find Bonilla before the Brits do. I reckon he'll be hugging the coast, and we should do the same. The Brits have a battle cruiser out looking for us—the HMS *Brilliant*—and I don't want to die in this damn rust-bucket."

Murmurs spread among the men.

"I know what some of you are thinking." Lee stared them down. "But if we cut-and-run and leave Bonilla to the Brits, or, worse, the Hondurans, this revolution is over." He smiled. "And you boys won't get your pay. Now, are we ready to go a huntin'?"

The crew responded in unison. "Yes, sir!"

"That's what I like to hear. Molony, mount a machine gun at the stern—just in case." Lee nodded to a couple of the Hondurans. "You two, pile some sandbags up either side. Captain,"—he looked at Captain Woods—"let's get the hell out of here. Point her south. Aim for Trujillo. We'll work our way back up the coast."

A couple of hours later, about eight hundred yards from the coast, Lee warned the captain not to get any closer. "Keep her steady. If Bonilla's around, we'll spot him."

It had become clear that every garrison town along the Caribbean coast had been notified about the *Centinella.* As they passed the town of Balfate, four hundred soldiers marched out to the strand as a show of force. Molony grabbed the binoculars. "General, a small vessel is approaching."

Lee followed Guy's line of sight, shielding his eyes from the sun. "A *cayuco*. It'll be a message." He turned to the captain. "Stop her dead. Let's hear what they have to say."

It was addressed to Lee, and was to the point: come ashore and surrender. He turned to his men. "Feel like surrendering today?"

"Hell no!"

He chuckled. "All right, then. Let's have some fun." He sat down to scribble a message in his barely legible hand. Grinning, he passed it down to the *cayuco.*

"What did you tell him?" asked Molony.

Lee smiled. "I invited him out to sea to settle the matter."

Thirty minutes later, the *cayuco* was back with a reply.

Lee opened it and guffawed. "This is swell. We've really got under his collar." He ran his finger under the jagged script. "I'm a *yanqui* something … a mercenary … a *gringo* something else—well, we knew all that! And I can make out his name this time: Pedro Díaz." He looked at Molony. "Give me those binoculars."

Lee peered out at the coast. "Yep, thought so." He turned to his men. "I know this guy. Short, fat, and ugly to boot. He almost killed his *tiente* one day after catching him in bed with his wife. I don't blame the poor woman. Díaz looks like he's never broken a sweat in his whole sorry life."

He hastily scrawled another message, handed it to the *cayuco* peddler, and turned to the ship's captain. "Start her up, nice and slow. We'll get Díaz sweating yet."

Under the noonday sun, the *Centinella* started moving, just a little faster than walking pace and parallel to the coast. The soldiers took turns peering through the binoculars, watching Díaz and his men struggle to keep up in the baking heat.

"Spread out some awnings over the decks," Lee told the men. "And let's get some of these coconuts open. It's getting *mighty* hot!"

The men lined up at the rail, relishing the sweet juice, laughing as the soldiers toiled in the heat to follow the *Centinella* all the way to Nuevo Armenia. Once there, Lee ordered the captain to stop. He stepped up to the rail and stretched, yawning in full view of Díaz and his troops. "Nice ride," he said, grinning. "But maybe it's time to head back."

To the despair of the soldiers tracking them, the *Centinella* turned and headed back where it had come from—at the exact same speed. Through the binoculars, Lee could see Díaz spitting and cursing. His soldiers roared in frustration, aimed their rifles at the *Centinella,* and began firing wildly. Much to the men's amusement, the captain hit the deck in mock terror and crawled to the sandbags that shielded the machine gun, despite the boat being well out of range.

He turned to Molony. "Time to give 'em a taste of your gun."

Molony took his position at the machine gun and kicked the captain. "You're in the way, you'd best move."

The captain looked up in fright. "I'm not going anywhere."

Molony chuckled. "On your head be it." He shifted the gun slightly so the red-hot casings would fall directly on the captain's head. Kneeling, he let out a short practice burst, just to get his range, and then got into position. With the next burst, he raked the white sand. The terrified soldiers ran straight into the bush. Even though the beach was now clear, Molony kept firing, amused at the yelps of the ship's captain.

By the next morning, they were back on Utila. Good news awaited them for a change. Bonilla and the *Emma* were safe—waiting at a small island just outside Puerto Barrios. "This is it, boys," said Lee. "In Guatemalan waters, the Brits can't touch us. We'll ship out at nightfall."

47

Lee and Molony paddled over to the island where Bonilla's men had decamped, and the Honduran embraced them both warmly.

"My general," he said to Lee, "good to see you again." Their disagreement had been forgotten in the face of a greater threat.

"If you're looking for a plan," said Lee. "I don't got one." He dug his toes into the sand.

"I do." A mysterious smile spread across Bonilla's face. "We surrender."

"Are you crazy?" yelled Lee. Lowering his voice, he added, "What the hell do you mean surrender?"

"Not to Davíla," Bonilla said. "Or the British."

Lee eyed him, confused.

"To Cabrera." Bonilla smiled once more.

It took a moment for it to sink in. Surrender to the Guatemalan authorities would be in name only, but would satisfy the diplomatic protocols that the British—with their battle cruiser—were so fond of. Lee allowed himself a smile before his brow creased with worry again. "What about the guns? The munitions?"

Bonilla tapped his nose and walked up to the tree line,

where a bunch of crates sat out of reach of the water. "*Tranquilo*," he said, kneeling in the dirt. "Everything has been arranged." The boxes had not yet been nailed shut, and Bonilla flicked one open with the knife from his belt. He held the lid while Lee peered inside. It was filled with sand and shells.

"Ingenious," said Lee, putting his arm around Bonilla. "But where do the real guns go?"

Bonilla pointed across the bay. "Our friends in Livingston."

Lee chuckled and called Molony over, pointing at the boxes. "Nail all these shut. Good and tight, now."

In the meantime, Bonilla divided up the remaining three thousand dollars of the revolutionary kitty to pay each man what he was owed. Lee watched in admiration, knowing full well that the men would have accepted less, given they had seen no *real* action. He also knew that money would be badly needed for the next attempt at winning back his country.

By the time Bonilla was done, the sun was peeking over the horizon.

48

Three days later, Lee and Bonilla sailed into Puerto Barrios and surrendered to Guatemalan authorities.

The Guatemalans did nothing, other than put them on a train to Guatemala City; there they met their old benefactor, President Cabrera, who gave them the freedom of the city.

Adelaide was happy to see him, but Lee sensed some residual frostiness. He was back earlier than planned, in one piece too, but she knew it was only a matter of time before he disappeared again. Sure enough, after Lee had been lying low for a few weeks, Bonilla sent a message. They were to travel to Puerto Barrios to meet *El Amigo*.

Lee found Bonilla on the train and took the seat beside him. They shook hands solemnly; no grand Latin embrace this time. "Who's *El Amigo* anyways?" Lee asked, leaning in close.

Bonilla raised an eyebrow. "What do you call him?"

He had to think about it for a moment before realizing whom Bonilla meant. He chuckled. "Why, the Banana Man, of course. Although, I'll admit *El Amigo* has a certain charm."

When they arrived at Puerto Barrios, an intermediary took them straight to the clandestine meeting place—a deserted storeroom in an abandoned hotel. Sam Zemurray sat alone at a table, two empty chairs facing him, clenching and unclenching his fists. Lee could tell Zemurray was tense and knew he was no wide-eyed *yanqui* mixing in matters he didn't understand. Zemurray couldn't afford for this revolution to falter either. He had too much invested in it. It was his only chance to level the playing field with competitors like Standard Fruit or the giant United Fruit Company.

Zemurray greeted them with a curt nod. "We have to be quick," he warned. "If this treaty goes through, I'm finished."

Bonilla did his best to calm him. "We have some time."

Lee lit a *puro,* as Bonilla continued. "Even if Dávila signs the treaty, it won't get through Congress—not on the first attempt, at least. Too many people have a *personal* interest to hand over the customs houses without a fight. And the people aren't happy with their *yanqui* cousins right now. As I said, we have a little time."

Zemurray nodded a few times, as if digesting the information with each movement of his head; then he looked to Lee. "What do you need to get things moving again?"

"Not much in the way of arms and munitions. We still have most of that stored safely." He took a drag from his *puro,* exhaling toward the ceiling. "But we need something else. A boat. I mean, a real boat—something fast enough to outrun the Hondurans."

Zemurray paused, nodding again. "I'll see what I can do."

Pretty soon, Lee was back to hustling for troops, selling the prospect of a grand adventure in Honduras to the many soldiers of fortune kicking around. When word got back to Washington, the Americans made known their displeasure. Their consul in Puerto Cortés had already alerted them that the whole northern coast was talking about Bonilla's return. To assuage them, Cabrera deported Lee and Bonilla to New Orleans.

Lee Christmas was on the way home again, but he didn't plan on staying long.

49

Lee stepped off the steamer, Bonilla right behind him, and scanned the crowd for Guy Molony. "Shouldn't be too hard to spot him," he told Bonilla, over his shoulder. "Damn kid is a giant."

Bonilla dug him in the back and pointed. Molony, towering over the thronging hawkers and gawkers, was waving at them, a goofy grin on his face. He reddened as Bonilla enveloped him in a full-throated embrace, cringing at the snickers of the stevedores who idled nearby. Lee grabbed Guy's hand and near shook his arm out of its socket. "Guy, we're gonna hit them again." He fixed him with a stare. "You hear me?"

"Well," said Molony, "that's the best news since I got word you were coming."

Lee smiled. "Miss me that much?"

"Honestly, I was more excited about getting the afternoon off."

"New job eating into your leisure time?" Lee poked him in the ribs.

"You sound like my boss," said Molony, before adopting a haughty tone. "The Otis Elevator Company doesn't tolerate daydreamers, Mr. Molony."

"Ouch," said Lee. "I'd probably knock his block off."

"Tell me about it." Molony winced. "It was worth it for the cover story, but I think that's blown now."

The smile vanished from Lee's face. "What do you mean?"

"Two men," said Molony, leaning in. "Over my left shoulder. The taller one followed me here. The other guy, I guess he was here already."

Lee scanned the crowd until he saw the two Molony was talking about. He dropped his voice to a near whisper. "They know you spotted them?"

"Don't think so."

"Then let's start walking." He picked up Bonilla's suitcase and handed it to Molony. "Don't pay them any attention."

Molony bent his head to Lee. "You still want to go to the place on Basin Street?"

"It's ready, ain't it?"

"Sure, I just thought—"

"We act as normal. Stick to the plan."

Once the trio had made their way through the crowded pier, they took the streetcar up to Toulouse. Bonilla craned his neck during the short journey, drinking in the sights and sounds of New Orleans. He got even more animated as they walked through the French Quarter, clapping at the brass bands that played on every street corner, and marveling at the tuba player who danced while hitting his notes, the instrument wrapped around his corpulent frame. And he gaped open mouthed at the painted ladies of Basin Street who flashed their skirts at passersby, trying to tempt them into their abodes of ill repute.

"Put the suitcase down," Lee told Molony once they were inside the safe house. Then he turned to Bonilla. "These are your digs," he said. "I'm staying with a friend."

Bonilla nodded and walked to the window to gaze out over the street. "Who was that following us?"

"US Treasury," said Molony. "I think, anyways. This treaty has been getting a lot of press. A lot of powerful people want this thing signed, and they don't want any revolutin' getting in the way. Not until it's signed, at least."

"Zemurray's backing will disappear if that treaty is signed," said Bonilla.

Lee smiled. "Well, then, we best act quick."

50

Two weeks later, Zemurray came through, and Lee hurried down to Lake Pontchartrain to inspect the vessel. He strolled along the pier until he came to the right boat—the *Hornet.* A figure tooling about on deck waved to him. "You must be Lee, Sam told me you were coming."

He reached up and shook the man's hand. "Captain Johnson, I take it."

"Please, call me Charles." He smiled. "Hop aboard and I'll show you around."

The boat's skipper was picking at some peeling paint when Lee joined him on deck. "She needs a little attention," he said. "But she's a hell of a vessel."

"I think she's perfect." Lee walked up to the prow and then gazed back. "Bigger than I expected too."

The skipper nodded. "She's big, all right. 'Bout one hundred and sixty foot, give or take." He walked up to the main mast and gave it a hearty slap. "Twenty-four foot beam too, but she'll still reach sixteen knots in good weather.

"That fast?"

"Sure," said the captain. "Once we're done refitting, at least. There's something else I think you'll like." He brought Lee down to the engine room and pointed to a bronze plaque.

He leaned in to get a better look. "1890?"

"Yep. Saw service in the Spanish–American war. Part of the mosquito fleet sent to blockade Cuba."

Lee knocked on the plating that surrounded the engine room.

"Navy must have put that in," said the skipper. "It was added after she was built."

Back up on deck, Lee spotted two men in trench coats leaning against their automobile. One of them was scribbling something down—probably the name of the boat. He turned to the captain. "Sam tell you about these guys?"

He chuckled and saluted the agents. "Don't worry, Lee." He clapped him on the back. "I wouldn't give them the steam off my piss."

Lee guffawed, hiding his relief. There were too many moving parts for his liking. Too many people who could spill with the right incentive. Or pressure. He stared down the agents, cracking his knuckles.

There was no point in them hiding their work. The constant shadow of the Secret Service proved the authorities knew what they were planning—not that it was hard to deduce, given the failed revolution some weeks back. The government took an extremely dim view of anyone launching a rebellion from US soil. Using an American-flagged vessel to target a friendly country would bring a strong reaction from Washington. But as far as anyone watching was concerned, Lee was a private citizen refitting a boat. And that was all.

After quizzing Captain Johnson about repairs, he took the streetcar back into town, tailed the entire way by the two agents. They parked outside as Lee entered Remy Klock's saloon; and they still sat there while he walked right through the bar and out the back door. When he got to Basin Street, he wanted to make sure he'd shaken the tail, so he walked right past Bonilla's place until he caught up with a newspaper boy. With the paper folded under his arm, Lee doubled back and spotted the tail on the other side of the street. *Screw it*, he thought, and went up to Bonilla's door anyway.

Half an hour later, Lee and Bonilla walked around the corner from Basin to Conti. As they passed the long row of dollar cribs, Lee could tell Bonilla was still apprehensive. He quickened his pace until they reached a bigger structure at the end of the street. He'd memorized the address from an ad in the *Sunday Sun*—No. 1304, a brothel run by Madame May Evans, which promised to be quieter than those on the main drag. A group of kids lounged at the entrance, peddling marijuana cigarettes, three for a dime. Lee scattered them with a glare and strode up the steps. The door opened before he could knock, and after a quick glance at Bonilla, he pushed inside.

Bonilla's brow furrowed as he took in the gaudy interior.

"It's perfect," Lee said, trying to reassure him. He handed a bill to the waiting Madame. "We just want a quiet place to talk."

She folded the note into her corset and led them into an adjoining room that was more muted than the parlor, if you ignored the gallery of nudes adorning the walls. "Will this do?"

Lee walked to the window and peered through the curtains at a perfect view of the street. He could see the two agents scoping out the building, one of them again taking notes.

"It's perfect," he said.

After the Madame left, Bonilla said, "I don't understand."

"It's simple. Those agents are gonna be on our tail no matter what. I tried shaking one today, and he picked up the scent in minutes. These guys are pros. Guy might have been right. US Treasury agents. Makes sense, anyways."

"What does this mean for the plan?"

"We change nothing," Lee said, sitting in one of the plush armchairs and indicating for Bonilla to do likewise. "They're watching all of us, even Guy. They know about the boat. And they've probably figured out what we're up to."

Bonilla sat down, finally, and sighed.

"There's more," said Lee. "Guy told me some newspapermen have been asking questions."

Bonilla let out a string of curses as Lee continued. "Now, we're probably going to get a lot of press attention. The government might be leaking the story themselves, getting more eyes and ears on us, seeing what the muckrakers can shake loose."

"You think anyone will talk?"

"I'm working on the assumption *everyone* will talk. This is a hot story. JP Morgan angling to buy up all the Honduran debt while putting the taxpayer on the hook for insurance. Everyone with two nickels to rub together suddenly has skin in the game—and they ain't backing our side."

They sat in silence for a moment until the Madame opened the door and slipped inside. "Sorry to interrupt your business, gentlemen, but I thought you'd like to know."

"Go on," said Lee.

"Fella came in. Fierce interested in joining you two."

"What you tell him?"

She smiled. "Private party."

Lee took out another bill, but she shook her head. "That one's on me. Never liked cops."

He raised an eyebrow. "Shoes," she said. "Can always tell by the shoes."

"Do me a favor," Lee said. "Let him in next time. I'd prefer to keep him in plain sight."

She nodded and grasped the door handle behind her. "Fetch you boys a drink?"

"That would be lovely, ma'am."

Lee turned back to Bonilla, noting the confused look on his face. "I'll explain in a minute," he said. "But before I forget, fill me in on Davíla."

Bonilla snapped his fingers. "Yes, the people are mad. They think he's selling the country off to the *yanquis*."

"That's what I wanted to ask," said Lee. "What's JP Morgan getting for clearing all those loans?"

"The customs houses."

"A percentage?"

"No," said Bonilla. "Running them directly."

Lee chuckled. "No wonder Sam is so keen to knock Davíla off." He thought for a moment. "Does he have the votes to push through the treaty?"

"It's hard to say. He and Sierra have a lot of influence. But with revolutions breaking out all over the country, everyone is watching his own back."

"Is there a chance Davíla will just ditch the treaty? Because if he does, Sam's backing will evaporate."

"He can't," said Bonilla. "His credibility depends on the treaty's passage. He sought it, he backed it, and he needs the money for his project. If that trans–oceanic railway doesn't get built, Davíla will get destroyed in the next election."

The Madame knocked and entered, leaving the door slightly ajar. "You boys must be getting thirsty. She clapped, and two scantily clad girls entered, bearing drinks. Lee saw Bonilla grin, but he shook his head, intercepting the cocktails. The Madame clapped her hands again and the girls scurried to the door, one stopping to pout at Lee.

He gave her a little wave of his hand. "Promise to be a little friendlier tomorrow night," he said. The Madame nodded and left.

"Tomorrow night?" asked Bonilla, arching an eyebrow.

Lee passed him his drink. "Oh, yeah. So here's the rest of the plan."

51

For the next three weeks, while the *Hornet* was being refitted, Lee, Bonilla, and Molony whiled away their evenings carousing in The District, which some were now calling Storyville, after the lawmaker whose legislation had created it. In an attempt to halt the spread of prostitution into every sector of the city, the council had designated a twelve-block area north of the French Quarter as a legal red-light district. In local parlance, it was a place where patrons of sporting emporiums could enjoy themselves without interference from the law.

Each night, the Treasury agents would dutifully tail Lee and his companions into Storyville and post a man outside the brothel. Lee ensured these ostentatious sessions would run late into the night, noting that the agents would often quit when the drinking got heavy or if it looked like things would go on until dawn.

The refitting of the *Hornet* was complete by mid-December, and she began loading up cargo immediately. Agents openly searched each shipment, finding nothing but coal. The Paredes–Knox treaty was getting a lot of press attention, as was anything that was seen as affecting its passage, especially Lee Christmas, Manuel Bonilla, and the

Hornet. The Honduran embassy protested again and again that the boat was to be used in an attempt to overthrow their government, and demanded that US authorities seize the ship. But the agents couldn't uncover any evidence of suspicious activity. On December 20, the skipper of the *Hornet,* Charles Johnson, finally received permission to clear the port. The vessel meandered the ninety-mile stretch toward the Gulf—agents following her all the way downstream and out to sea before they were satisfied.

The following evening, when Molony returned home from work as usual, his sister passed on a short telephone message from Christmas: *Tell Guy it's tonight.*

Molony said nothing. He went to his room, packed his belongings, and returned to the kitchen with a note for his mother. *The plant owes me eight dollars*, he wrote. *I won't be here to collect.* He left to meet Bonilla and Christmas at the corner of Canal and Royal.

The agents had doubled their watch—probably extra suspicious now they had found nothing on the *Hornet.* Lee, Molony, and Bonilla were tailed right to the door of May Evans's sporting emporium, where they had frittered away the past few weeks. As soon as they were inside the parlor, Lee summoned a boy and took him to the front window. They peered out the shutters. "See those three." He pointed across the street. "The ones walking real slow, pretending not to look this way."

"I see 'em," said the kid.

Lee pressed a coin into his hand. "Keep an eye on them. If they quit watching this place, come back and tell me straightaway."

Soon after the boy left, a stranger entered. Lee raised an eyebrow at Molony, who gave a curt nod. Bonilla's eyes narrowed.

Good, Lee thought, *they've pegged him too.*

Bonilla sprang into action, ordering champagne for everyone. Lee set a fierce pace, chugging back glass after glass, whereas Molony, after a long day at his regular laboring stint, needed only a couple before he was soundly asleep in the corner.

Lee could see he would have to shoulder most of the burden for keeping this party going, but there was no better man. He drank and danced, and flirted with the girls. Bonilla ordered bottle after bottle. Lee drank glass after glass. In the corner, Bonilla clapped his hands along to the tinny, mechanical piano, which he kept feeding quarters. "*Muy alegre amigos! Muy alegre!*"

The party continued past midnight, the music and dancing increasing in intensity. By two-thirty, the stranger was done and made an abrupt exit looking like he was about to puke. Once he had cleared the building, the party ground to an abrupt halt. Lee waited anxiously by the door, watching as the agents got into their cars and drove away. A few minutes later, the boy reappeared.

"I was right on the corner where they were waiting," the kid said. "The man that was in here now came over and said this was just another of those drunken parties they've been having. He said he was sick and tired of it, that you ain't going nowhere tonight. Then they all hightailed it."

Lee paid the boy and returned to the parlor. Bonilla

looked at him hopefully. Lee said nothing, instead reaching into his pocket for a *puro* and taking his sweet time lighting it. He smiled. "Well, *compadre*, I've heard of rags to riches, but this here's the first time I've head of someone going from the whorehouse to the White House."

52

Lee shook Guy awake. "It's time," he said. As Bonilla settled the bill, Lee spied out the shutter once more. He turned to his companions. "Cars are outside."

Molony and Lee piled into the second car, gripping each other as it took off at an almighty pace, bouncing along the rutted streets on the way north to Lake Pontchartrain. Lee pulled himself forward and hollered in the driver's ear. "You sure this thing is safe?"

The driver laughed in response, as a pothole sent Lee flying into Molony's lap.

Guy grimaced. "I'm none too crazy about this either."

They made their way beyond the city limits, up to where Bayou St. John entered the lake, and the driver slowed a touch. He leaned back to look at them. "First time in an automobile?" They nodded. "Can always tell," he said.

But something else was bothering Lee. Nearby was the old Spanish Fort. He thought back to the day he had spent on the surrounding fairground. Kissing Mamie on the Ferris Wheel. Goofing around at the shooting gallery. Both of them filling the silence with nervous chatter, both scared and anxious about their planned elopement.

He hung his head.

"There it is," said Molony, elbowing him in the ribs. The car skidded to a halt, its headlights illuminating a boat: Sam Zemurray's private yacht, which would ferry them to their maritime rendezvous with the *Hornet*. The banana magnate and sponsor of this revolution was already aboard, dressed in the simple garb of a deckhand. He waved at their automobile and drew a finger across his throat. The driver cut the lights.

Molony helped Lee from the back seat and steadied him as he tried to find his feet. For a second, Lee thought he was going to puke. All those bubbles sloshing around in his stomach had become a dagger stabbing at his intestines. But after a couple of deep breaths, he straightened up. When Lee was a few steps away from the car, it revved its engine and sped away, spraying dust and dirt and fumes. That time, he did puke.

"Now I'm glad I dozed off," said Molony, stepping onto the boat. Lee wiped his mouth with the back of his hand. After making sure they weren't tailed, Sam Zemurray introduced his brother, already at the wheel of the yacht, and they cast off as soon as Lee sat down, Sam's brother sailing the yacht out across Lake Pontchartrain. They turned east toward The Rigolets, where they watched the sun rise over breakfast, before turning in for a well-earned nap.

It was dusk before they reached Ship Island, off the coast of Biloxi, dropping anchor on the Gulf side, where the island shielded them from any prying eyes on the mainland. After dinner, they took turns keeping watch, but the *Hornet* never showed. When the sun rose on December 24, they cast anchor and crossed to the mainland, knowing the *Hornet* wouldn't attempt another rendezvous until nightfall. Zemurray went ashore, alone, to provision the boat, having warned Lee and Bonilla to keep below deck. Their photographs had graced enough newspapers recently. While he was gone, the rest turned to poker to occupy their minds. As Lee dealt the first hand, with a *puro* clenched between his teeth, he chuckled when he realized their table was a case of rifles. He was less happy when Bonilla walked away with the pot.

After the sun set, Zemurray's brother maneuvered the boat out toward the back of Ship Island. Lee stared out at the horizon.

"Don't worry, she'll come." A voice came from behind him. It was Zemurray. "If she knew she wasn't going to make it here before dawn, she would have turned back. She'll come, though. I'm sure of it."

"I hope you're right." Lee lit up another *puro*. "It will be a sorry Christmas if she doesn't." By the time the vessel rounded the western tip of Ship Island, Molony and Bonilla had joined them on deck. Zemurray let out a whoop, pointing at the signaling lights of the *Hornet*, some twelve miles distant, safely in international waters.

They pulled alongside and began transferring boxes of rifles and ammunitions. Once the munitions were stored safely in the hold of the *Hornet*, the banana magnate made his goodbyes, wishing the men luck.

"I've bet the farm on you," he said, removing his jacket and passing it over the rail to Bonilla, who shivered in the icy December wind. "I might as well bet the coat too."

Lee tried to get some sleep while the *Hornet* cut across the Gulf of Mexico, envious that Molony had dozed off instantly, and Bonilla too. Lee just didn't feel tired. His body ached, but his brain was working through all the permutations of the next few weeks. All of the plans of attack. All of the things that could still go wrong.

He must have dozed off at some point, for when he awoke, their sleeping area was already bathed in light. Scratching his stubbly chin, he sat up and pulled on his boots. He stretched, slowly, yawning all the while, and then went up on deck. Captain Johnson turned from the wheel and nodded, taking a swig from his mug.

"Don't suppose that's coffee," said Lee.

The captain shook his head, a smile tugging at his lips. "Don't you know what day it is?"

"Uh." Lee counted his fingers. Before he could figure it out, a groan came from below: Molony and Bonilla getting up. The captain checked the horizon and then clapped Lee on the back. "Let's go down to the others. There's something I want to show you."

As Bonilla stretched and Molony rubbed his eyes, Captain Johnson dug around in the hold. "I had to hide it away. Couldn't risk you finding it." He carried a keg into the center of the room, already tapped. "But I couldn't help myself this morning." Molony and Lee grinned at each other.

"Merry Christmas," said the captain.

Lee chuckled. "Well, I'll be damned." He eyed the captain. "Hope you've got more than one mug."

53

The *Hornet* docked out of sight of the Guatemalan authorities at Bahia Graciosa, reuniting with the *Centinella*, which had been passing as a fishing boat during their absence. Lee glowered when he saw it; he was sure it was jinxed. Bonilla ignored him and sent for the arms and men at Livingston. As soon as the machine guns arrived, Molony set up a lantern so he could work through the night. He wanted to strip and reassemble each piece before their first engagement; it would be dawn before he was done.

While Molony busied himself, Lee surveyed the men under his command. Some were Honduran—supporters of Bonilla before he was deposed—but many others were mercenaries, soldiers of fortune, mostly from America. There were criminals and jilted lovers, young runaways seeking adventure, and older heads seeking more tangible rewards. He knew many of them from his time in Guatemala and immediately made officers of those he trusted best: Joe Reed, Ed McLaurie, and Guy Molony.

The men arriving from Livingston huddled around Bonilla immediately. Lee watched Bonilla's face pinch with concern before the exiled Honduran leader beckoned him over. "The *yanquis* aren't happy," he explained.

"Well, we did give their hotshot agents the slip there in New Orleans."

"Quite," said Bonilla. "And now they've dispatched a cruiser—the USS *Tacoma*—to patrol the area."

"They gonna intervene?"

Bonilla took a breath. "The *Hornet* is still flying an American flag. Anyone on board could be charged with piracy if they take part in an engagement."

Lee thought for a moment. "We mightn't be bunched just yet," he said. "Can't we change the registration here? Or maybe Puerto Barrios?"

Bonilla shook his head.

"What if we dump all the guns first?"

"Not going to help," Bonilla said. "Cabrera's happy to turn a blind eye to what we're doing here. We're out of sight, giving him plausible deniability. But if we fly a Guatemalan flag into battle…"

Lee cursed, as Bonilla spread his hands and continued, "And we can't take Puerto Cortés without the *Hornet*."

"Goddamn it," said Lee, before calming himself. "Okay. What are the options?"

Bonilla shrugged. "Wait."

"But if we wait, Davíla will have conscripted half the country."

"What do you suggest?"

Lee remembered the island he'd captured last summer. "What about Utila? We can take it without breaking a sweat and change the registration there."

Bonilla snapped his fingers. "Not Utila," he said. "But Roatan. The Bay Island's governor has his office there. All we need to do is convince him to change the registration."

"I can be very persuasive." Lee smiled, fingering the machete at his belt.

Roatan lay twenty miles northeast of Utila. It also had no real strategic value, so resistance would be light. Flying the Honduran flag should keep the Americans out of their hair, and that damn cruiser. After a moment's thought, Bonilla gave the order.

The *Hornet* slipped into Dixon's Cove around midnight, concealed by the headland from the principle settlement, Coxin's Hole. A direct assault would have succeeded, but Bonilla was anxious to avoid casualties and minimize property damage. He didn't want to give the Americans any pretext to intervene.

The raiding party disembarked from their vessel as quietly as possible, directly opposite a short trail through the jungle, which should lead them straight to the governor's office and the *cuartel.* Lee wasn't taking any chances, however. There was no telling whether the garrison had been beefed up. He ordered Molony and his machine gun up to a bluff overlooking the harbor, to provide cover for their advance.

The rest of his men, he gathered at the shoreline as he issued instructions for the attack on Coxin's Hole.

54

Lee stood opposite the path to the governor's mansion and looked up at the headland. In another ten minutes, Molony would be in place, and the rest of the men could move out. A cry went out from a scout, and Lee's troops raised their weapons, training their sights on the entrance to the jungle path. A lone figure emerged waving a torn bedsheet—the white flag of surrender.

"Hold your fire," barked Lee.

Bonilla's first victory on Honduran soil hadn't even cost him a bullet, let alone any blood. The fortress was turned over to the rebels, and the governor affected the transfer of the *Hornet* with Lee barely needing to wave his pistol. Government soldiers defected as the Honduran flag was raised on the *Hornet*, bringing the number under his command to one hundred and thirty. It wasn't an army, but it was a start. On top of that, he now had a foothold on Honduran soil. But he was twitchy, and his men too—all riled up for a shooting match only for the enemy to surrender.

As Bonilla took care of the formalities, declaring himself President and establishing his temporary seat of government in Roatan, Lee realized it was New Year's Eve. He made his way down to the house where Molony and Ed McLaurie had been billeted, finding them both relaxing on the porch. "Boys, I've just had a hell of an idea. I wouldn't mind spending New Year's Eve over on Utila. How about we sail over and capture the joint?"

"All right." Molony nodded.

McLaurie looked between the pair, raising an eyebrow. "What about Bonilla?"

"Aw, don't worry about him. He told me I earned a holiday and can do whatever I please. Besides, he was just complaining that Dávila has put a real *hijo de puta* in charge of the island after what we got up to last year. The whole of Utila is under martial law. Name's Jackson. Some American. Working for a fruit company. A real hard-ass, by all accounts. I sure would love to get rid of him. Me and Molony had a fine time there—real decent folk. And the women…"

Molony let out a low whistle. "He's not wrong, Ed."

"Don't you need orders?" asked McLaurie. "Something official? We can't just walk in like bandits."

"I'll get whatever papers we need." Lee put a hand on his shoulder. "Come on, Ed."

McLaurie thought for a moment. "Well, all right."

"With us three, I'll need seven more. Round up some volunteers." Lee made to leave. "And be down at the dock in an hour."

"Before you go, Lee," Molony called out. "You planning on taking the *Hornet*?"

"Why?"

"Bonilla mightn't be too happy."

"Leave it to me, boys."

By seven o'clock, Molony, McLaurie, and seven eager

volunteers arrived at the dock.

Lee waved from the deck of the *Centinella*. The group groaned—by then, everyone shared his view that the boat was jinxed.

"Come now, boys. She ain't all that bad!" He ignored their jeers. "I'm going to break this miserable old grease-barrel's jinx if it takes a leg." He grinned. "Now, git aboard and do your cussin' on the way."

They reached Utila just after two in the morning, half a mile east of the only lights on the island: the *cuartel*. At first, it appeared the lights were flickering, until they made out a guard pacing back and forth. They drew closer, noticing another building that loomed from the darkness. Voices drifted out from within. Lee crept along the corrugated iron wall, toward the entrance. His men assumed position on either side of the door and took aim. Lee knocked twice and then stood back, drawing his weapon.

A man stuck his head out. "Yes?"

He lunged forwards, grabbing the man in a headlock. "What the hell is going on here?" he growled.

The guy didn't struggle. "A simple prayer meeting," he said. "I swear."

"I'm Lee Christmas." He waved his troops down and released his hold. "These are my men. And we're taking the island."

The man clasped his hands together and looked heavenward. "Our prayers have been answered." Several more congregants stepped out into the night—men, women, and children.

Lee's brow furrowed. "Why are you praying at night? I

don't get it."

"It's the *comandante*. He has forbidden public assemblies. We always pray the New Year in, but he wouldn't allow any exceptions."

"We'll see about that." Lee turned to Molony. "Set up your machine gun on that ridge above the *cuartel*. Be ready." He gestured to the rest of the men. "Keep quiet, and for God's sake no smoking or fooling around. Don't shoot until I say." He faced the congregation. "Can one of you show me where Mr. Jackson's house is?"

Guy Molony set up on the ridge, as ordered, and trained his machine gun on the door of the *cuartel*. The rest of the men flanked him … and waited … watching the sentry pace out his shift, bathed in lamplight.

A shriek in the distance made the sentry reach for his weapon.

Another shriek followed, this time closer. The sentry peered into the distance, the direction in which Christmas had disappeared. As the din grew nearer, the men could make out a voice. Between cries of "*Viva Bonilla*," a man shrieked in pain. Dropping his rifle in fright, the sentry ran into the *cuartel*.

A man wearing a nightgown came into view, with Christmas right behind him kicking him in the rear, propelling him toward the *cuartel*. "Say it again!" he roared.

"*Viva Bonilla!*" shouted Mr. Jackson, only to be booted again by the general.

"Say it again!"

The men collapsed into laughter. Christmas glowered at them, pointing to the *cuartel* below them. "Supposing they made a charge?"

"*Viva Bonilla!*" bawled the stricken *comandante.*

"*Viva Bonilla!*" replied the men, in unison.

Christmas gave him one last taste of the boot for good measure, and then grabbed him roughly around the neck, twisting his head to face the *cuartel.* "Now, go down there and tell your boys you have surrendered the island to us." He shoved him down the hill, toward the enemy.

55

The garrison of Utila was only too happy to surrender and defect; the islanders were not alone in despising Mr. Jackson. Lee appointed an interim *comandante* until Bonilla could pick his own man, and then supervised the distribution of the armory among hand-picked locals—in case the *cuartel* had any funny ideas about switching sides again once he sailed out of view. Lee and his men were treated to a breakfast feast by the people of Utila, delighted to be out from under the yoke of the dictatorial Jackson.

Back aboard the *Centinella*, on the return journey to Roatan, Lee needled Mr. Jackson. "Don't worry, *comandante*, I have some pull with Bonilla. If I speak to him, you won't be tortured before you are shot."

The men had to suppress their laughter, enjoying the goading.

When Bonilla heard about Lee's teasing, he was furious, and set Mr. Jackson free immediately. He was tense for another reason, in truth. Dávila was pulling out all the stops to get the Paredes–Knox treaty through Congress. Bonilla's sympathizers on the mainland were plaguing him with anxious messages, urging him to make his move, and rumors were widespread that the United States would step in and put down their little revolution once the treaty was ratified.

A few hours after Lee returned from Utila, another ship docked at Roatan—the USS *Tacoma*. Commander Archibald Davis rowed ashore and immediately demanded proof that the *Hornet* wasn't engaged in anything it shouldn't be. Bonilla showed him the Honduran registration, but Commander Davis wasn't satisfied. He remained at Coxin's Hole, pledging to keep an eye on proceedings.

Bonilla's anxiety grew over the next week as the messages from the mainland became increasingly frantic. But his hands were tied while the *Tacoma* was in the bay. He couldn't risk seizure of the *Hornet*—the only vessel quick enough to outrun trouble. Meanwhile, boatloads of volunteers poured into Roatan, all sympathizers from the mainland, eager to help Bonilla regain his rightful place in the Presidential Palace.

The deposed Honduran leader looked out at an army of women all stitching blue denim uniforms, assembling blue-and-white hat bands, fashioning ammunition belts, and tearing sheets into bandages, and then he paced back over to the table, his hands behind his back. Lee waited for his friend to gather his thoughts.

Bonilla peered at the map on the table, frowning. He stabbed a finger at Puerto Cortés. "Since our failure last summer. Puerto Cortés has been fortified, and the *cuartel* has been stuffed with Davíla loyalists. In short, it's now very well defended." He jabbed his finger sixty miles east. "La Ceiba too."

Lee watched Bonilla trace a finger down sixty miles of

coastline. "Trujillo, however, is another matter. My spies tell me it is a much softer target."

"Makes no difference to the plan," said Lee. "We just work our way west rather than east."

"Good." Bonilla nodded. "Now all we need is for this American cruiser to disappear." He banged the table. "Damn *yanquis*." He looked up at Lee with a wry grin. "Present company excluded, of course."

A few days later, on January 8, Bonilla finally caught a break. The USS *Tacoma* abruptly departed, and Lee was ordered to gather his men. As he looked over the troops assembled at the pier, he held his hands aloft, waiting for silence.

"It's time to move the fight to the mainland, boys." He grinned. "We're gonna come down on them like a buzzard on a sick steer."

56

Once the USS *Tacoma* disappeared over the horizon in the direction of La Ceiba, the *Hornet* pulled out of the harbor with the *Centinella* and a sloop in tow. Bonilla looked at his flotilla, his *yanqui* commander-in-chief, thirty officers, and one hundred and fifty soldiers all decked out in their new kit, all speeding toward the mainland. Below deck the boat carried even more spare uniforms; he was expecting plenty of new recruits.

The captain killed the engine just shy of Trujillo at dawn. "Let's go over the plan again," suggested Bonilla.

Lee chewed the inside of his cheek, waiting for his temper to calm. "You know the plan," he said. "We've been over this."

"I want to hear it again." Bonilla picked up a rifle. "Because I'm coming with you."

Lee cursed and grabbed him by the elbow, marching him up to the stern, out of earshot of his men. "What the hell, Manolo?"

"San Martín fought beside his men. Hidalgo too. And Bolívar." He exhaled through his nose. "I must take part."

Lee wrenched the rifle from his grasp. "If you can be disarmed that easily," he said, "you've no place on the battlefield. And I don't know who the hell those guys are, but what are you thinking?"

"A real leader fights with his men."

Lee bit his tongue. It wasn't the time for a shouting match. "A leader's job is to *inspire* his men, and there's more ways of doing that then charging the enemy. Didn't you see all those volunteers pour into Roatan? Haven't you been getting frantic messages demanding your arrival on the mainland?" He put an arm around Bonilla. "These men believe in you. And you need to place the same faith in them: that they'll get the job done."

Bonilla pouted. "So I cower out here while all of you take bullets in my name."

"You're smarter than this," Lee said. "You should understand the alternative. If you're the one taking bullets, this revolution ends. Everyone else is replaceable. Even if I go down, goddamn it, Guy will do a fine job in my place. But if you get shot…"

Lee trailed off as Molony approached. He looked to Bonilla, and then Lee. "Everything all right?"

"What do you want?" Lee growled.

"Nothing," said Molony, holding up his hands. "It's just … I've got seventy-five men back there raring to go, and if we don't move out soon, I'm afraid they might start shootin' each other."

"I'll be there in a minute," said Lee.

Molony saluted and walked off.

"If you really want to make yourself useful." Lee turned back to Bonilla. "Sail around to the bay and distract that cannon. Just stay out of range of the damn thing." He placed a hand on Bonilla's shoulder. "We need you alive."

He was following Molony to the stern when Bonilla called out after him. "General," he said, "what's the range of that cannon?"

57

Lee and seventy-five of his toughest men waded ashore one mile east of their target: the town of Trujillo. Once everyone had hit the beach, Lee called Molony and McLaurie to him. "Split the men into two groups." He put a hand on McLaurie's shoulder and pointed at a narrow strip of land running under the cliffs that separated them from Trujillo. "Ed, you lead your boys along this little beach here, right to the base of those bluffs yonder. That should bring you right in front of the town, but wait until we get there."

He looked to Molony. "You're with me. We're going to head up the western bluff there, and see if we can take out that cannon. Once we cross that river, there's a hill where we can set you up—"

The siren of the *Hornet* drowned him out. Instinctively, the men turned to face the noise, even though the vessel was out of sight. Then came the roar of the cannon, and once more the siren blared. Lee raised his hands and addressed both groups. "Settle down now, you hear? That's just Bonilla toying with them."

The relieved group broke into smiles.

"Now, while he's zigzagging back and forth, driving that cannon crazy, they're all gonna be looking the wrong way. So let's do this." He clapped McLaurie on the back. "Move 'em out."

"You heard the man," Ed said. "Let's get movin'."

A river separated them from the incline approaching the cannon, but Lee and his men forded it without difficulty. Pedro Gonzales—a Honduran recruit who was very eager to join the fray—was first across and immediately broke into a run up the slope on the other side. The rest of the men couldn't hope to keep up, not lugging Molony's machine gun and all its ammo.

"Guy, set her up here," Lee instructed. "The rest of you, follow me!"

Lee charged up the slope, his men desperately trying to keep up. When, panting, he reached the cannon, he saw that two of the crew had been killed and a third wounded. But there was no sign of Pedro Gonzales. He counted the bodies as the rest of his men caught up. "Pedro must have chased the rest of them back toward the town."

He signaled down to Molony to shift the gun up the hill, hoping to cover their advance on the *cuartel*. The machine gun in place, Lee ordered the charge. He combined with McLaurie's forces at the base of the bluff, and advanced street by street toward the wide-open plaza that fronted the *cuartel*. Lee was just about to order his men into position when he took one last look at the target. He couldn't believe his eyes. Gonzales, alone, was accepting the surrender of the garrison, directing the enemy soldiers to lay their arms against the wall.

After signaling Bonilla for the *Hornet* to come ashore, Lee grabbed Pedro Gonzales. "What the hell happened?"

"I don't know," he said, with a slight smirk. "As soon as

I hit the other side of that river, I just started running."

"Guess you forgot about the machine gun we were hauling," growled Lee. "And my orders to keep together."

"I know," said Gonzales. "I didn't mean to go any further than that hilltop."

Lee rolled his eyes. "And yet…"

"I must have surprised the team manning the cannon."

"Surprised them? You surprised me!"

Gonzales nodded. "Shot three before they knew what was happening, but two of them ran down toward the town, heading for the *cuartel*."

Lee grunted, as Gonzales continued, "It was too late then to wait for reinforcements." The Honduran smirked again. "Or orders."

It still didn't make sense. "How did you get the entire *cuartel* to surrender?"

"I chased those *hijos de putas* all the way into town. They'd ditched their weapons, so they were moving a little faster than me. I let off a couple of rounds, hoping they'd hit the dirt, but they just kept running." He shrugged.

"Then what?"

"Well, I had to keep going at that point, so I chased them all the way through town, across the plaza, and right into the *cuartel*." Lee shook his head in amazement as Gonzales continued. "The *comandante* surrendered on the spot. Guess they thought I had an army right behind me."

Lee slapped his leg. "Shit. If we don't get a real firefight soon…" He embraced Gonzales, but growled in his ear. "Now don't do that again."

Not only had Lee captured Trujillo without the loss of a

single life, he had increased the rebels' stores by adding one cannon, four hundred rifles, and twenty thousand rounds of ammunition. Bonilla entered the town to a surge of recruits, and several businessmen also pledged their support. He'd left Guatemala two weeks beforehand with an "army" of thirty officers; now, his *gringo* general commanded four hundred men.

It was looking promising—until another American warship, the USS *Marietta,* sailed into the bay of Trujillo.

58

Aboard the USS *Marietta,* Commander George Cooper beckoned his first officer. "When does Christmas get here?"

"Sir?"

"The damn mercenary," snapped Cooper.

"He's on his way."

"Good. Anything on the wire?"

"Yes, sir. An army of Bonilla sympathizers that had been hiding out in El Salvador has raided across the border, striking at several small towns. Dávila estimates their numbers at several hundred. He has dispatched five hundred reserves to drive them back. He has also instituted the draft in La Ceiba and Puerto Cortés. Every Honduran male of military age is required to report to their local barracks. Our local consul reports increasingly frantic requests for US intervention."

Cooper nodded. "I just wish Washington would give us some clear orders."

"Sir?"

"Never mind. I'm taking the matter in hand. Let me know as soon as Christmas comes." Cooper retired to his State Room, always preferring to negotiate amidst its gilded splendor. Opulence had a funny effect on people. Some men grew weak-kneed just going in there, especially after walking the length of the deck and seeing the firepower at Cooper's command.

He didn't know much about this mercenary, Leon Christmas. The file was alarmingly thin, his Washington contacts had informed him. From what he could tell, Christmas was just a hired goon with a knack for being in the right place at the right time. He'd had no formal military training, despite seeming competent enough in the field, and Commander Cooper had been around long enough to respect Napoleon's maxim about lucky generals.

His thoughts were interrupted by a knock on the door, and his aide slipped in. "General Christmas is here, sir."

"Send him in."

The mercenary stepped inside, smiling, and then strode over to Commander Cooper and gave him a hearty handshake.

"Damn," said Christmas, taking the room in and beaming at Cooper. "Nice digs."

As Christmas gaped at the room's finery, Cooper took the opportunity to examine him. He cut an impressive figure, Commander Cooper had to admit, despite being a little rougher around the edges than expected.

Uninvited, Christmas dropped into a chair opposite Cooper's grand mahogany desk. "Been roughin' it the last few weeks." He smiled again. "But I won't bore you with the details."

"Drink, General?" Cooper didn't wait for a reply, instead taking a bottle and two glasses from a drawer.

Christmas held the glass to his nose and inhaled. "Much

as I like Hondurans, they have no clue about whiskey."

"I'll say." Cooper clinked glasses with the man before taking a sip. He let the smile fall from his face. "Let's get down to business."

Christmas drained a considerable measure in one gulp, and wiped his mouth with the back of his hand. "Ready when you are." He grinned.

"Bonilla won't let me put a guard aboard," said Cooper. "I don't want to leap to conclusions about your actions, but that does make me suspicious."

"Would you?" Christmas smiled again.

The mercenary's demeanor was putting Cooper off his stride. "Would I what?"

"Let us put a guard aboard your vessel."

Commander Cooper eyed the man for a moment. "That's what Bonilla said. The reason I asked you here was to urge you, in the strongest possible terms, to await the decision on the status of the *Hornet* before engaging in any further revolutionary activity. You must convince Bonilla."

"And who makes that decision? Washington?"

Cooper nodded.

"It will be next year before those blowhards make up their minds."

Cooper suppressed a laugh. "Look, Lee, I'll be frank. I think you're engaging in activity that your country—the United States of America—does not desire. I also think you pulled a fine ruse getting the *Hornet* out of New Orleans. But the game is up."

Christmas produced a small cigar and lit it, inhaling deeply. "The *Hornet* is a transport vessel, nothing more." He blew a circle of smoke across the desk toward Cooper, exhaling the rest through his nose. "You've searched her for arms," he added. "She's clean. And she's flying the Honduran flag. You have no lawful reason to impede her operation."

"Let's be absolutely clear." Cooper tried to keep an edge out of his voice. "This treaty *will* be signed. And the Hondurans *will* ratify." He stood, his knuckles on the desk, leaning toward Christmas. "Once that happens, any of your mercenaries in the field will be considered enemy combatants." He leaned in further. "American or not."

Christmas exhaled another circle of smoke. "We prefer the term 'soldier of fortune'." He stubbed out his *puro* in the whiskey tumbler. "And I'll take this damn country before you get your boots wet, Commander."

59

The Americans were going to put a stop to the revolution—or such were the rumors after the Paredes–Knox treaty was signed in Washington. However, it was still unclear whether the Honduran Congress would ratify the treaty. Bonilla and his rebels would need to capture the entire northern coast before a vote was held; yet the rebels weren't quite ready to launch an attack on La Ceiba. Recruits were still pouring into Trujillo, and Bonilla wanted them equipped and trained first. With the Americans on his back, he figured he'd only get one chance. Instead, he dispatched Lee to seize Iriona, fifty miles further down the coast.

Lee took Ed McLaurie and thirty men and seized the town with minimal resistance, the only blow being their first casualty. But the rebels were bolstered by the contents of Iriona's customs treasury, the ammunitions in its *cuartel*, and another surge of recruits.

Once the fallen Honduran recruit was given a proper burial, Lee ordered everyone back aboard the *Hornet* with as much of Iriona's armory as the vessel could safely hold.

"Spare no fuel," he told the captain, anxious to see if Bonilla would finally grant permission to move on La Ceiba.

Just short of Trujillo, a sloop bore down on them at top

speed. "Hand me those binoculars," said Lee. As he brought the vessel into focus, he could tell it was crowded with men—Bonilla's men, waving rifles and machetes, desperately trying to get their attention. "Kill the engines." He turned to the skipper. "Now!"

The *Hornet* sat dead in the water, waves bobbing it from starboard. McLaurie came up on deck, swearing. "Something up?"

Lee pointed to the sloop. "We got trouble."

McLaurie turned to bark orders down to his men, but Lee grabbed his arm. "Not that kind of trouble, Ed."

They watched as the smaller vessel drew alongside and lashing ropes were thrown across. He sought out the sloop's captain. "What the hell is going on?"

The skipper came to the rail. "Bonilla sent us," he said, as his men tethered his boat to the *Hornet*. "Trouble with the *yanquis*. All weapons must be transferred to us."

Before Lee finished cursing, McLaurie had organized a chain of men from starboard to the bowels of the ship, passing up crates of rifles and boxes of ammo until the sloop looked as if it might sink under the weight. The men worked as fast as they could; if that American spotted them before the transfer was complete, they could lose everything. As soon as the last crate of rifles was on the deck of the sloop, Lee ordered the ropes untied.

The sloop took off in the opposite direction, and the *Hornet* sailed around the headland and into the bay of Trujillo, right into the path of both the *Marietta* and the *Tacoma*.

She was seized before she could even dock, and Lee's men ordered ashore. Together, they stood on the pier with a mixture of relief and despair, watching the *Tacoma* tow their vessel toward Puerto Cortés. They may have lost the *Hornet*, but they would likely have lost their inspirational leader, too, had the Americans caught them with all of those rifles.

60

Losing the *Hornet* was a blow, but it had served its purpose: gaining Bonilla's men a foothold on the Honduran mainland. Lee couldn't dwell on it. He had bigger fish to fry. With the Americans ratcheting up their interference, he'd finally been granted permission to march on La Ceiba. He set out from Trujillo with a force of five hundred men.

The small town of Nuevo Armenia was in their path, but scouts had already confirmed that any government troops stationed there had high-tailed it, probably retreating to La Ceiba. The rebels took the town unopposed, and Lee was happy to give his men a rest and a proper meal. The next morning, while he was checking supplies with Ed McLaurie, a sloop delivered a letter from Bonilla. He cursed as he read its contents. "Goddamn it!" He kicked over a crate of bananas.

"What's up?" asked McLaurie, beginning to place the fruit back in the box.

Lee didn't answer for a moment, instead pacing back and forth. "New orders from Bonilla."

"Uh-oh."

"Yep. We gotta stay put."

"Goddamn it." McLaurie flung the bananas to the

ground.

"That's what I said." Lee smiled momentarily, and then a frown furrowed his brow. "It's not that bad. Apparently some army of partisans is making its way down the mountains. They've joined up from all over. Bonilla wants us to arm them and bring them with us."

"How long have we gotta wait?"

"A couple of days," he said. "But I don't like it."

He waited, nonetheless, all the while fretting that something else would further delay their attack and worrying that the defenders of La Ceiba would perceive his stalled advance as indecision or trepidation.

His mood soured when Molony walked into the *cantina* Lee had requisitioned as his headquarters, accompanying a messenger under a truce flag. "It's the Brits this time," said Molony, handing Lee an envelope. "He insisted on delivering it in person."

"This should be interesting." Lee knifed through the waxy seal. As he scanned the contents, his face darkened. He dismissed the messenger.

"What is it?"

"These bastards are trying to trip us up any way they can." Lee curled his lip.

"Who is it from?" asked Molony. "What does it say?"

"The captain of a British ship, this time, sticking his oar in. The *HMS Brilliant*." Lee tilted his head back, sticking his nose in the air. "Captain Woollcombe relies on me to prevent my men from endangering the lives and property of British subjects."

Molony shook his head. "Does he now?"

"Yeah, and it gets worse. He says it's 'in our best interests' to follow certain rules he's got laid down. And if we don't, he has a force of men in La Ceiba that will drive us off."

"What rules?"

Lee opened the convention, read the contents, and then spat on the ground. "Rat bastards. They don't even recognize Bonilla." He waved the document in Molony's face. "The local garrison commander has agreed the rules of engagement with this British captain. Both their names are signed below." He pointed at the bottom of the page. "Look."

Molony's face scrunched up. "I'm not sure I understand."

"It's about respect. They agree the rules between them, don't ask Bonilla, and don't put his name on the bottom."

"What rules?"

"They're making it next to impossible for us to launch an attack. They've established some kind of 'neutral zone' where no fighting can take place, or they'll get involved. The Americans too. The *Tacoma* is guarding La Ceiba along with the British." Lee examined the document once more. "Listen to this crap," he said. "If any bullets even pass through this neutral zone, they'll sound their ships' sirens. If fighting doesn't cease, they're gonna open fire on *both* armies. This is horseshit. I'm sending a reply."

Lee grabbed a pencil and scribbled an angry letter, denouncing the lack of consultation, the withholding of proper recognition of Bonilla's standing, and accusing the British of breaching their neutrality by affording the defenders of La Ceiba their protection. He declared they were one day's march from La Ceiba, and he was proceeding with his assault regardless.

He read the letter back to Molony, who winced. Thinking better of it, Lee crumpled the page. With a sigh, he handed the communications from the British to Molony. "Have this wired to Bonilla in Trujillo."

Later that day, he received Bonilla's response, ordering him to send a far more respectful reply that promised to obey the rules of war.

Guy Molony avoided the *cantina* as much as possible over the next two days. Lee was like a cat on a griddle, liable to spit at anyone who so much as looked at him. Instead, Guy busied himself with stripping and reassembling his machine guns and trying to teach others the finer points of handling such a weapon.

Lee's mood broke on January 22, when he got the go-ahead from Bonilla, and Guy joined the rest of the officers in the *cantina* for the briefing. With the plan of attack agreed upon, the rebels moved out that evening, in better spirits now that they were finally closing in on La Ceiba. It was only supposed to be a day's march, but the incessant tropical rains hampered their progress. Guy marveled at how much water could fall from the sky, reminding him of the downpours in Manila, which could last for a week. Three days of squelching through the jungle later, the rebels finally reached the mouth of the Cangrejal River, just short of their target.

Before they could even set up camp, another emissary approached under a truce flag. This time, Guy let McLaurie take the messenger up to Lee. When Ed returned, Guy raised an eyebrow.

"US Consul wants to meet Lee before he attacks La Ceiba," McLaurie said, before smiling. "Or, should I say, the 'Honorable General Christmas'."

Guy spat. "I'd say he liked that."

"Yup." McLaurie chuckled. "Consul offered to come unarmed, only with his assistant, and Lee said he could bring whoever he damn well liked."

Guy gave McLaurie a wry grin. "This should be fun."

The next morning, Guy was up by the mouth of the river—where the land jutting out past the jungle afforded a view of La Ceiba—trying to determine the best spot to place his machine gun. His first job tomorrow would be covering the rebels as they crossed the river. Gazing back at the town, he spotted a launch puttering out from the wharf, and he hollered back for some binoculars. When he was able to take a closer look, he saw the boat was filled with officers. He'd never seen so much gold braid or so many unearned medals. His lip curled in disgust. "They're coming," he yelled.

Ten minutes later, the dignitaries disembarked on the rebels' side of the river mouth and marched up to Lee's command post. Guy watched as they were all introduced: the US consul, the British vice-consul, Commander Cooper of the USS *Marietta*, and Captain Woollcombe of the HMS *Brilliant*, as well as a host of lesser officers and flunkies.

Molony guessed it was an attempt at a show of force, and he watched Lee stifling his laughter, especially when shaking hands with the pompous British captain. They carried a whole host of agreements they wanted Lee to sign. Aside from the restrictions regarding the neutral zone, the rebels were forbidden from launching an attack that afternoon, and from initiating one at night whatsoever.

By the final stipulation, Lee had clearly had enough. "What the hell? Is this going to be fought under the Queensbury rules? President Bonilla is a gentleman. And I'm ready to be reasonable, but goddamn all these rules!"

Guy had enough too, and slipped away quietly. If his time in the Philippines had taught him anything, it was that this was no time to be sitting around listening to these guys jabber on. He took three men, all armed with shovels, and headed for the riverbank. They begin digging, relentlessly urged on by Guy when they took a breather.

"Here! You really mustn't, you know!" One of the British naval officers ran toward the digging crew.

"Mustn't what, exactly?" Guy sneered.

"Fortify your position," replied the Briton in a haughty tone. "We're here under a flag of truce. You really mustn't. It's just not cricket."

He dropped his spade and balled his fists. "I'll give you cricket." He pointed to La Ceiba. "Tomorrow, it's me they're going to be shooting at, not you." He picked up his shovel once more, jabbing its blade at the Brit. "Besides, I'd like to see anyone try and stop me."

Their raised voices attracted the attention of the truce party, who approached, their numbers restoring the British officer's bravery. "Don't you see?" He addressed Guy in a shrill tone. "You are preparing a fortified position under our flag of truce. The town's defenders can't fire on you while we are here, and you are taking advantage. That trench is going to be very useful to you tomorrow."

Christmas caught up and winked at Guy. He clapped the

haughty British officer on the back, almost a little too hard; he nearly slipped into the trench. "We won't be here long enough to use it," he said. "We'll be in La Ceiba before dinner."

"Laid out, and covered with blankets," said the officer. "Ready for burial."

Christmas grinned. "In that case, make sure to pick out a dry spot for us, because we're wet enough now to last through hell."

His mood brightened by this interchange, Christmas signed all the documents requested of him. A few hours after they departed, he received one final message from the delegates, reminding him of his responsibility under the rules of war to request the town's surrender before launching any attack.

Molony stood back as Christmas turned the air blue.

61

On the morning of January 25, 1911, Lee gathered his officers in the tent at the mouth of the Cangrejal River, just short of La Ceiba. Terms of surrender had been rejected the night before, meaning the rebels had finally satisfied the Byzantine conditions of the British and American naval officers. Lee went over the plan of attack one more time with his officers, a gentle breeze passing through the tent as he spoke.

"We have two main problems here," he said, "aside from being outnumbered, of course. But we're used to that. Luckily, some of you can take whole towns on your own."

McLaurie slapped Gonzales on the back, as Lee continued. "The neutral zone—as I've explained already—cannot be breached, no matter what." He paused, eyeing the men in turn. "I'm serious about this. The Americans and the Brits are itching to get involved, and believe me when I say they won't be joining our side."

"I wouldn't mind havin' a pop at that Brit," said McLaurie.

Lee chuckled. "Guy, too, I'd imagine." He stopped and looked back over the assembled faces. "Where's Molony?"

McLaurie yanked a thumb in the direction of the river

mouth. "Still digging that trench."

"Still?" He waved a hand. "Anyway, you'll both have plenty to shoot at later on. But before I get to that, between here and La Ceiba is this jungle." He indicated the dense foliage on the other side of the river. "If you try to cut through it, you'll get all tangled up before you know what's what. Only one road through it. Crosses the river by a ford a little bit inland."

He looked to one of his commanders. "Leiva, you'll take your men up to that ford. They're dug in on the other side, and I'm guessing that's where most of their troops will be—that's where they'll expect us to attack, at least. But all you'll need to do is keep them engaged."

Leiva nodded. "Yes, sir."

"I mean it," he said, his eyes darting to Gonzales. "Don't attempt to push through unless they start falling back. We just need you to keep 'em busy."

"As ordered, sir." Leiva shared a grin with Gonzales.

"Meanwhile, me, Ed, Joe, Pedro, and Guy will take a detachment of men along the strip of beach fronting the jungle." He took a deep breath then exhaled. "It's gonna be tricky. The beach turns into mud pretty quick—a swampy marsh they've strung eight lines of barbed wire across. They've got some fortified trench down there with a Krupp gun covering the whole thing, probably a company of men also. Not too many, though. They think it's impregnable," Lee smiled, "but we'll find a way through."

He drew himself up to his full height. "Boys, I want this fight over quickly. They might outnumber us, but a lot of their men have been conscripted and have sympathies with our side. If the tide turns quickly in our favor, I think they'll lay down their guns. But if it gets drawn out, they may take a liking to their side after all. Got that?"

"Yes, sir!"

"Anyone I spoke to beforehand, follow me. The rest of you, go with General Leiva. And I'll see you in La Ceiba."

He walked out of the tent, down toward the *cayucos*, looking back up at the trench—the digging of which had so antagonized the British. His men piled into the dugout canoes, leaving Lee last to step aboard. As they pushed off, he looked back once more in Guy's direction. "Hope he's ready," he said.

"He's been digging all night," said McLaurie. "If he ain't ready now…" He shrugged.

Lee switched his attention to the opposite bank. "Keep your eyes peeled, boys." There were more dangerous elements of the plan, but nothing that left them quite so exposed. He noticed a few of his men muttering prayers as they paddled across. To his relief, they reached the other side without incident, the first *cayuco* of troops taking position while the rest landed and pulled their boats ashore.

He signaled back to Molony. The ditch wasn't needed after all. After waiting fifteen minutes for the machine gun crews to make their way down and paddle across, Lee was desperate to get into position before Leiva's men engaged the main body of La Ceiba's defenders, so much so that he almost yanked Molony out of the *cayuco*.

"Take a couple of men and start out ahead of us," he instructed. "Keep your eyes peeled. We don't know exactly where this trench is yet. Find a position to bed down. Two machine guns and the Hotchkiss should do the trick. Take out that Krupp gun first chance you get."

Molony squinted back at him. "When?"

"What do you mean *when*? Now!"

"I've been in that trench all night. I haven't had a damn thing to eat."

Lee reached into his pocket and withdrew some stale animal crackers. "You've got to be kidding me," said Molony, stuffing his face, crumbs coating his stubble. "I mean *real* food."

Lee smiled and nodded toward the town. "There's plenty of good grub in there."

Before Molony could respond, gunshots rang out in the distance. "That must be Leiva." Lee turned back to Molony. "Git going!"

62

Guy Molony started off along the beach with the other gunners and their crews, still sore about missing breakfast. He heard the crackle of defensive fire almost instantly. Something slapped his face and he looked around, confused; none of the others were close enough to have struck him. Pulling his hand away from his cheek, he noticed the blood. *Must have been grazed by a bullet.* Further rounds kicked up sand far behind him. "Hit the deck!" he bellowed.

Once Guy got his bearings, he figured the enemy was firing high because they were behind some kind of tall embankment. He propped himself up on his knees. When no fire came, he ordered his men to do likewise and rigged up his machine gun on the spot, aiming it at the origin of the enemy fire on the other side of the marsh and letting off a few short bursts. Silence was the sole response, punctuated by distant gunfire from Leiva's inland engagement of the enemy. Molony looked back to see Christmas, McLaurie, and the rest of the men advancing toward their position, only to come under heavy fire. When Guy went to lay down cover, his gun jammed; he cursed.

The dense scrubland around the swamp screened the enemy from view, and the barbed wire ran right out into the water. He couldn't get enough of a fix on the enemy's position to take them out with the Hotchkiss. Guy's palms blistered on the searing-hot gun barrel as he tried desperately to un-jam it, while Gonzales braved a hail of bullets to wade out and try to get eyes on whatever was halting their advance.

Running back from the water, bullets splashing all around him, Pedro dove onto the sand beside Guy. "Enemy position," he panted. "Fortified. Maybe one hundred and fifty yards ahead." Gonzales held a hand up as he gathered breath. "Barbed wire only goes a few yards into the water. We can wade around it and charge them."

"Like hell, we're supposed to…" Guy paused, snapping his fingers. "Did you say a hundred and fifty yards?"

Gonzales pointed. "Right there."

He whooped, and called out to Joe Reed. The three of them hauled the Hotchkiss into position and aimed six shots, one after the other, right where Pedro reckoned the trench was. That was enough for Gonzales; he charged toward the water, wading until he could circumnavigate the first of the eight fence posts where the barbed wire terminated.

Guy sighed, picked up a rifle, and turned to Reed. "Watch these guns." With four recruits in tow, he raced after Gonzales, holding his weapon high, out of the tide. For a moment, he thought the splashing of the men trailing him was a hail of enemy bullets, and he braced for the inevitable. It was a couple of seconds before he realized, somewhat sheepishly, that the enemy wasn't shooting at all. He caught up with Gonzales, and they rounded the last fence post and looked back to see Christmas leading the remaining men into the water.

The six in the advance party charged the trench, yelling and hollering, only to discover it abandoned; the front of the fortifications had been completely blown away. He turned to Gonzales, grinning. "One of those potshots got lucky." He looked around, remembering something. "Hey, where's their gun?"

"Maybe they hauled it away."

Guy shook his head. "Wouldn't have had time. These guys beat it in a hurry." At the waterline, he spied a dark shape lurking below the surface. "They dumped it. Come on." Molony beckoned to the others. "Help me with this thing."

It took all six of them, but they managed to haul the Krupp out of the ocean. Guy smiled. "They left the ammo too. Come on, boys, let's swing this 'round and point it at that there *cuartel*."

Before they could move into position, Christmas burst out of the water, hurtling toward them, a panicked look on his face. "Guy, are you okay? We heard the shooting stop…" He caught his breath, placing his rifle at his feet. "We thought you were a goner." He tilted his head, examining Guy. "Hey, they got you."

"Huh?" Guy's hand went instinctively to his jaw. "Aw, just a lucky shot. Only grazed me. No big deal."

Christmas gave him a stern look. "Try ducking next time."

He grinned. "Why—"

"Enemy approaching," screamed McLaurie, raising his weapon. "And I don't think they're surrendering."

"Get to the barricades." Christmas stooped low, grabbing his gun. "And start shootin'."

Across the railroad track that separated the trench from the outer streets of La Ceiba, enemy soldiers advanced, ducking in and out of doorways, firing on the group's position. Molony and the rest of the men laid down a withering response. The enemy began retreating. A gray mule rode into view, bearing an officer who urged his men forward, convincing them with the flat of his machete. Without Christmas giving the order, a dozen bullets tore into the officer's torso. They watched in disbelief as he wheeled his beast around and sought cover in a side street. Before Guy could react, Lee clambered out of the trench and raced after him, with Pedro Gonzales right on his heels.

Christmas stopped at an abandoned machine-gun placement—a newer model too.

"She jammed, but I can fix her." Guy kneeled down to examine the weapon. "No ammo, though."

"Maybe in the *cuartel*."

They kept moving, following the rest of their men, edging through the town, securing each side street as they passed. The *cuartel* was directly in front of them. When they charged, they found the enemy had already retreated and that Pedro Gonzales controlled the building. He was haranguing the sole occupant—the terrified warden of the arsenal, whose hands shook as he handed over the keys.

They immediately began loading up the machine guns with all of that fresh ammunition, and when they were done Christmas noticed Gonzales had disappeared again. He nudged Guy. "Pedro must have gone to liberate Puerto Cortés." Their peals of laughter had only just subsided when Gonzales returned, red-faced and panting, triggering another laughing fit.

Gonzales tapped his foot, waiting for them to quit. "Found the rest of them," he said. "They're all in a trench on the other side of that cemetery we saw on the way up here. Only thing is, they're right in front of that Neutral Zone." He winked at Christmas, smiling. "And Pedro Díaz is with them."

Christmas clapped his hands together. "This couldn't have worked out better." He turned to Guy. "You take Pedro and that fancy new machine gun and pin Díaz down in that trench. Just be careful with those bullets. I don't want to give anyone an excuse to stop this fight. Me, Reed, and McLaurie will stay right here. I've got a feeling that group engaging Leiva's men might start retreating this way—they've nowhere else to go, and we've got to hold this *cuartel*. Díaz won't be able to go anywhere. He's backing right onto the Neutral Zone."

They set up their machine gun right at the edge of the cemetery, using a tombstone for cover. Guy fed a belt into the gun as he surveyed the scene. The enemy was dug into a long trench at the back of the graveyard, firing occasionally from the top. Just behind them, in front of a row of houses, was the Neutral Zone—or so he guessed, given that it was fronted by a line of British marines with bayonets drawn. Guy trained the sights low. He didn't want to draw those bastards into the fight.

After each withering burst of fire, the enemy was temporarily cowed, and Guy and his crew crept a little further forward. The pace of the advance was interminably slow for the likes of Gonzales, whose constant demands to charge the trench became too much for Molony. After another vicious blast from his machine gun, Guy turned to him. "Shut up, Pedro. I don't want to hear it."

"You don't have any *huevos*, you know that?" Gonzales stood. "If I had that gun, I'd charge right over there, shove it down the throat of Don Pedro Díaz and—" His tirade was cut short by a bullet whizzing through the air and tearing through his upper arm. Gonzales looked down at his wound, furious, but he still didn't take cover. "*Hijo de puta*!"

Guy smiled. "Best take yourself back to the *cuartel*, Pedro. That looks nasty." As Gonzales trudged away, Molony called over his shoulder. "Don't worry! I'll try not to have too much fun." He followed his comment with a lengthy burst of fire, as Gonzales sulked back to Christmas and McLaurie.

The defenders of the trench had suffered enough. They poured out, attempting to retreat, only to run into a wall of marines that wouldn't let them pass. Guy held his fire, watching the spectacle unfold through his sights. There appeared to be an argument of some sort. Several men were getting right in the face of one British sailor, who didn't even blink. Then the government forces dropped their weapons at their feet, raised their arms in the air, and walked into the Neutral Zone.

"All right, boys," said Molony. "Let's pack her up. We're going back to the *cuartel*."

He found Christmas in a heated discussion with British and American officers. His face darkened as he looked up to see Molony. "What are you doing here?" he growled. "I told you to keep 'em in that damn trench!"

"They ran out," replied Molony, shrugging.

"What do you mean 'they ran out'? Where to, goddamn

it?"

"The Neutral Zone," said Guy. "They surrendered. The damn trench is empty, and there wasn't anything I could do about it."

"Now, gentlemen." Lee returned his attentions to the naval officers opposite. "You see?"

They nodded reluctantly. Guy watched as Christmas pressed home the point.

"Here are the facts," he said. "I control the beach, the *cuartel*, the graveyard—the whole town from here up to the Neutral Zone. The only enemy troops that haven't surrendered are down by the river. Their *comandante* is wounded, and Leiva should break through shortly." He paused. "If you don't go down there and ask them to surrender, I'll take the rest of my men and attack their rear. They won't have a chance." Christmas spread his hands. "We could have a slaughter on our hands."

Guy was impressed. He knew it was a bluff—they had no idea how Leiva was faring, and he didn't sound like he was going to break through any time soon—but the sadness on Lee's face looked so real that he was almost moved. The assembled naval officers stood as one and marched down to the remaining Dávila troops, insisting upon their surrender. Only afterward did it become clear that the disarmed government forces were far more numerous than the rebels they had surrendered to. Leiva had suffered numerous losses, and was in quite some difficulty toward the end.

But by two o'clock in the afternoon, La Ceiba had fallen.

63

The former *comandante* of La Ceiba succumbed to his wounds that night and was buried the next day with full military honors. Lee ordered the release of all captured prisoners, so they could show their respects at the funeral—with one exception, Pedro Díaz. Díaz had made many enemies during his stint in the Honduran army. With a large number of his ex-subordinates having defected to the rebels, the British felt it prudent that Díaz remain captive.

The somber drinking that followed the service took on a more festive air as night fell, but Lee and his officers retired to the *cuartel* to share a bottle in private. Bonilla now controlled the Bay Islands, two lucrative customs houses, and the coastline from Iriona to La Ceiba. Lee's forces had won a genuine battle, showing tenacity and ingenuity in the face of greater numbers. Desertions from the government side would increase, and yet more new recruits would flock to the rebels' banner. And he had a whole barracks full of guns and ammunition to arm them.

The pick of the bunch were the five new machine guns and two old Gatling guns that Molony began disassembling as soon as the bottle of *aguardiente* was passed around. McLaurie winced as he took a swig. "How you boys ever got used to this rotgut is beyond me."

Lee guffawed and grabbed the bottle, making a big show of swallowing a huge gulp without so much as blinking. "Never show fear in the face of the enemy." He mopped his brow and passed the bottle down to Molony. "Even if you're crying inside."

"I knew it," said McLaurie, slapping his thigh. "Tell you what, though. Questionable local hooch aside, I'm of half a mind to settle down here when we're done knocking off this Davíla."

"Oh, yeah?" Molony hadn't even noticed the bottle beside him.

"Sure," said McLaurie. "Why? What you planning to do after the war?"

"This ain't done yet," growled Lee. "And it's bad luck to talk like it is."

Molony stopped tinkering and glanced up at Lee. "Sure, but with all these new weapons … I can't wait to set them up in the field."

"And the income from this customs house here will go a long way," said McLaurie.

Molony nodded. "We pretty much own the Caribbean coast now, once we take Puerto Cortés."

"Quit jabbering." Lee kicked Molony. "And drink up."

Once Guy was done, Lee grabbed the *aguardiente* from him. "Like I told you already: you'll jinx us." Lee fumbled in his pocket for a *puro*, and took a swig from the bottle before lighting the cigar. "Anyway, who knows what the Americans will do next."

McLaurie got a faraway look in his eyes. "I think I'd like

to be a coconut farmer." Lee and Molony erupted in peals of laughter.

After a full minute, Lee wiped his eye. "Shit, Ed, that was a good one."

"I'm serious." He grabbed the bottle from Lee. "I could do it, too."

Guy and Lee burst into laughter once more.

"What?" demanded McLaurie, pouting.

Molony calmed himself. "Sorry, Ed. I shouldn't laugh. It just sounds funny—a coconut farm."

"Okay," said McLaurie. "A plantation then."

"That sounds better," Molony conceded. "But do they do that? I just assumed they grew wild everywhere."

"Sure they do," he said. "There's big money in it."

Lee raised an eyebrow. "Really?"

Before McLaurie could respond, Pedro Gonzales burst through the door, red-faced and sweating.

Lee threw his hands in the air. "We surrender! Don't shoot us!" This time they all roared with laughter.

"*Hijos de putas.*" Gonzales grabbed Lee's arm. "Listen, an urgent letter just arrived on the Guatemala steamer." He handed it to Lee.

The group fell silent as Lee tore it open. While he scanned the contents, the three men edged closer.

"What is it, Lee?" asked Molony.

A grin spread across his face. "Where's that damn bottle?"

"What is it?" repeated Molony.

"A girl." He beamed and grabbed the *aguardiente* from McLaurie. "A baby girl. Born this morning."

Guy and Pedro congratulated him while McLaurie shook his hand. "Does she have a name?" he asked.

Lee took a swig. "I'm gonna call her Ceiba."

64

When Bonilla arrived to survey the famous victory, he saw it had come at a heavy price. General Leiva's losses during the conquest of La Ceiba left barely half of his six hundred men fit for duty. Within a day, however, spurred on by Bonilla's arrival and the air of unstoppable momentum, some seven hundred new recruits joined the revolution.

The surge in volunteers was welcome. Capturing Puerto Cortés would be a much trickier proposition. While Molony, Gonzales, and McLaurie ensured the new recruits were equipped and given at least some basic training, Christmas and Bonilla discussed tactics in the *cuartel.* "Remind me why we can't just march on Puerto Cortés?" asked Bonilla, pinching the bridge of his nose.

"I don't know how long it was since you were last there, but any time you visited it was probably by train." Lee leaned in to the map. "And it's not well marked here but this *laguna* which wraps all the way around the back is actually saltwater." He pointed at the edge of town. "This is a bridge, a long trestle bridge, not a strip of land. We would be cut to pieces trying to attack down there."

"Even with numbers?"

Lee puffed up his chest. "Me and a handful of others

held off the whole San Pedro garrison there a few years back."

"I think I heard something about that." Bonilla smiled. "But that's not the only access point."

"That trestle bridge over the *laguna* is just for the banana train. There's a road bridge on the other side of town, but you'd have to march by the rest of Puerto Cortés just to reach it. And those who weren't picked off on the approach would face the same problem trying to get across that bridge."

Bonilla stifled a yawn, holding up his hand by way of apology. "And we can't attack by sea."

"Nope," Lee said. "Pretty much suicidal now, with the *Hornet* gone and the Americans and British guarding the harbor."

Bonilla stared at the map, rubbing one eye and then the other. "What are the options?"

"Only one, far as I can see." Lee leaned over the map. "The harbor of Puerto Cortés is protected by this headland." He traced his finger away from the town. "On the other side is this beach. It's more exposed, so the seas are much wilder, but we should be able to land there."

"Could be dangerous if they expect it."

Lee nodded. "They will expect it," he said. "And it will be dangerous. We'll have to hit the beach pretty hard, gain control as quickly as possible. Then we'll hold it while the rest of the troops disembark, and then move on the town itself."

Bonilla stretched. "I'm sorry Lee, I need to get some sleep. We'll continue tomorrow."

"Can I start planning the beach landing?"

"Talk to your officers. Draw up a detailed plan for taking that beach. I'll look at it, but I haven't made any decisions."

Lee stayed in the *cuartel* as Bonilla left, staring at the map of the Caribbean coast of Honduras that was stretched over the table. He tapped his finger on Puerto Cortés and remembered stepping off that banana boat, unknown, without a penny to his name. *Hell*, he corrected himself, *I remember stepping on that damn steamer, drunk, not even knowing where it was headed.*

And now he would arrive as liberator.

The next morning found him poring over the map once more, discussing with Molony and McLaurie how many men they should commit to the first wave. He relished the task, excited to have another chance to test himself in battle. But he was surprised when Bonilla arrived two hours early.

"We're not quite done yet," said Lee.

Bonilla waved a hand. "Never mind that."

"Huh?"

"Davíla's men have abandoned Puerto Cortés," said Bonilla, his eyes dancing.

McLaurie and Molony congratulated Bonilla, but Lee ignored them. "What do you mean by 'abandoned'?"

"I don't know," admitted Bonilla.

"Did they retreat? Are they waiting for us in the bush? Did they all defect?"

Bonilla furrowed his brow. "We have reports they retreated up the railway track to San Pedro." McLaurie whooped, but Lee shot him a fierce look as Bonilla continued. "But I haven't confirmed anything yet."

Lee slammed a fist on the table.

"General," said Bonilla. "I know you wanted your battle, but there's a town there for the taking. Maybe we could…" He spread his hands.

"Shit," said Lee. "Of course." He turned to Molony. "Find Joe Reed. Gonzales and Leiva too." He punched Ed in the arm. "You get down to the pier and round up the skippers." Lee smiled. "Tell 'em we move out in two hours. No excuses!"

Lee may have been denied his battle, but he wasn't denied a hero's welcome as the population of Puerto Cortés thronged the streets to welcome the rebel army and its *gringo* commander. In the crowd, Molony spotted his old friend, fresh off the Guatemala boat—the guy who'd tipped him off about the Honduran gig in the first place, Sam Dreben.

After the rebels had marched through the town and back again, Lee headed to the *cuartel* to see if the garrison had left anything useful. Gonzales intercepted him with a message from Bonilla. He wanted to talk. Alone.

Lee made his way down to the banana wharf—the same spot where he'd winded the brother of his second wife, and the place he had eloped from with his third—and waited while Bonilla dealt with the entreaties of a pair of local businessmen. On seeing Lee, Bonilla made his apologies to them and summoned Christmas forward.

"New friends?" Lee asked, with a wry grin.

"My least favorite part of the job." Bonilla picked at a loose thread on his sleeve. "But forget that." He looked up. "I have big news."

Lee swept his arm back toward Puerto Cortés. "Bigger than this?"

"No." Bonilla laughed. "Well, maybe. You wanted to know why Davíla beat such a hasty retreat?" He tapped his nose. "I think I have the answer."

"Go on."

"I still have eyes and ears in Congress. Presidential Palace too. It seems Davíla got desperate after the fall of La Ceiba and telegrammed Washington."

Lee raised an eyebrow.

"He promised to sign the treaty and push it through Congress if they intervened."

"I'm still waiting for the part with the good news," said Lee.

"President Taft told him to get the treaty passed first, and he'd have all the backing he wanted."

Lee rubbed his thumb and forefinger together.

"Quite," said Bonilla. "But he must have been desperate, because he called the entire chamber into his private office, one by one, and begged them to vote for the treaty."

"Did they hold the vote?"

"They did, all right. And they voted no!"

"The treaty is dead?"

Bonilla grinned. "The treaty is dead, *amigo*."

65

That night, Puerto Cortés threw the wildest *fiesta* it had seen in living memory, helped on by Bonilla forking over a significant portion of the revolutionary budget to keep the rum flowing. The party spilled over into a second day, and a third, with only a rudimentary watch posted at both bridges—and they were just as drunk as everyone else. Festivities finally calmed on the fourth day, when Bonilla received further news. The United States was inviting both sides to attend formal peace talks aboard the USS *Tacoma.*

"Peace talks!" Lee yelled when he heard, livid at the news. "You should damn well tell 'em to shove it."

"*Tranquilo,*" said Bonilla.

Lee continued pacing. "This war is over, goddamn it. It's only a matter of time." He shook his head. "Davíla has no chance."

"I know, and so do the Americans."

"Why are they pushing so hard now anyways? The treaty is dead."

"Lee, listen to me." Bonilla stood in his path, forcing him to stop pacing. "This isn't a negotiation. Davíla needs to save face. And probably wants safe passage out of the country."

Lee snorted. "So we'd be discussing his surrender?"

Bonilla smiled slightly and waggled his hand. "More or less."

The peace talks began three days later on the deck of the USS *Tacoma*. Lee recognized a couple of faces, nodding at Commander Cooper who looked less at ease on the deck of someone else's vessel. A diplomatic fuss erupted when Davíla arrived and refused to sit at the same table as a mercenary. Lee was sorely tempted to knock his teeth out, but Bonilla squeezed his arm. "Give us a moment," he whispered.

Lee lit a *puro*, gazing out at Puerto Cortés over the rail of the *Tacoma*.

"Isn't this a crock of shit?" Commander Cooper joined him.

Lee turned and smiled, surprised. "Ain't that the truth."

"Got another one of those?"

"Sure."

Cooper took his time lighting it. "I'll tell you exactly how this is gonna go," he said, exhaling through his nose. "Davíla's guys will say some shit, then Bonilla will refuse. Then Davíla's guys will ask for the same concession in different words, and Bonilla will refuse again."

Lee nodded, wondering where he was headed.

"Which is his right," Cooper said. "Davíla's in a position of weakness."

"The war is won." Lee sighed. "Didn't see the point in coming here in the first place."

"Right," said Cooper. "I'd be saying the same thing, in your shoes. But Davíla needs to save face. If the newspapers report that he signed away his presidency after ten minutes, he'll look like a coward. So he'll drag this out as long as he can." The commander took another puff. "Davíla's only got one card to play. He can go now, or he can prolong the war. Either way, he's gonna lose."

"That's not worth much." Lee cracked his knuckles on the rail. "We ain't near tired yet."

"Right," said Cooper. "He's already got safe passage. Davíla knows we've pretty much guaranteed that already."

"What's he going to push for, then?"

"Oh, he'll try for whatever he can get. I'm guessing a compromise candidate as interim president, followed by an election."

"Bonilla would win in a landslide."

"Exactly," said Cooper. "Davíla's job here is to push the date for that election out as far as possible, giving him a chance to regroup."

Lee sighed again and Cooper clapped him on the back. "Politics, my friend." He stubbed his *puro* on the rail and flicked the butt into the ocean. "I must say, though, didn't think you'd get this far."

Lee smiled. "Was never in doubt, Commander."

"I see that now," said Cooper. "Come on, let's rejoin them. We can make faces at each other from either side of the table."

He chuckled. "I'm not welcome, remember?"

"Don't mind him." Cooper waved a hand. "You take your seat at that table. I watched your performance at La Ceiba. Those interlocking fields of machine-gun fire." He shook his head. "Brilliant." He clapped Lee on the back once more. "And if Davíla has a problem with it, I'll throw the bastard overboard myself."

The talks didn't conclude until sundown, Bonilla showing far more patience than Lee. The agreement was simple. Davíla would resign, and the revolutionary forces would stand down with immediate effect. A compromise candidate, Dr. Manuel Bertrand, would be installed as president until an election could be held later in the year.

In the end, Davíla didn't even contest the October election, and Bonilla defeated his opponent in a landslide. He was inaugurated four months later, on February 1, 1912, and finally reinstalled in the Presidential Palace that had been wrested away from him by force. To ease the transition, Bonilla named Bertrand his vice president.

Stability, however, would remain out of reach.

66

Two days after President Bonilla was sworn in, a revolt broke out along the Salvadoran border. Bonilla stayed Lee's hand when he wanted to quash the rebellion personally, making excuses Lee couldn't understand. In the end, local commanders snuffed out the threat before any troops could be dispatched from Tegucigalpa.

Despite how briefly the insurrection flared, it was enough to spark another. One of Bonilla's old adversaries, Valladares, sailed from Costa Rica to El Salvador and began gathering recruits. Since the peace talks aboard the USS *Tacoma*, Valladares had been sending forth vicious screeds, pamphlets decrying both Dávila and Bonilla as *yanqui* stooges. It was only a matter of time before Valladares crossed the border, and Lee was itching to have a crack at him.

Two weeks later, Lee sat outside Bonilla's office, fidgeting with his epaulettes. His foot began tapping again and the sound echoed down the hallway. He placed his hands on his thighs and bit his lip. He had been waiting for almost an hour. If Bonilla was trying to cool him down, it wasn't going to work.

Eventually, the door to Bonilla's office cracked open; Lee barged in straight away. "What's all this about?" he bellowed as he pushed open the door. "Guy told me you've appointed Durón in my place."

Bonilla waited until his aide had left. "Lee," he said, indicating to a chair opposite. "*Por favor*, sit."

"Like hell, I will."

"I know you're angry. And you have every right to be."

Lee bit his tongue and let Bonilla continue.

"But I can explain. Please," Bonilla said. "Sit."

Lee reluctantly slumped in the chair. "This better be good," he growled.

Bonilla picked up a pen from his desk, eyeing it for a moment, before setting it down. His voice was almost cracking as he spoke. "You know I have the utmost respect for everything—"

"Aw, cut the crap, Manolo." Lee waved a hand. "Give it to me straight. You owe me that much."

Bonilla nodded.

Lee felt a lump form in his throat. "You want me gone?" He half rose from his chair. "Because if you do—"

"No!" Bonilla jumped to his feet and rounded the table. "You are my commander-in-chief, and there's nobody I would have in your place."

"Then why did you appoint that drunkard Durón? I could have Valladares licked in a week."

"I have no doubt about that." Bonilla put his hands behind his back. "You are my greatest commander." He walked to the window. "But there are … extenuating circumstances here."

"Don't give me that crap."

"You've read his pamphlets." Bonilla turned to face

him. "I'm a *yanqui* stooge, and you're a spy for Washington."

"Nobody buys that horseshit."

"There are things…" Bonilla trailed off, searching for the right words. "The *yanquis* are sending Philander Knox next month."

"Why?" asked Lee, this time rising from his chair. "I thought that treaty was dead."

"It is. He's touring all of Central America."

"That's not gonna help the situation. He's the one American politician the people know by name."

"*Exactemente.*" Bonilla perched himself on his desk. "And now I can't meet him here in the Palace. It looks bad for me, and bad for Honduras. I have to go down to Tigre Island and meet him off the boat, so his arrival doesn't spark an uprising."

"Hardly your fault."

Bonilla smiled. "This is where my job is different to yours. I have to clean the shit anyway. It's the secretary of state. Making arrangements like this makes it appear I can't even control my own country."

Lee said nothing, finally understanding Bonilla's predicament. "And this *yanqui* crap Valladares is running with…" He sighed. "Valladares picked up quite a few recruits with that rhetoric. If I put you in the field, it might inflame the situation. I want to end this now."

Lee chewed his lip. "At least tell me he's gonna to take Molony's gunners."

"Durón is keen to see this new unit in action. How many has he got now?"

"Fourteen, plus their crews. They're young, but they'll

get the job done." He looked down at his hands and then back to Bonilla. "You know," he said. "I never did get my final battle."

"You think this is the last of it?" Bonilla laughed.

Lee chuckled along with him. "True. And I suppose La Ceiba was pretty good."

"You won me the country, General." Bonilla stood, extending his hand. "And I'll never forget it."

Lee looked sideways at the offered hand. Then, he grabbed it and shook hands vigorously. He couldn't help grinning. "I did, didn't I?"

67

Colonel Guy Molony booted Durón's hammock once more, but the groggy general waved him away, muttering curses before dozing off again, still cradling his bottle of *aguardiente* like a babe. Guy curled his lip and spat in the dirt. He strode back to his team of gunners, surveying the chalk-white hill of El Horno in the distance.

Although night had fallen, the full moon hanging overhead lit up Valladares and his men like New Orleans on Mardi Gras. Guy grimaced. "Damn fools."

"Sir?"

Guy pointed toward El Horno. "Tell me, what do you see?"

"The enemy, sir."

"Exactly," he said through gritted teeth. "This isn't a fight. It's target practice." He turned to his men. "Line 'em up, boys." It gave him no pleasure, winning like this. Guy blessed himself. "Aim." He watched the cadets train their sights. This would be over in seconds. *Well*, he thought, *they had their chance to surrender*.

"Fire!"

The sound was deafening—fourteen machines of death in perfect concert. His eyes readjusted after the muzzle flash as the gun smoke began to dissipate. White puffs of dust kicked up by their stray shots escaped up into the night. On El Horno, Guy saw nothing but a string of dead men.

Durón appeared at his shoulder, rubbing his face. "Is it done?"

Guy stood aside to let Durón see for himself. The corpses had begun bleeding out, staining the pale hill. "*Bueno,*" said Durón. "Send someone over to make sure Valladares was among them."

"Already done."

When the spotter team eventually returned, they brought disturbing news. They'd clambered all over that glowing outcrop, checked all the faces of the fallen, even scoured the undergrowth at the base of the cliff, but Valladares was nowhere to be found.

68

To soften the blow of moving him aside for the operation against Valladares, Lee received another appointment: *comandante* of Puerto Cortés and Inspector-General of Northern Coast. The latter was an especially lucrative position, adding plenty of side-benefits to Lee's three existing salaries. Traditionally, the inspector-general creamed a good deal off the top, which wasn't considered corruption but rather a perk of the job. Everybody expected it. But Lee was running other things on the side, too—activities that would have put him on notice with the *comandante*, if he didn't also hold that position. And he didn't plan on opening an investigation anytime soon.

With his newfound wealth, Lee purchased a thousand-acre coconut plantation with his new business partner, Ed McLaurie. And he didn't stop there. When the old Louisiana Lottery Building came up for sale, he bought that and remodeled it, opening it as the town's newest attraction—the Palm Hotel—which soon became the social center of Puerto Cortés. On any special occasion, such as the president's birthday, the anniversary of his victory at La Ceiba, or even the Fourth of July, Lee would throw an incredibly lavish affair, advertising in the local newspapers that there would be free champagne to all comers.

One afternoon, while smoking a *puro* in the door of the hotel bar and nodding to passersby, Lee spied McLaurie exiting the general store at the opposite end of Calle de Linea. He waved his hat until he caught Ed's eye. Flicking his smoke into the street, he hollered at the bartender. "Open one of those bottles now, Alberto."

He embraced McLaurie at the door. "You heard the news?"

"No. What?"

"Valladares is dead."

McLaurie grinned. "Shit, I was beginning to think that guy was charmed."

"You and me both," Lee said. "Come on, raise a glass with me." McLaurie muttered excuses, but Lee steered him by the elbow up to the bar. "So, what brings you into town? Saw you coming out of the general store."

Ed waved a hand. "Just getting some supplies."

"Anything I need to know about? Send me the tally, and I'll pay my share. You know that."

"It's nothing, honestly. Only cost a few bucks. Just needed some stakes for a new fence. Critters getting in."

"Let me know if you need any help." The bartender finally returned, and Lee raised an eyebrow at the wait.

"Had to find a cold one." The bartender placed the bottle on the counter.

"Well, git her open," said Lee, smiling at Ed. "This champagne won't drink itself."

Lee picked up both flutes and handed one to Ed. "To the Republic." He raised his glass.

McLaurie smirked. "And all who sail in her."

Lee held his glass away. "No," he said. "Let's do this right." He raised his glass again. "To the Republic. Finally at peace."

After he took a sip, McLaurie set his glass down. "Really think that's the end of it?"

"He was the last one with any hopes of toppling Bonilla."

"How'd they get him anyway?"

"Don't know all the details," Lee said. "But they caught up with him in some one-horse town. Tatumbla or something. He was shot resisting arrest." They both fell silent until Lee noticed the bartender hovering and turned to him.

"Want me to leave the bottle?" he asked.

Lee raised an eyebrow, but Ed shook his head. "Wish I could stay and tie one on, but I gotta get back."

"Finish your glass, at least." Lee gestured to the flute before turning to the bartender. "Top us up, and keep the rest for punch."

Ed groaned at the mention of it.

"You don't like my punch?"

"Don't get me wrong." McLaurie covered the rim of the flute with his hand when the bartender went to refill him. "It tasted great. That was the problem."

Lee chuckled.

"What goes in it anyway?"

"Bottle of rum," Lee said. "Bottle of champagne. A few slices of whatever's lying about, banana, papaya, pineapple…"

Ed's eyes bulged. "And you're telling people it's not a *hard* drink?"

"It's got fruit in it," Lee protested.

McLaurie shook his head and finished what was left of his champagne, leaving Lee to his thoughts.

Needless to say, Lee's considerable largesse increased his already widespread popularity. He wasn't just a hero in Puerto Cortés; he was hailed everywhere he went: La Ceiba, Trujillo, and Tegucigalpa. When he rode the rails up to San Pedro Sula, his old comrade and the new *comandante* of the city—General Leiva—put on a public concert in his honor.

But despite being a friend to half the country, Lee never could get along with any of Bonilla's ministers. For his part, he simply didn't trust them. And he guessed they were jealous of his close relationship with the president. Anytime one of their spats got out of hand, Lee would simply telegraph his resignation to Bonilla, who would summon him to Tegucigalpa and beg him to remain.

Lee always caved.

69

Lee sat in the bowels of the steamer, feeling some old excitement return as they approached the port of New Orleans. Things were going well back in Honduras—frustrating squabbles with politicians aside—yet the pull of this city was strong.

He and Adelaide had fought before he departed. Lee had invited her to come with him, but she was shrewd enough to sense his reluctance. Their shadow argument consisted of Lee insisting his wife come along, and Adelaide insisting her husband go alone, when in truth both of them wanted the exact opposite. He knew the root cause, too. On many occasions Lee had expressed his desire to bring all of his estranged children to Puerto Cortés. Now that he'd made a name for himself and had money rolling in, Lee felt increasingly desperate to make up for lost time and broken promises. And he was advancing in years, he supposed. His wife never expressed any objection to the idea—except when he threatened to actually do something about it. In the end, though, Lee was glad he was returning alone. Adelaide was jealous enough whenever he so much as mentioned his first wife. He didn't want to find out how she'd act in Mamie's presence.

In fact, when he thought about it, Adelaide had only really hit the roof when he had mentioned he planned a trip up to Memphis. He was still mulling that over when the steamer blared its siren and the passengers began shuffling toward the exit. As he queued with the rest, clutching his suitcase and shivering at the slight chill in the fall air, Lee thought back to the last time he was home, wondering if any agents would be shadowing him this time. *Maybe a newspaperman looking for a quote. More likely,* he conceded, *I've been forgotten altogether.*

He stepped off the boat and was swarmed right away. A scrum of reporters crowded around him, shouting questions, trying to get his attention. "Lee, Lee, over here!"

"General Christmas, a quote if you will."

At first, Lee tried to shield himself with his suitcase and push through, but there were too many. He held his hands up to stop the yelling. "Anyone here from the *New York Times*?"

The assembled hacks grumbled at the mention.

"No one brave enough?" he asked. "Well, someone better tell those guys I'm still alive. You got proof now." The reporters chuckled as Lee continued. "I know you guys got deadlines. But you should always wait until the fighting's done before filing your story."

The newspaper men laughed along with him.

"Although," he continued, "being a ghost made it a little easier to slip out the last time." The newspapermen scribbled notes.

"How does it feel to be back in New Orleans?" one shouted.

"This city," he said, growing wistful. "I dunno. I guess

you never really leave this place." He tapped his breast. "You always carry it with you."

Questions were shouted one after the other, but Lee shushed them all. "If you'll excuse me, boys, I've a fierce thirst. Any of you who want another quote are gonna have to follow me up to Remy Klock's saloon and match me drink for drink." He picked up his suitcase. "And you're buying." He pushed his way through the crowd.

The swarm of reporters followed him all the way up to Poydras Street, where he stalled them at the door of the bar. "Do me a favor, boys." He paused. "Give me a minute on my own."

A reporter stepped forward, grabbing a pencil off his ear. "Why's that, General?"

He smiled. "'Cos it will be a hell of a lot funnier if I take a seat at the bar quietly and y'all pour in after."

The reporters chuckled as he put a hand on the door and raised a finger to his lips. He tried to slip inside quietly, but as soon as Remy Klock saw him, he boomed, "Well, I'll be damned. America's most famous soldier of fortune!"

Lee guffawed, shaking hands with Remy. "Only 'cos you ain't heard of Machine Gun Molony yet." He mimicked a gun and planted several bullets in Klock's chest.

Remy laughed and plucked a bottle from the shelf, but Lee shook his head.

"What?" Remy asked. "Gone off the whiskey now?"

"The expensive stuff," Lee said, pointing.

"Who's buying?" asked Remy with a smile. "Because I'm pretty sure I've an unpaid tab from the last time you went to the top shelf."

The door burst open, and the newspapermen streamed in, surrounding Lee. He winked at Remy. "They are," he said.

Lee spent the next few days visiting every bar in the Third Ward, and half of them in the French Quarter too. Each morning, he cut out the stories from all the papers and mailed them back to Adelaide. Once the attention died down, he boarded the train to Memphis, and was again swamped by reporters before he'd even left the platform. Once he'd satisfied their need for snappy quotes and dramatic photographs, he found that his estranged children had all married, and his first daughter with Mamie had already made him a grandfather. As for Mamie, she had re-married. Lee kept a respectable distance, much as it pained him.

On his return to New Orleans, he finally caught up with his old friend Boyd Cetti, sharing a drink in Tom Cook's bar.

"I was actually in Remy's place the night you swanned in with all those reporters." Boyd confessed.

"Shit," said Lee. "Why didn't you say hello?"

"I tried." Boyd took a sip of his whiskey. "They were three or four deep around you. I went to get something to eat, and by the time I got back, Remy said the circus had moved on."

"Sorry about that Boyd, but those guys are vultures. If you don't feed 'em something, they'll pick your bones clean."

"I get it." Boyd held his hands up. "No need to explain." He gazed around the quiet bar. "Prefer it like this anyway, when we can talk without hollering."

"And drink." Lee clinked his glass to Boyd's and took a swig.

"How was Memphis?"

"Great to see the kids," Lee said. "Really great." He paused, and then answered the unasked question. "Didn't see Mamie. Or, should I say, Mrs. G.F. Hanson." He grimaced.

"Yeah. Didn't know if I should write you. Figured…"

"Aw, it's all right. I expected it to happen at some point. She's a fine woman." His eyes glazed over. "If she's happy, then I'm happy for her. The kids say he's a good man."

"How they all doing?"

"I'm a grandfather," said Lee.

"Hell. Really?"

"Hattie had a baby girl. Cuter than you'd believe."

"They grow so fast," said Boyd.

"You're empty," Lee said, fighting back tears and motioning to Boyd's glass as a distraction. "Grab a bottle off Tom and tell him to stick it on my tab."

Boyd made his way up to the bar. Lee looked up at the ceiling, trying to keep his emotions in check. He felt as if he could blink and his entire life would be over; he'd be nothing but a distant memory. A face in a faded photograph. A name in a yellowing newspaper, boxed away in someone's dusty attic.

"You okay?" Boyd plonked the bottle down.

Lee dabbed at his eyes with a handkerchief. "Getting old, is all." He smiled. "And maybe a little sentimental." He took a deep breath as Boyd refilled his glass. "Shit, let's change the subject."

Boyd took the hint. "Hear about your cousin?"

"No."

"Making a real name for himself. Some kind of pilot."

Lee struggled to follow the details, but it seemed his

cousin had designed a new kind of plane—something called a monoplane. As Boyd filled him in, Lee's mind exploded with possibilities. They got through half the bottle as Lee listed the different governments in Central America he could hawk one of these newfangled planes to. "There's millions in this, Boyd. Millions."

Such money would come in handy. On the back of impressing his old friends and showering gifts on his ever-growing family, Lee's cash had run out. He was forced to take a loan from the Honduran Consulate in New Orleans just to afford passage back to Puerto Cortés.

70

Lee was in a foul mood all the way back to Honduras, thinking about Mamie, his kids, and having missed them grow up. He wasn't looking forward to seeing Adelaide either, nor the bullshit dance he'd have to do when she got pissed off about something innocuous and he'd have to figure out what she was really mad about. Seemed like that was their sole form of interaction these days—dancing around a fight, making up after a fight, gearing up for a new fight. Lee had always liked people who were straight with him, but most of the time, his wife was too gummed up to tell him what was actually bothering her. It was draining. And with his short fuse, it was a recipe for trouble.

He was embarrassed when the *cuartel* band greeted his arrival, especially because he'd telegrammed ahead to explicitly state he didn't want a fuss; he waved the band away as soon as they started playing. His mood didn't improve when he sat down at his desk to review the correspondence that had piled up in his absence. One peevish communiqué from Bonilla's ministers after another. Cursing each of them, he crumpled the pages and tossed them across the room. Then he wrenched open his desk drawer and grabbed a bottle.

I can't go home to Adelaide like this, he told himself. He sucked the *aguardiente* down. Then he put his head in his hands and cried.

When he was done, he felt a little lighter. He lit a *puro* and happily puffed smoke over the remaining pile of messages. Woozy, he tipped some *aguardiente* over the letters and set them ablaze, sweeping the flaming pile off his desk. The embers died out on the floor, little wisps of burnt paper floating and sinking in the air. Then he penned another resignation letter to Bonilla. Before he wrote the final line, he took a heavy gulp of *aguardiente*, wincing as it burned down his throat, into his stomach, and right down to his toes. "And this time, I mean it," he scrawled.

The reply from Bonilla came by telegram. It was curt and to the point. "Come to Tegus now stop," it said. "This time I mean it stop."

Lee was half-considering ignoring the summons when he caught two sentries gossiping about Bonilla's rumored resignation. Without saying goodbye to Adelaide, he took the train up to San Pedro before switching to horseback, riding that poor mount to near death.

He arrived just as Bonilla transferred his powers to his deputy, Dr. Bertrand. Lee fought his way through the flunkies and vultures, getting as far as Bonilla's private quarters before being intercepted by the palace guards. In all the commotion, with Lee becoming increasingly aggressive about his attempts to gain entry, Guy Molony appeared and pulled him inside.

"It's bad," Guy whispered before berating the guards for not recognizing their commander-in-chief.

As they entered Bonilla's room, Lee saw a shriveled figure in the bed.

Bonilla weakly raised an arm to salute his old *gringo* general.

"What the hell, Manolo?" Lee stepped forward and clasped his hand.

Bonilla blinked away the tears. "I'm dying, Lee."

"You ain't dead yet," Lee said. "I'll get you some real doctors. I know a guy in San Pedro. Better than anyone here."

The president shook his head. "It's too late. Nothing can be done."

"There's gotta be some way we can—"

"Bright's Disease," said Molony. "Advanced."

When Lee started to speak, Bonilla squeezed his hand. "It's over." He wheezed. "I've made my peace with it."

Manuel Bonilla died a few hours later with his loyal *yanqui* general and Guy Molony by his side. The whole of Honduras went into mourning.

Six leading figures were eyeing the Presidential Palace, but Lee's position was safe enough. While his quarrels with the ministers continued, so did the pleas not to resign, this time from the new President, Dr. Bertrand. He needed Lee close to him, and knew Lee Christmas could be trusted. Besides, with an election looming, it didn't hurt to have the hero of La Ceiba around.

71

Lee was like a man with a pebble in his shoe. This should have been his peak. He was rich, powerful, and respected. Feared too, by some, but loved by many more. However, as he made plans to move his children south to Honduras, his relationship with Adelaide disintegrated further.

Bonilla's sudden death made him even more aware of his own mortality—something he'd avoided wrestling with after being shot point-blank in the chest, dashing across the plain of Maraita against a entire army, or even when he had driven headlong into an oncoming train almost twenty years before. Dr. Bertrand had been keen to stress he still wanted Lee around, but they didn't have the same rapport. In short, Lee wanted his children around while he was still important, before he became old and useless or went the way of Manolo.

Fighting with Adelaide was near constant. It was as if each minor slight ripped open every old wound. Each squabble aired every historical grievance. Lee began dreading going home, often staying in the *cuartel* later and later into the night, desperately trying to postpone the inevitable. It wasn't all her fault; far from it. He was a proud man with a quick temper, and he rarely backed down when he felt wronged. But the end result was the same, nonetheless: the two of them at each other's throats. Sometimes, it got so bad he wouldn't go home at all, preferring to pass the night in one of Puerto Cortés' *cantinas*. More often, he'd drink alone in his office, or take a bottle down to the wharf and gaze out at the endless ocean.

On one such night, he returned home well past midnight, hoping to tiptoe into bed and slip out the next morning without encountering his wife at all, if possible.

"Where have you been?" Adelaide was waiting up for him, drinking coffee in the kitchen, drumming her fingers on the table and staring at the clock, just as Mamie's old battle-ax of a mother had used to.

"Out," he said, leaning on the table for support.

"You're drunk."

"What of it?"

Adelaide sipped her coffee, but Lee could see a vein pulsing on the side of her neck, fit to pop.

"Where were you drinking?" she asked.

He paused for a moment, wondering if there was any way to avoid the argument. *Screw it*, he thought. "What's it to you?"

"I asked you a question."

If Lee was sure about anything, it was that he couldn't bear to tell Adelaide that things had gotten so bad he'd prefer to be alone than come home to her. "The *cantina*," he said.

"Liar." She stood, jabbing a finger across the table. "I went down there—"

"You did what?"

"Asked around, too." She smiled, but there was no humor in it. "No one had seen you all evening."

Lee was flummoxed. "What I meant to say was, I was planning on going down there—"

"Bullshit."

The silence was punctuated by the ticking clock, louder than he'd ever noticed.

"What's her name?" demanded Adelaide.

He was struck dumb.

"I knew it." She slapped the table.

"But—"

"Save it." Adelaide made to leave. "I don't want to hear it." She paused in the doorway. "And don't even think of following me upstairs."

Lee sat at the kitchen table for hours, wondering why he hadn't defended himself. When he got drowsy, he headed to the *cuartel*, hoping to catch some sleep in his office. He plonked himself in his desk chair and closed his eyes. Sleep, when it did come, was fitful. The rest of the time, he tormented himself with the irony that this was the one time he had truly respected the matrimonial vow.

He was still angry when he woke, shivering despite the early morning heat, his blanket having slipped to his feet. After rubbing his face awake, he stood and shook his legs and then marched all the way home, determined to set Adelaide straight. When he got there, she was still seething. Again, he didn't deny her accusations, although he had the opportunity.

Her nostrils flared. "I'm going to Guatemala for a few days. The children are coming with me. And you better shape up or you'll be out on the street."

Lee didn't even try to stop her. As soon as she left, he went straight down to the Palm Hotel and got roaring drunk, telling everyone he'd packed Adelaide and the kids away so he could have a good time. Only the intervention of his staff prevented him from getting into several brawls. When he sobered up, a couple of days later, he telegrammed his wife in Puerto Barrios, beckoning her home, promising her the moon.

Two days later, he waited patiently at the wharf for the delayed Guatemala steamer. When it eventually arrived, he spotted his three children on deck and waved. "Where's Mommy?" he asked as they disembarked.

His oldest daughter, Leah, handed him a letter. "She's going to stay with uncle for a while."

"Uncle?" he asked, confused. "What uncle?"

He tore open the letter. Adelaide was leaving him, running away with her lover to Nicaragua—out of his reach. He was furious, but when he finally calmed down, he realized his pride was bruised more than his heart. He sued for divorce.

As his soon as their *decree nisi* was granted, Lee had a bead on number four.

72

The year was 1914 and the most eligible bachelor in Puerto Cortés, the *yanqui* General Lee Christmas, head of the Honduran Army, *comandante* of the garrison, and inspector of the northern ports was fifty-two years of age. He had made good on his Memphis vow. Living with him in Honduras, enjoying both his fame and largesse, were eight children from three different marriages, ranging from a girl of two to the mother of a five-year-old. Even had his children not been there, their father's pursuit of a sixteen-year-old girl would have raised eyebrows, more due to his advanced age than her tender years. But the fact that his children were all much closer in age to the object of Lee's affection brought their distance in years into sharper focus.

It began as a flirtation, nothing more. Lee was friendly with the Culotta family, fellow New Orleanians who had moved south to work for Sam Zemurray, and Ida had caught his eye for some months. He knew any potential match would arouse resistance, not least given his reputation for extra-matrimonial dalliances, so he had to tread carefully. He studiously avoided any direct contact until his divorce from Adelaide was finalized.

While waiting down at the banana wharf for the Puerto

Barrios steamer, Lee spotted Ida accompanied by her older sister, both of them seeing off a friend. He decided to test the waters and took advantage of the jostling crowd to maneuver her to one side. He leaned over her, eyes twinkling, and spoke in a hushed tone. "Know why I'm going to Guatemala?"

"No," said Ida, smiling. "Tell me."

"To buy a present for my sweetheart. Want to come with me? You could help me pick out the gift…"

"Maybe some other time," she said. The steamer blared its warning, and their conversation was cut short.

Lee returned a week later. He was sitting in the bar of the Palm Hotel when he spotted Ida and her sister passing by on their evening stroll. He leaped from his chair, asking permission to accompany them. At the end of their walk, after exchanging the usual pleasantries, Ida's sister called on a friend. Alone with Ida for the first time since their last conversation, Lee took his chance. "I brought back a present for my sweetheart," he said. "Know who it is?"

"Well," said Ida, with a mischievous smile. "Could be any girl in this town."

Lee frowned. "I mean you." He produced a pearl-handled fan from his inside pocket, offering it to her. She paused for a moment, glancing over her shoulder, worried her sister might return, before accepting the gift. Lee took her hand, squeezing it softly. "Let's tell your parents we want to be together."

Ida gasped at his forthrightness. "General—" She collected herself.

"I told you already. It's Lee."

"Lee, I think it best if I speak to them first. They still see me as their little girl—"

"But you're—"

She held up a hand. "I know. But we must be careful." Ida looked toward the house. Footsteps could be heard heading toward them. She hid the fan in her purse. "Wait until you hear from me. Please."

He nodded, and then doffed his hat as Ida's sister came out onto the porch. "Ladies, you must excuse me. Thank you for your company."

Lee's patience only lasted a week. Without any further word from Ida, he resolved to call on the Culotta home and make his intentions clear.

73

Lee put on his best suit—a crisp white linen affair topped with a brand new panama hat—and gazed at his reflection. *Molony never did get me that hat*, he remembered. *Rat bastard.* He chuckled and then strode out the door, down Calle de Linea in the direction of the Culotta house. In his excitement, he'd forgotten to check his pace, so he was sweating furiously as he approached. He stopped short, fanning himself with his hat before losing his patience again and knocking on the door.

Mrs. Culotta led him into the drawing room where her husband was already seated. He raised his glass in salutation, greeting Lee heartily.

"A drink, General?" asked his wife.

"Plain ol' Lee is fine, ma'am." He removed his hat. "And a whiskey, if you have it."

Mrs. Culotta opened her cabinet, poured the drink, and placed the tumbler at his side. "I'll leave you two alone."

"Ma'am," said Lee, "you'd best stay. I'd like to speak with both of you, if I may." He saw the confusion on Mrs. Culotta's face, and the surprise on her husband's, and drew a breath. "It's about Ida."

Mrs. Culotta perched herself on the arm of her

husband's chair. "What has she done?"

"Is my daughter in some kind of trouble?" asked Captain Culotta.

Lee smiled. "I hope not."

"Please explain, General," said Mrs. Culotta.

"It's Lee, please. I'm not here on official business." He paused. "This is a social call."

Captain Culotta's brow furrowed. "I don't understand, Lee."

Lee bit his lip, searching for the right words. His right leg began tapping. "I want to make Ida my wife," he blurted.

Mrs. Culotta's hand went to her mouth. She turned to her husband, who had almost dropped his tumbler, her eyes bulging.

Captain Culotta replied with a short, sharp shake of the head. Then he turned back to Lee. "I'm sorry ... you caught us off guard."

"I apologize for that," he said. "But there's no way to say it other than to come right out and say it."

Captain Culotta took a sip of whiskey, his hand trembling slightly as he lifted the glass. "I consider you a dear friend," he said. "But this is my daughter, and I must be frank. You're thirty-five years her senior."

"She's sixteen years old!" said Mrs. Culotta.

Her husband gave her a severe look. "I'll be straight," he said. "This is *never* going to happen. You're a soldier of fortune, an adventurer. I'm sorry to say this, Lee, but you'll probably get yourself killed one day. Ida would have no one to support her."

"And you're not a Catholic!"

Captain Culotta squeezed his wife's hand. "Yes, there is that. Plus, there's the small matter of three previous marriages and several children."

"I'm a man of means," protested Lee. "And I always provide for my family. All of 'em."

"There are other considerations." Mrs. Culotta fixed Lee with a queer look, letting her unspoken accusation hang in the air. He knew what she meant. She didn't have to say it outright. His reputation was well known around the town.

Captain Culotta drained his glass and placed it on the side table. "I'm sorry, Lee, but I absolutely forbid this. She's my youngest daughter. It's my responsibility to look after her. You must drop your attentions at once."

Lee left the house fuming. Not only was he to end his pursuit, Mrs. Culotta had made it clear that Ida would be forbidden to have any contact with him whatsoever. But Lee wasn't one to give up easily.

He purchased the general store on Calle de Linea, right opposite their home, and he spent his days gazing across the street, scheming. And then it came to him.

Ida, like most young people in Puerto Cortés, liked to go for an evening stroll along the seafront. Lee was banned from accompanying Ida … until he devised a ruse to get her out of sight. The popular route for such a walk followed the curve of the bay. Beyond the headland, after the banana wharf, it swung around to the wilder shores of the beach that faced the open sea. The path then looped around a thicket of jungle above the town before returning to town.

At night, Lee and his soldiers worked their machetes to carve a secret path through the loop of jungle. When Ida took her usual evening stroll with friends, she passed along the bay, as usual, and then the banana wharf. When he saw her, Lee would rise from his chair, mount his horse, and race off in the opposite direction, past the *cuartel.* Once out of sight of the Culottas, he would bank toward the edge of town, enter his secret pathway through the jungle—obscured from prying eyes by a false screen of foliage—and gallop to the other side, popping out on the beachfront and beckoning Ida for a secret rendezvous.

74

A standing tradition in Puerto Cortés, and indeed all of Central America, was the serenade. A young buck would engage musicians to call on the house of his intended and serenade the girl on his behalf. Indeed, a lady's beauty was often measured by how many such serenades she received. Given the small size of the port town, the only band capable of performing a task without embarrassing the tradition was that of the *cuartel.*

As *comandante*, Lee was also in charge of the band. Whenever he received a request from some besotted lothario, he would march his troops to the respective house. That summer, however, he took to adding a stop: the Culotta residence. The band's old Spanish waltzes routinely filled the air outside their windows. So as not to arouse the suspicion of Ida's parents, a stooge was found—some kid called Álvarez, who lent his name to the charade. Lee would stand smartly in his white dress uniform, fulfilling his duty, watching young Ida out of the corner of his eye. If her parents were absent, Lee and Ida would even share a brief dance. Such moments were rare enough. Mrs. Culotta, increasingly watchful, kept a close and suspicious eye on her daughter's sudden happiness.

One afternoon, Lee sat in the shade of his porch,

hollowing out the inside of a champagne cork. When the hole was the requisite size, he folded a note and placed it inside.

"Pssst. Armando." Lee beckoned a neighbor's boy who was playing in the street. "*Ven por aquí*." He handed him the cork without further instruction.

Later that day, when Ida saw Armando tossing the cork on the street, she called him over. After retrieving the hidden message, she secreted in her purse, scrawled a reply, and inserted it in the cork's chamber. Patting the confused Armando on the head, she then headed back inside.

All summer it continued: furtive glances and surreptitious messages followed by secret picnics and stolen kisses. The town gossips suspected a romance. The barflies knew someone had turned Lee's head; he only avoided the *putas* when he was in the first flush of love, they argued. When he began tinkering with the engine of his motor launch, rumors intensified. He was to elope once more and marry the Culotta girl before her parents could stop him. The giddy talk must have reached Ida's parents, for they barred the windows of their home and added new locks to their door. Captain Culotta muttered something about burglars, but everyone knew it wasn't his possessions he was worried about.

Once Lee saw the newly barred windows, he decided to act.

75

Taking a leave of absence, Lee took the toy train up to San Pedro Sula and then rode the remaining distance to the capital. Salvatore Culotta—Ida's older brother—was working in Tegucigalpa as a manager for one of the fruit companies. Lee felt more than a little nervous going to Salvatore's home. He'd tried to convince him to meet in a *cantina*, but Ida's brother had insisted. As Lee approached the house, he once more wished the meeting was taking place on neutral ground, somewhere he could control the flow of liquor to ensure enough kept coming to soften his edges.

"I can see you are a practical man," Lee said, sipping coffee in Salvatore's living room. He'd noted the clean but Spartan house on entry. "I'll state my case plainly."

"I would appreciate that." Ida's brother was giving nothing away.

Lee set down his cup. "You're aware of the situation with me and Ida?"

"I'm aware that my father won't countenance a match, and that my mother has forbidden any contact."

"And I've respected that," said Lee. He paused, trying to figure this guy out. "More or less," he added, waggling his hand.

Salvatore allowed himself a brief smile. "I'm not sure what there is to discuss."

"I have a proposal."

The man's face darkened. "If you think you can buy my sister." He stood, balling his fists. "I'll lick you right here and now. I don't care who you are."

Lee remained seated, holding up his palms. "That's not what I was suggesting at all," he said in the most soothing tone he could muster. "I should have chosen my words more carefully."

Salvatore's face flushed with embarrassment. "I'm s-sorry," he stammered. "I thought—"

"It's all right," interrupted Lee. "This is a delicate matter." He waited while Salvatore sat back down. "But I promised to speak plainly, so here it is."

Salvatore nodded.

"I'm not giving up the chase," he said. "This isn't some kind of passing fancy." He cleared his throat. "I'm in love."

"And Ida?"

Lee shook his head. "I don't know, to be frank."

"Well…"

"But she seems to reciprocate. At least, I know she cares for me."

"It might be nothing more than an infatuation," said Salvatore.

"True," conceded Lee.

"Girls grow up quicker than boys," he said.

Lee nodded, giving him room to say his piece. "She might just be flattered by the attentions of a powerful man."

"All of this is possible," said Lee, noting the surprise on

Salvatore's face when he agreed with him. "Which is why I'm also keen to tread as carefully as possible."

Salvatore held his gaze, considering what Lee had said. He tapped his chin with his forefinger. "You mentioned something about a proposal back there, before I got ahead of myself."

Lee chuckled, waving a hand. "Understandable," he said. "But my proposal is this." He set his cup down. "The only way we'll find out if this is an infatuation or whether those feelings are real is if me and Ida are allowed spend time together."

Salvatore shook his head.

"Strictly chaperoned, of course," Lee added.

Ida's brother pursed his lips.

"We've hardly had a chance to talk since I asked for her hand." Lee paused, deciding to risk it. "You know what women are like. Deny them something and they'll want it twice as much."

Salvatore went to speak, but Lee raised his hands to forestall him. "All I'm talking about is taking an evening stroll together—under strict supervision, as I said. Maybe dropping by the house for dinner." He could see Salvatore's resistance waning. "Nothing more."

"It's not my decision."

"I understand that." Lee decided to press the matter. "But this is the only way to see if there is a serious basis for the relationship." He paused. "And, of course, your father would still have to agree to any match."

Salvatore stood, hands on his hips. "I'm not making any promises. I don't even know how I feel about it myself. But I can see you're a decent sort." He smiled, finally. "Persistent, too. And I respect that you came to talk to me."

"I appreciate your time." Lee put on his hat.

"I'll pass on what you said, but it is out of my hands." He walked Lee to the door.

With some reluctance, the Culottas welcomed Lee back into their home. He was permitted to see their daughter, but only under strict supervision. He called for dinner, breaking bread with the family around their small dining table. In the evenings, he took Ida for an evening stroll, always accompanied by a relative. However, when it was her sister's turn to accompany them, she gave them plenty of time on their own once out of sight of the town.

When he felt the Culotta's anger had dissipated, and that they had begun to accept him as a genuine suitor for Ida's hand, he pressed for a commitment. Finally, after Lee agreed to be baptized into the Catholic Church, a date was set: December 2, 1914.

76

Though Lee had been thrice married, none of his previous nuptials had been marked with a formal ceremony. Determined to make it the biggest celebration Puerto Cortés had ever witnessed, he spared no expense. He sent diamonds to New Orleans to be set into a wedding ring for Ida, and, finding the bakers and florists lacking in expertise to match his exacting demands, he arranged for a giant cake and a huge shipment of flowers to arrive by steamer the day before the ceremony. He also chartered two ships to ferry in friends from La Ceiba and Puerto Barrios. To entertain all of the guests, an orchestra was hired from San Pedro Sula, and a *marimba* from Guatemala. Lee's daughter Sadie was making the dress for a bride who was several years her junior.

Guy Molony arrived the day before the ceremony, although he hadn't responded to the invitation. "Aw, you knew I was coming anyway," he said. "Why waste the stamp?"

Lee chuckled and led him down to the *cantina.* "Hotel's kind of busy at the moment," he explained. "Besides, every time I show my face there, something else seems to go wrong."

Guy stood aside to let Lee walk through the door first. "Best get in there and get hidden, then." He clapped Lee on the back.

"Spit it out," Lee said, eyeing Molony as they sipped their first drink.

"What?"

"You've had something on the tip of your tongue since you got here."

Molony allow himself a smile and punched Lee on the shoulder.

"Now spill, goddamn it."

He waved a hand. "It's nothing."

"Spill."

"Just curious if this is it for you now."

"What do you mean?"

"I'm sure I'm not the first to say it, but this is wife number four."

Lee eyeballed him, waiting for him to finish.

"Two more and you got the set," said Guy.

"What's that supposed to mean?"

Molony cradled his glass. "Met this guy in the Philippines. Dunno what his name was, but everyone called him Wolfy."

Lee wasn't sure where this was going.

"Anyway," Guy continued, sipping his drink. "Can't remember what age he was, but he was younger than you." Molony smiled. "And he already had five ex-wives!"

"Damn," said Lee.

"When I was on shore leave with him, he'd spend half his time chasing tail, always using the same line."

"Which was?"

Guy smirked. "Wanna be my next ex-wife?"

Lee chuckled.

"See, he had this dream. His coffin getting carried out of the church, borne by his six ex-wives." Guy paused. "All of 'em weeping."

Lee grabbed him in a headlock and slapped him playfully in the face.

Molony squirmed free. "Not sure you want a black eye, what with your big day tomorrow and all."

Lee paused. "Good to see you again." They clinked glasses. "Even if you are a rat bastard."

"Thought I'd find you here," said a voice behind them. They turned to see Ed McLaurie. Guy jumped out of his seat. "Shit, Ed. How long's it been?"

"Not long enough." He jabbed Molony in the ribs.

"How's the coconut farm?"

"Plantation," corrected McLaurie, before they all laughed. He turned to Lee. "They're looking for you back at the hotel."

"What's new?"

"Some problem with the ring."

Lee jumped up and darted out the door, running all the way to the hotel, only to find his well-laid plans unraveling. The boat had arrived without either the flowers or the cake. Worse again, the messenger sent to New Orleans, the one who'd been carrying all those diamonds, had absconded. Lee was absorbing the disastrous news when Ed and Guy caught up with him at the hotel. After he filled them in, the boys offered their help. Lee sent Ed to find a local pastry chef and press-gang him into service.

"Whatever it takes," said Lee. "But I gotta warn you,

he's already sore he didn't get the gig in the first place." McLaurie nodded and headed out the door.

He turned to Molony. "Get up to the *cuartel* and send someone on the banana train to San Pedro." He thought for a moment. "Can't remember her goddamn size, and I'm not bothering her with any of this." He tapped the bar, trying to jog his memory. "Screw it," he said. "Tell 'em to get two plain gold bands."

"No diamonds this time?" asked Molony.

Lee almost swung at him.

"I'm kidding," said Guy, backing away toward the door. "Kidding."

Lee turned to the bartender. "Alberto, get a few helpers and head down to the seafront. You know them gardens with all the nice flowers?" The bartender nodded. "We'll have to make our own bouquets."

Lee took a breath.

The ceremony wasn't as grand as originally planned, but everyone pitched in to make sure things went smoothly. Lee didn't sleep at all the night before, and he was still fretting and sweating as he stood at the head of the assembled guests in the Palm Hotel. As he fidgeted with his cufflinks for the umpteenth time, Guy leaned in. "You got the rings, right?"

Lee turned to him, ready to explode, struggling to keep his voice down. "Damn it, I ask you to do one—"

He was cut short by the band launching into the wedding march. Lee turned his head to see Ida entering on the arm of her father. His legs quivered as he took in the sight; he'd never seen her look so beautiful. Captain Culotta began to lead her down the aisle, and Lee turned back to Molony.

"Kidding," he said. "Just kidding."

Lee shook his head, and turned to face the still-smirking priest.

77

Lee's lengthy pursuit of Ida had distracted him from the turmoil brewing in Honduras. Bonilla's replacement, Dr. Bertrand, faced opposition to his candidacy in the upcoming vote. Several powerful factions had their eye on his office, all pointing to a potentially bothersome clause in the Constitution that precluded a president from succeeding himself. Dr. Bertrand's supporters countered he was merely completing Bonilla's term and so remained free to contest the election. With figures in both parties jockeying for position to undermine Bertrand, one of Lee's sidelines began garnering attention—an informal lottery in Puerto Cortés, in competition with the government's own efforts.

Popularity became its downfall. Everyone knew the government lottery was rigged; as soon as an alternative appeared, the starry-eyed dreamers toughing it on the plantations bought tickets in their droves. After losses spread among the banana pickers and stevedores, one of Dr. Bertrand's ministers—a prickly fellow Lee had tangled with before—had the perfect excuse to shut the lottery down. Lee flew into a rage and immediately telegrammed his resignation to Tegucigalpa.

The following morning, he dallied at the kitchen table,

Ida glancing at the clock and raising an eyebrow. She took the coffee pot from the counter and topped up his cup. Lingering beside him for a moment, she put a hand on the back of his head. "What's going on in there?"

"Huh?"

"For starters." She placed the pot back down on the counter. "You're stirring that cup like nobody's business, even though you haven't put sugar in." Lee shot her a foolish grin and reached for the sugar. His wife glanced at the clock once more. "Plus, I couldn't normally pay you to stay past nine."

"Aw, that's not true," said Lee.

"Sure it is." Her eyes dancing, she opened the top button of her blouse. "No matter how I might try to dissuade you." She unbuttoned the next.

Lee smiled, sipping his coffee. "You better cut that out before you get yourself into trouble."

"Really?" She grinned impishly as she popped the next button, exposing a glimpse of bodice. "I'm sorry. It's just *awfully* hot this morning." She turned her face up to the ceiling fan, letting the air ripple through her blouse.

Lee's mouth hung open as Ida popped the second-last button. She moved toward the door. "In fact," she said, stepping through the frame, out of view. "It's so hot, I think I'll go lie down." Ida held her blouse through the doorway, and then dropped it.

Lee was out of his chair before the fabric hit the floor.

After they made love, Lee and Ida lay on the bed, letting the fan wash cool air over their naked bodies. He felt her take his hand, and squeeze it. "What's worrying you?"

He exhaled. "The resignation."

"I figured as much. But you've been here before."

Lee propped himself up on his elbows. "You know, every time I resigned before, I always had a little voice in my head wondering what I'd do if they accepted. But deep down, I always knew I was safe. This time?" He shook his head. "I don't know. I haven't been in Tegus for a while. Things are changing, and I'm out of the loop." He turned on his side, leaned his head on his palm, and gazed into her eyes. "And I've got a bad feeling about it."

She matched his stare for a moment. Smiling, she said, "What's the worst that can happen?"

Lee flipped onto his back and blew through his lips.

"I mean it." Ida leaned over him, gazing at him intently. "What's the worst that can happen?"

"They could accept."

She laughed and sat up in bed, turning to face him. "And would that be the end of the world?"

Lee struggled to respond, but she tapped him on the nose. "Silly." She swung a leg over to straddle him. "And I'm sure a man of your considerable talents, and energy, will find a use for himself."

He blinked. "Even if it means leaving here?"

She nodded and leaned down to kiss him. "Long as we're together," she whispered.

The news still hit him hard. When he reached the *cuartel* later that morning, there were no telegrams summoning him to Tegucigalpa, no pleas to reconsider from Dr. Bertrand. Instead, a short message from his cabinet secretary formally accepted his resignation. Lee was informed that a temporary *comandante* was en route, and he would be relieved of duty that afternoon.

He began clearing his desk.

78

Lee carried a box of his possessions down to the Palm Hotel and deposited them in a corner, immediately signaling the bartender for a drink. Instead of approaching the bar as usual, he took a table near the box at the back of the room, where he was less likely to be spotted by passersby. The bartender hovered beside the table. Lee took a sip and then looked up at him. "What's up?"

"That's the last of the whiskey.

Lee put a *puro* between his lips. "I signed an order two weeks ago."

"You did," said Alberto, backing away slightly. "But the distributor must have misplaced it. I've reordered more, but we'll have no whiskey for a couple of weeks."

"Goddamn it." Lee took the unlit *puro* from his mouth and threw it on the table. "What else? There must be something else, or you wouldn't still be hovering there."

"Room Twelve," the bartender said. "Someone tipped over a pail, and it leaked into the room below."

He sighed. "What's the damage?"

"We'll have some plastering to do, but can't tell how much until it dries out."

"Okay." Lee took a gulp of whiskey. "Can we stick the

guest for any of the damages?"

Alberto paused. "He's already checked out."

Lee smacked the table. "Didn't I tell you guys to check the rooms before the guests check out?"

"He checked out late," the bartender said. "Claimed he was running for the steamer."

"All the more reason."

The bartender nodded. "Of course, but the guest in Room Eight arrived at the same time to complain about a leak, and by the time—"

"Not your fault." Lee waved a hand. "I'll be up to take a look in a minute."

The bartender nodded and shuffled away.

As Lee inspected the damage, he realized the minutiae of running the Palm Hotel now bored him. He decided to put the place on the market and accept the first half-decent offer. And the general store, too. He'd been letting things slide there anyway, having only bought the place to spy on Ida's house during their secret courtship.

He signed the documents in the bar of the Palm Hotel, shaking hands with the new proprietor, before doing the same with Alberto and thanking him for his service.

"One piece of advice," Lee said to the buyer, jabbing his thumb back at Alberto. "He might be the bartender, but he really runs the place. If you've any sense, make him manager." Then he left and rejoined McLaurie in the *cantina.*

"Happy?" asked Ed.

He nodded. "It's the right move. I'd stopped caring about the place. Not even sure why I bought it."

Ed pointed to his empty glass. "Probably for the free

booze."

"True," said Lee, laughing. "But you always pay for it one way or the other."

"Ain't that the truth." Ed waggled his glass again, and Lee got the hint. When he returned with two fresh drinks, McLaurie leaned in. "So what are you gonna do now? Heard you've put the general store up for sale too."

"Why? You interested?"

"Hell, no." Ed took a sip. "I've enough to keep me busy. But you must have a plan. You always have some kind of plan." He smiled. "No matter how crazy."

"Not really. Was talking to Ida last night. With the kids heading back to America, what with this war in Europe, I was thinking of doing the same."

"Think we'll get pulled in?" asked McLaurie.

"Dunno." Lee swirled his glass. "Some say it could be over in six months. But the longer it goes on…" He spread his hands.

McLaurie raised an eyebrow. "Back to New Orleans?"

"Maybe not straightaway," said Lee. "Ida's keen. She hasn't been back since she was small, and she's heard me talking enough."

"It stays with you."

"Sure does. But she made a good point. Said New Orleans ain't going nowhere, and maybe we should see what's cooking in Guatemala first."

McLaurie seemed to consider that for a moment. "Know what? She's got a point. You resigned. You weren't fired in disgrace."

"Gee, thanks."

"What I mean is, your stock is pretty high right now, despite what's going on. Might as well capitalize on that down here while you can."

"Shit, Ed. You might actually be talking some sense. You okay?"

McLaurie took Lee's hand and put it on his own forehead. "Must have one of them tropical fevers. Am I burning up?"

Lee guffawed.

79

In April 1915, after the general store found a buyer, Lee and Ida took the steamer up to Puerto Barrios. Lee had always enjoyed the mixed crowd on this journey. Most routes went direct from New Orleans to Puerto Cortés and then made their way back north, calling at smaller towns like Puerto Barrios. It meant a real spread of passengers on the boat—wide-eyed adventurers like Lee in his younger days, businessmen seeking opportunities among the proliferating cash crops, holidaymakers, revelers, and those visiting friends and relatives just over the border.

While he left Puerto Cortés under something of a cloud, Ida's enthusiasm for their new adventure soon banished any foreboding—even if she spent half the voyage dealing with seasickness. They went straight to the station in Puerto Barrios, catching the passenger train up to Guatemala City, where they checked into the Imperial Hotel.

"Can we stay here forever?" She flopped onto the luxurious bed and batted her eyelashes. "It's darling."

Lee smirked. "A while maybe."

"But I *love* it," she said.

He was about to point out the nightly rates when she bolted from the bed and ran to the bathroom. When she emerged minutes later, Lee raised an eyebrow. "Still seasick?"

"I should see a doctor," she said.

Later that day, while Ida rested, Lee hit the town, buoyed by the news that they were expecting their first child. It seemed the perfect blessing for their new start, a sign their best days were still ahead of them. As he walked through the streets of Guatemala City, seeking out all of his old contacts, he could see a lot had changed since he lived there with Magdalena Talbot. President Cabrera maintained his iron grip on the country, but his popularity was sliding. Dissent was widespread, and rumors about his mental fragility persisted. At first, Lee thought them nothing but smears put about by Cabrera's opponents, but given the pervasiveness of such talk, and in quarters normally loyal to Cabrera too, Lee began to wonder if there was something to it.

He kept such concerns from Ida. She still wasn't right following the steamer trip and often complained of dizziness and shortness of breath. The ever-present nausea was taking its toll on her already slight frame at a time when she should have been putting on weight, rather than shedding it. In October, after another round of cajoling, she agreed to see the doctor once more.

At the clinic, Lee paced the length of the corridor for what seemed like hours. He was contemplating barging into the doctor's office when the door opened.

He wheeled around. "Give it to me straight, doc."

"She's not well, and this altitude is doing her no favors. You need to get her down to sea level immediately." The doctor put a hand on his shoulder. "If you don't, she may lose the baby."

The decision was made immediately. He accompanied Ida back home to her parents' house in Puerto Cortés. The following month, a healthy baby boy was born: Dominicio. The birth was free from additional complications, but the doctors stressed that Ida's weak state required a lengthy convalescence. While Ida regained her strength, Lee found himself with time on his hands to plot his next move.

80

Lee was forever dreaming up get-rich-quick schemes. He plagued the Honduran government for an exclusive shark-fishing license and a ten-year exemption from taxes to get his new enterprise off the ground. The tax concessions were granted right away, and Lee hurried to the Culotta house on Calle de Linea to share the good news. "It's gonna be something else, Ida," he said.

"I'm not sure I follow," she admitted.

Lee nodded. "I get that a lot, but picture this … a flotilla of boats under my command. Hauling their catch back at the end of each day. Skinning them huge bodies on the beach."

Ida made a face.

"You don't have to watch that part," he chuckled.

"Sounds disgusting."

"Has to be done," he said. "We'll be sun-drying the hides and exporting the leather." He snapped his fingers. "Imagine walking sticks carved from backbones. Wouldn't that be something?"

"Can you eat the meat?"

Lee shook his head. "Could be good fertilizer, though."

"And there's money in this?"

"Not really," said Lee. "We'd need a pretty tight

operation just to cover costs."

"Maybe I'm just tired, but what's the point if there's no money in it?"

"The liver." He beamed.

Ida stared at him blankly.

"If the rest of the operation breaks even, we get the liver free, more or less."

"Okay," she said. "But what good's that?"

"Shark oil."

"Did you say 'shark oil'?"

"I've a contact in New Orleans," Lee said. "Reckons he can process shark oil into a high-quality lubricant for precision instruments."

"And there's money in that?"

He beamed. "Millions."

As unlikely as the enterprise was, Lee could not be dissuaded. He had no savings salted away, so was forced to return to the government with his tail between his legs and beg for a job to raise the capital. He got one of his old roles back. Even if being the inspector-general of the northern coast didn't quite have the same cachet as the others, it paid handsomely and it demanded little of his time. The income took the pressure off, but he still needed more money. He knew Ed enjoyed running the coconut plantation, but selling his share was the only real option. He only hoped Ed would be able to buy him out so Lee wouldn't have to force him to sell.

One evening, while mulling over the best approach in the *cantina*, Ed surprised him at the bar. "Glad to find you here, Lee. I have something I need to discuss with you."

"Funny you should say that. So do I."

They walked back to Lee's table and took a seat.

"You first," Ed said.

"No," said Lee. "I insist."

Ed sighed. "It's the war. Got a letter from Guy. You know he's back in New Orleans?"

"I didn't hear that."

"Just back, I think. He's sure we're joining the war, and he wants to sign up as soon as they formally announce."

"I guess it's only a matter of time." Lee chewed his lip. "You thinking of enlisting too? That what this is about?"

"Thinking about it."

"I wouldn't think twice," said Lee.

McLaurie nodded. "All things considered," he said. "Might be wise to sell the plantation now, while we can still get a good price. Who knows how this thing will spread?"

"War's been going on more than two years now, and it looks further away than ever from finishing." Lee thought for a moment. "I was keen to hold on to the plantation. Was a nice, stable income. But I see what you're saying."

"Thanks, Lee. I knew you'd understand." Ed took a sip of his drink. "Now what did you want to ask me?"

He smiled. "Same thing."

"Ya big lug." McLaurie punched him in the arm. "That's for making me sweat."

A buyer finally met their valuation in early 1917. Part of the payment was a vessel—the *Taft*—and Lee had the beginnings of his shark-fishing flotilla. Once he had settled up with Ed, Lee had around twelve thousand dollars to set up the rest of his empire.

Before he could even get it going, the United States of America finally declared war on the Central Powers and began shipping troops to the battlefields of France. Lee had already discussed the matter at length with Ida. As he had pledged, he didn't even have to think twice. He mothballed his shark-fishing enterprise, quit his job as inspector-general, packed up his belongings, and took his family on the next steamer north to New Orleans, planning to offer his services to the US Army.

As the American mainland came into view, he wondered if his rank in the Honduran Army would be recognized. He was confident, though. He felt like a returning hero.

81

Lee stepped off the steamer with Ida and Dominicio, surprised no newspapermen were waiting to ambush him. He'd figured that America's most famous soldier of fortune returning home to pledge his services was worth a few column inches, and he had warned Ida about the expected clamor at the port; now, he felt more than a little foolish.

They went straight to the place Lee had arranged on Magazine Street. Ida reminded him of his departed friend Manuel Bonilla, the way she craned her neck at the street-corner musicians and gaped at the ever-present drunkards and prostitutes. When Lee explained he had to leave for the recruiting office, she almost pushed him out the door.

"I know why we came here," she said. "And it's fine. Go do what you have to do. Just remember you promised me a stroll through the French Quarter tomorrow."

"Wouldn't miss it for the world." He pecked her on the cheek and headed downtown.

The recruiting officers were a welcoming pair, helping him to fill out his application and only stalling when it came to the matter of his age.

"I'm fit as a fiddle," protested Lee. "And I could lick the pair of you with one arm tied behind my back." That brought a smile, at least, but when he inquired whether his rank in the Honduran Army would be recognized, things got bogged down.

"That's not always as straightforward as you might think," one said. "What was your rank? I'll attach a note to your application."

"Commander-in-chief," said Lee, smiling.

The recruiting officers were taken aback for a moment, as if unsure whether Lee was messing with them. "Uh," the other said, looking back at the portrait of President Wilson. "That *particular* position might be taken."

"Figured as much," said Lee, tapping the forms. "But you best send this straight to the War Department in Washington. They've a file on me, probably an inch thick. They know who I am."

He left the office a little disappointed. He hadn't expected an officer's commission on the spot, but he hadn't predicted such prevarication either. He decided to swing by Tom Cook's saloon on the way home, to shake his mood.

The place hadn't changed much. Old Tom was still hanging in there behind the bar, surly as ever, but Lee didn't see any familiar faces in the crowd. Tom poured him a whiskey and slid it across the counter. "You back for long?" he asked.

"Hope not," said Lee.

Tom smiled. "Good to see you, too."

Lee chuckled and took a sip of his drink. "Signed up today," he said.

"Don't know why we're getting involved." Tom wiped the counter, even though it seemed clean. "Should leave them to it, if you ask me."

Lee was about to object, when he caught Tom's expression, sadder than he'd expected. "Your boys signed up?"

"Damn fools," Tom said. "Wouldn't listen to their Pa." He glanced up at Lee. "Fella your age should have more sense."

"Maybe," said Lee.

Tom muttered to himself while arranging the bottles on the shelf. He turned back to Lee. "Know what they've gone and done now?"

Lee shrugged.

"Shut down Storyville," he continued. "Orders from the navy." Tom smirked. "Guess they were worried their boys wouldn't ship out if they got too distracted."

"I'll be damned," said Lee.

"Course, it won't stop nothing. Just drive it underground. But the government never had much logic to it."

"Well, if the army turns me down, there goes Plan B."

Tom's brow furrowed. "Didn't think running a cathouse was your style."

Lee puffed up his chest. "I figured the well-to-do ladies of this town would pay top dollar for some prime beef."

Tom guffawed. He pointed to Lee's empty glass. "Another?"

"No thanks," said Lee. "Big day tomorrow."

"Oh, yeah?"

Lee paid Tom, and winked. "Hot date."

82

Lee cut the short clipping out of the newspaper and placed it in an envelope, ready to mail back to Ida in New Orleans, disappointed that all he could find was a single mention. *General Lee Christmas, soldier of fortune and prominent figure in many Central American revolutions, offered his services yesterday to President Wilson. The President told him he would like to talk to him later.*

He had left Louisiana when the army perfunctorily informed him that he was unable to enlist as a general officer, and had hurried to Washington to plead his case. With the distractions of war, the press had no need to clamor around him. And his extensive contacts failed to obtain him a meeting with the president, despite the article making it sound like he'd stormed the Oval Office. The secretary of state heard him out, but made no promises, palming him off with the excuse that the army board that decided such matters was an independent body, and he couldn't be seen to interfere. The senator for Louisiana bagged him a couple more meetings with the secretary of state, but it brought no further advancement of his case. Eventually, Lee returned to New Orleans to await the outcome of the army board's hearing.

While waiting for the decision, he returned his

attentions to his shark-fishing enterprise, opening an office above a shoe store on Charles Street. A pair of businessmen pledged fifty thousand dollars, on the condition that Lee could prove the scheme's viability. Promises were made to furnish them with samples of his wondrous shark oil.

It was October before he received word from the War Department. They curtly informed him that his application was void, on the grounds that he had failed to complete an officers' training course. Lee knew it was bureaucratic bullshit. He threatened, through the media, to whip the entire board for turning him down. He was fifty-four years old, but he still felt in the prime of his life. Bitterly disappointed by the government's refusal to let him serve his country, he took his family and what little he had left of his money, and headed down to the docks.

83

Back in his adopted homeland, Lee set to work building up his shark-oil empire. He spent his mornings out in the bay aboard the *Taft*, hunting for sharks with a young native boy as his only assistant, and his afternoons on the beach at Puerto Cortés. The narrow strip of sand around the headland from the banana wharf, the very same spot he once planned to land an assault on the town, was his outdoor factory. There, they skinned the sharks and hung the hides to dry in the relentless sun. Giant hunks of shark flesh were cut free from the cartilaginous backbones and boiled in an outsized iron pot. Lee stirred the concoction with a broken wooden paddle, his helper feeding the fire beneath. As he gazed out to the ocean, absentmindedly puffing on his *puro*, his mind wandered, incessantly calculating the innumerable riches his enterprise would bring. He didn't even notice the putrid stench of rotting flesh.

Once he'd manufactured several bottles of his miraculous shark oil, Lee sent two samples back to his prospective business partners in New Orleans. Not needing to wait for their reply, he immediately left for Guatemala to secure the exclusive shark-fishing license that had eluded him in Honduras. Once he proved the viability of his scheme, he was sure the waters would be teeming with competitors. He needed to corner the market, in advance, for himself.

After greasing all the right wheels and pocketing the requisite license, he returned to Puerto Cortés to face yet another hurdle: the twelve grand he had received for his share of the coconut plantation was all but gone. He had frittered away a fortune. Some of his old friends in the Honduran army offered to get him a position, but Lee felt he couldn't accept, not with the United States at war. He still held some outside hope the US Army would reconsider, that there would be some kind of public outcry, that the media would whip up a firestorm and demand the army find a place for a man of his talents.

In January 1918, while casting around for a salary, he received a telegram from one of his Guatemalan contacts. The president himself was requesting Lee's assistance. On Christmas Day, Guatemala City had been leveled by a powerful earthquake; a second, in January, had finished off the remaining buildings. Lee was needed to head up part of the relief effort. Delighted to make himself useful once more, he left on the first boat to Puerto Barrios, which happened to be a steamer from New Orleans, whose route first took it to Puerto Cortés.

Aboard the vessel, Lee got chatting to the occupants, as was his way. He met a fellow called Mr. McDonnell—an architect with a New York lumber company that specialized in building the mobile barracks being deployed in war-torn France. The discussion put Lee in sour form, but his mood brightened when the fellow asked him to spill some war stories. When Lee mentioned he was heading to Guatemala

City to help with relief efforts, McDonnell explained his own situation.

"My employers, J.H. Burton & Co., have already been contracted by the Guatemalan government."

Lee's nose twitched, sensing an opportunity. "Is that right?"

"That line of mobile buildings I was telling you about … we landed a contract to build several thousand portable homes."

"Makes sense." He nodded. "I haven't seen the devastation for myself yet, but reports indicate it's going to be months, at the very least, before they re-house all the families made homeless."

"Say, how did you get involved with the relief effort anyway?"

Lee tapped his nose. "I know plenty of people in town." He leaned in and dropped his voice to a conspiratorial whisper. "Cabrera requested me personally."

"That so?" McDonnell thought for a moment. "So you know the lay of the land fairly well?"

Lee filled him in on the various spells he had spent in the country over the past twenty years, and gave him a rundown on President Cabrera and the finer points of doing business in Guatemala City. Seemingly impressed with Lee's grasp of local affairs, McDonnell excused himself momentarily. When he returned, he asked Lee to accompany him, pointing to a gentleman smoking a pipe at the rear of the ship.

McDonnell introduced him to his boss, Mr. Burton, the founder and owner of the firm.

Burton offered his hand. "Good day to you, sir," he said between clenched teeth, before pocketing his pipe. "I'll get right to the point, if you don't mind. We're in need of an interpreter, Mr. Christmas, preferably someone who is *persona grata* with the government, if you will. Mr. McDonnell here has informed me that you know the place well, and I would be terribly grateful if you could recommend somebody you could trust. Preferably an American."

Lee thought for a moment; then he smiled. "I know just the guy."

They agreed a salary of two hundred and fifty dollars a month. Lee would represent the company during negotiations and oversee things in Guatemala City when Mr. Burton and his staff had departed. After reaching the capital by railroad, Lee saw the full extent of nature's devastation. Only a handful of buildings remained intact. Those that hadn't been completely demolished were clearly unsafe for habitation, and the only accommodation Mr. Burton and his party could find was a temporary camp in a park—a row of army cots surrounded by boxes of dry goods.

Lee was able to arrange a meeting with President Cabrera right away, impressing Mr. Burton. However, after numerous meetings, it became clear Cabrera would not be able to establish credit to their satisfaction. Ten days after their arrival, J.H. Burton & Co., Inc., finished constructing what would be the only temporary home they would build in Guatemala City—for themselves. Determined not to let the trip be wasted, Mr. Burton surveyed numerous plots, investigating the possibility of opening a lumberyard in the country. Once a suitable site was identified, Lee was appointed manager, and Mr. Burton and his staff returned to America.

Free of the watchful eyes of Mr. Burton, Lee set about seeking new investors for his shark-oil project. The consortium in New Orleans had inspected the samples and summarily pulled out, failing to see the value in the scheme. To get over his disappointment, and now that a regular salary would keep him in Guatemala City for some time, he telegrammed his wife. Happily, Ida had recovered and was eager to join him. She arrived two weeks later with Dominicio and moved into the portable home.

84

Lee's role in the lumberyard wasn't particularly demanding. While waiting to hear back from potential investors in his shark-oil empire, he toyed with a new project. With too much time on his hands, he found himself recollecting his life, considering all of the choices he'd made—for good or ill—and the curious path his life had taken. He was still reminiscing when he left the lumberyard and headed home to Ida, the train wreck outside LaPlace, more than twenty years ago now, weighing heavy on his mind.

Ida, having seen his brow crease with worry, greeted him at the door and reached up to press her thumb against his forehead. "You'll dig a hole right down to your brain, if you keep that up."

Lee couldn't help smiling. He took her in his arms. "I'm so lucky to have you," he said, kissing her cheeks.

"Take your boots off and get comfortable." She took his hand and led him inside. "I'll fix you a drink."

"Thanks, Mamie," he said, before realizing his error. He stared up at his wife in horror. "I meant … sorry, Ida."

She raised an eyebrow. "Maybe I'll let *Mamie* fix you that drink."

Lee hung his head, until he felt Ida's finger under his

chin, lifting his eyes to hers. "I was *kidding*. Now are you gonna tell me what's up, or do I have to beat it out of you?"

Lee smiled, putting his arms around her. "Like to see you try."

"You're lucky you're still getting that drink." She wriggled out of his grasp. "But don't get any ideas."

He flopped into a chair. "Been thinking a lot about that train wreck." He looked at his hands. "Must have been why I called you Mamie."

Ida handed him his drink. "Why would you waste your time thinking about that?"

"Keeps coming back to me. Wondering if there was some way it could have been prevented."

Ida poured herself a smaller measure. "I can think of one or two," she said, raising her glass and smiling.

"Sure." Lee chuckled. "But the other day I heard about a guy who had a heart attack and keeled over on the throttle. Two died in that crash. Seems like there should be a button or switch." He took a sip of his drink and watched a smile play across his wife's lips. "What?" he asked.

She smirked. "Pretty hard to flick a switch when you're dead."

"That's it!" said Lee, slapping his hands together with such force that Ida almost dropped her tumbler. He jumped up from his chair and strode over to Ida to kiss her full on the lips. "I've got it."

"I don't—"

Lee held up a finger while he paced the room. "One second," he said. "Need to get this straight in my head." After a full minute of pacing, he stopped. "I know you've never been at the throttle of a locomotive, not a real one, but you saw that toy train in Puerto Cortés. Principles are the same."

Ida nodded.

"Now, to engage the throttle, you gotta push it forward." He indicated with his hand. "Like this."

"Okay."

"And what happens when you die?"

"Huh?"

Lee chuckled. "Sorry, let me try again. What if the throttle would cut out if you weren't pressing on it?" He watched Ida think through the implications.

"What if the driver scratches his nose? You can't have the train skidding to a halt."

"Right," he said. "But I'm not talking about the brakes. Without the throttle engaged, the train just slowly comes to a halt."

"So if someone passes out…"

"Or has a heart attack…"

They both fell silent. Ida finally spoke first. "Could it work?"

"Sure," he said. "Bunch of ways you could do it."

She smiled. "Hot damn."

"This could make me a millionaire."

"Really?"

"Think about it," he said. "As soon as those newspapermen get wind of this, they'll whip up a panic until this device is the law. Installed on every train in America." He smiled. "Then the world."

"How much do you know about making this … thing?"

"That's the beauty of it," said Lee. "You don't need to

know anything."

Ida raised an eyebrow.

"Just the basic concept."

"You sure?"

"What I mean is, I don't need to know nothing about factories or any of that. There's a firm of patent attorneys in Washington. Once I send them the sketches, they register the patent and then no one can steal the idea. Then I can shop it around."

Ida thought for a moment, sipping her drink. "Well, you better get to it."

"Only one question left to resolve." He kissed her cheek again.

"Oh, yeah?"

"How we'll spend all those riches."

Ida gave him a playful shove. "You know I don't care about that. I'm just glad to see you happy. That's all I need."

Lee sent the sketches off to Washington, only to receive disappointing news from New York. Mr. Burton informed him that their Guatemalan lumberyard wasn't as profitable as he had anticipated. It was to be liquidated. But Lee's indomitable spirit shrugged it off. He toyed with one far-fetched scheme after another until one idea came to him clear and fully formed.

Oil.

After learning the ropes prospecting for a season with W.M. Bancroft, another New York outfit, Lee had the bug. Gone were his schemes to earn millions. Now, he could dream in billions. But for today, he had to content himself with becoming a cattle-buyer, just to get himself through until his investors came on board. If only he had the capital! He had the ear of two presidents, both of whom presided over countries sitting on *oceans* of oil. Lee knew he could finagle and browbeat his way to concessions and land grants and anything else he needed. He sailed down to Puerto Cortés to call in some favors, en route to New Orleans, where he would begin beating the bushes for rich investors. Ida had gone a couple of days ahead of him, eager to spend a time with her family before they moved to America.

On the voyage to Puerto Cortés, Lee mingled as much as he could. Much had changed in Honduras in his absence, he learned. Dr. Bertrand had attempted to cling to power by appointing his brother-in-law at the end of his term, invoking powers derived from the martial law that his declaration of war against Germany had enabled. The inevitable revolution had sent him out of office, and into exile. Lee didn't even recognize the new president's name, but one thing was for sure: he'd have no pull with the new guy. He mulled this over as the steamer pulled into Puerto Cortés. The first thing he noticed was a bunch of soldiers hanging around the banana wharf; that in itself wasn't unusual, but these guys were alert. And armed.

Passengers began disembarking, and the soldiers formed a phalanx, forcing people through them in pairs. Lee made his way toward the exit. When he reached the front, the soldiers became animated, signaling their *tiente*. It wasn't simply that Lee had no pull over the new leader; he wasn't even allowed to enter the country.

Lee refused to re-board the steamer, and the *tiente* ordered his men aboard the boat to force the captain to wait.

It took the intervention of the local consul to diffuse the situation and grant Lee temporary permission to enter Honduras, gather his family, pack up his belongings, and leave the country for the final time. On the boat to Puerto Barrios, Lee Christmas watched his adopted homeland disappear over the horizon, and he despaired.

He only remained in Guatemala long enough to catch the next steamer to New Orleans, barely speaking to Ida on the journey back.

What a hare-brained fool I must look, he thought. *When we first met, I was the hero of La Ceiba. The whole damn country even. A man of means. Prospects. But now?*

The shark-oil business was dead. His patent was going nowhere. His military career was finished. And, of course, he was flat broke.

Despite his brooding, he hadn't given up hope. Once he financed the oil exploration, he would be swimming in it. And he was looking forward to seeing his old friend Molony. Lee smiled at the thought: Guy Molony, chief of police in New Orleans. He shook his head. *How things change.*

85

Lee went over the sketch one more time. "Come on, Guy. I know policemen are supposed to be dumb, but pay attention. When the rat steps on this panel here, the arm of the contraption fires down." He slammed the desk. "Crushing him."

Molony considered this for a moment, examining the trap in detail. "And what's this on the side?"

"When the arm is deployed, that triggers the release of the poison, which kills all the fleas before they get a chance to infest anything else. I'm telling you, every ship in America will buy hundreds of 'em. Ports will order them by the thousand."

Molony raised an eyebrow.

"You might be skeptical, but listen to this. I know someone who's close with the surgeon general. If I can mock up a model, he's going to take a look. And if he likes it? Well, then he'll recommend the Public Health Service adopts it, and that will be an order of a million traps—at least. I'm giving them a great deal. I only want fifty cents a trap. They can keep the rest of whatever they decide to charge."

"That's very generous of you," said Molony, smiling.

"But once the foreign governments get wind of this, I'll have orders coming in from all over the world. And then I can finance my own oil exploration."

"That's some plan." Molony nodded to himself. "What's the next step?"

"I sent the drawings to my patent attorneys in Washington yesterday," said Lee. "I expect to hear back in a couple of weeks."

"And what happened with that device for cutting the throttle?"

He waved his hand. "Aw, don't ask."

Lee left Molony's office and headed back to the little house he had rented with Ida on Chestnut Street—by happenstance, the very same street where he'd proposed to Mamie all those years ago. He couldn't help feeling a twinge of envy at how well Guy had done. As the man had said, there was a lot of luck involved. He had come home a war hero just at the time that reform-minded politicians were back in fashion, promising to clean up the city. Anyone with a link to the past was tainted.

Lee tilted his head back as he walked, closed his eyes, and took a deep breath. He felt the sun warm his face, and he reached into his pocket for a *puro*. Puffing away happily, Lee increased his pace. *I wouldn't like to be trapped behind a desk anyhow.*

Lee was waiting to hear back from his patent lawyers about the poison-spraying rattrap, but was never one to let the grass grow under his feet. He pressed every contact he could, telling them all about the richest oil lands in the world, and how he was the key to unimaginable wealth. One of his friends, Forrest Pendleton, the old head of the New Orleans Federal

Bureau of Investigation, offered to put him in touch with a friend in New York. "His name is Bruce Bielaski."

"What's he doing in New York?" asked Lee.

"President of the Richmond Levering Company."

Lee whistled. "Sounds fancy."

"Let me put it this way," said Forrest. "If you make a good impression, you'll have all the money you need." He stood Lee a hundred dollars to see him to New York.

When Lee got there, Bielaski saw a lot of potential in his plan. He forwarded Lee a cash advance, promising a lucrative contract with Richmond Levering if Lee could secure the necessary concessions. On his return to New Orleans, Lee barely had time to inform Ida and the kids of his plans before he left behind once more and sailed for Guatemala.

He got a meeting with Cabrera right away. The president agreed to everything Lee wanted: land concessions, and, crucially, the enactment of legislation that would allow drilling and waive taxes. He cabled New York immediately to tell them the good news.

There was only one problem. Lee was so desperate for the plan to work that he failed to spot something rather obvious: President Cabrera, after twenty-two years as the leader of Guatemala, was losing his mind. On April 8, 1920, Congress declared him unfit to govern the country and appointed a replacement, someone with whom Lee Christmas had no influence whatsoever. Unable to face telling Ida that his dream was dead, he decided to remain in Guatemala City, in case some opportunity came his way.

And it did.

86

Cabrera had been officially deposed, but he wasn't shuffling off the political stage without a fight. He took shelter in the imposing fortress of Las Palmas, overlooking Guatemala City, and army commanders still loyal to him flocked to his position, bringing their men and munitions. Lee assumed Cabrera was just flexing his muscles, hoping to win safe passage out of the country, perhaps seeking guarantees regarding his commercial interests … until Cabrera's artillery began shelling the city below.

For five long days, the mad bombardment continued. Nowhere in the city was safe from indiscriminate attack, the sole exception being the American Legation. Even a half-crazed Cabrera wasn't foolish enough to risk a US invasion. Once word spread, most Americans in the city headed for the Legation, Lee among them—more out of the hope he could make himself useful than any fear for his safety.

One of the people he met there was a young lawyer from New Orleans, called Max Shaumberger. They had plenty in common and struck up an instant rapport. Shaumberger had worked for pretty much all of the fruit companies at some point, and had also been a member of the clandestine network of State Department spies, reporting on potential German activity in the region during the Great War. He didn't say so straight out, but Lee could read between the lines. "If there's anything I can do," Lee told him, "I'm ready."

The following day, Cabrera's murderous shelling of the city continued. Shaumberger and Lee debated whether further artillery units had defected, or whether he had simply got his hands on more ammunition. But one thing was clear: the continued bombardment of Guatemala City was putting American lives and property at risk.

Shaumberger pulled Lee to one side. "You asked if there was anything you could do."

"Name it," said Lee.

"It's dangerous."

Lee smiled. "More dangerous than twiddling my thumbs and waiting for a stray shell to land on my head?"

Shaumberger spread his hands. "Honestly … yes." He explained that the American Legation desperately needed to inform Washington of the situation on the ground, but Cabrera had already knocked out the wireless tower.

Lee didn't even blink. "What do you need from me?"

"Get our wireless operator up to the next tower in the chain."

"No combat experience, I'm guessing."

Shaumberger shook his head.

"Where's the tower?"

"That's the tricky part," he said, smiling.

An hour later, Lee met the wireless operator in the ambassador's office.

Poor guy looks like he's gonna piss himself, Lee thought.

Shaumberger handed Lee the messages. "Keep them

safe until you get to that tower. He'll do the rest."

"Why not give them to him?"

"If he gets shot, you must abandon the mission and get back here."

Lee raised an eyebrow. "And what if I get shot?"

"Well, then he's screwed anyway." Shaumberger smiled.

Lee nodded and clapped the wireless operator on the back. "Don't worry, son. I don't plan on dying today."

Darting through the city, the messages in his pocket and the wireless operator cowering behind him, Lee and his companion dodged bullets fired at them from the heights above. But he got his man to the wireless tower safely, and soon the USS *Niagara* arrived to put an end to proceedings.

The heroic dash through town reinvigorated Lee, who set about trying to rebuild contacts with the new administration. Shaumberger seemed close to many of the new players, so Lee hired him as his attorney, and they lobbied Congress together for the necessary changes in legislation. He was making headway, such that Richmond Levering put him on a retainer of five hundred dollars a month, plus commission on production when it started. Despite several setbacks, toward the end of 1922 the petroleum laws were adopted. For his New York bosses, Lee had won the exploration rights for almost a million hectares.

He was back.

87

All the sacrifice had been worthwhile. All the time away from Ida and Dominicio was about to pay off. Lee wasn't exactly sure how big a million hectares was, but he knew it was big enough that they should find *something*. Ida might not crave the finer things in life, but he wanted to make sure she was provided for. He was still conscious of their difference in years, especially now he suffered nagging health complaints he just couldn't shake.

Giving him the most bother was an intestinal problem, which put him in great discomfort and severely restricted the carousing of old. Just as Ida had been ordered to the coast when she was pregnant seven years beforehand, the doctors warned him that the altitude was exacerbating his condition. Lee knew they were right, but he also knew that incalculable riches were within his grasp. As a compromise with his medical team, he agreed to spend weekends down at Puerto Barrios.

On the last weekend in December, disaster struck. A revolution overthrew the new government that Lee had worked so hard to ingratiate himself with. Within a month, the new administration ruled the concessions granted to Richmond Levering invalid. Lee had just turned sixty, was away from his wife and children, and his prospects seemed dim. But he had some friends in the new government, so he began his campaign anew. Richmond Levering viewed it as a setback, nothing more, and the company kept him on the payroll. What he didn't tell them was that his health had declined further. He spent days confined to his hotel room, plagued with what he suspected was dysentery. Lee sent Molony a photograph of himself sitting in a chair, wearing a nightgown, with his face pale and drawn and his muscles wasted away. Underneath, he inscribed: *Once A Merry Christmas!*

By March, after a severe attack that hospitalized him for a fortnight, Lee resolved to return to America, both to confer with his employers and to seek more skilled medical attention. He got the latter sooner than expected. His condition deteriorated so badly on the steamer to New York that he had to be stretchered off the boat in Manhattan and carried up to St. Vincent's Hospital on Twelfth Street. To make matters worse, while trapped in his hospital bed, he was told Richmond Levering had decided to mothball the Guatemalan oil concern. They promised to retain him if they ever decided to explore the idea again, but, for now, Lee's dream of billions was dead.

He wired Guy Molony, who forwarded money so Lee could return home. On the train back to New Orleans, he realized he hadn't seen his family in over a year. They met him at the station, but he was so weak he had to suffer the indignity of his wife helping him from the carriage. For once, he was glad there were no reporters … until he realized Lee Christmas just didn't matter anymore.

Finally, under the care of attentive professionals, his condition was properly diagnosed. Lee was sitting up in bed when the doctor entered the room.

"Good," the physician said. "You're awake."

"Hey, doc. Get anything from those blood samples?"

"Yes, actually." The doctor pushed his glasses back on his nose. "We don't see cases like this too often, but we're pretty sure it's a tropical sprue." He looked at Lee as if that explained everything.

"You're gonna have to help me out here, doc."

"Sorry. It's a disease borne by a yeast parasite. It's serious." The doctor removed his glasses and smiled. "But treatable." He stepped forward to Lee's side. "And certainly explains your yellowing pallor. That had us worried."

"So I'm not going to die?"

"It's not terminal. But you're not out of the woods yet." The doctor continued, but Lee didn't register most of it. He was just relieved someone had finally figured out what was wrong with him, and that he could lick it. He was anxious to get back to working on his business ideas. All these medical bills had to be paid, and he wanted Ida on a secure financial footing in case anything happened.

Guy Molony visited regularly and helped out with the bills. One day, he brought Lee the latest edition of the *Encyclopedia Britannica*, which featured what Guy thought was an amusing error. In their entry on Honduras, they had an account of the Battle of Maraita in which they claimed that "Lee Christmas was killed," citing no less of an authority than the *New York Times*. Lee flew into a rage, remembering their attempt to break out, the mad charge across the field, taking on an entire army. He remembered watching General Barahona and his *tiente,* Reyes, get hit, as well as hearing what had happened to poor old Fred Mills, only along for the adventure and shot like a dog.

"I'm going to sue them, Guy. I'm going to clean them out."

"Really?"

He pointed to the offending entry. "This is slander."

Molony was taken aback. He closed the book and went to put it away.

"Leave it," said Lee. "I'll need to copy this and send it to my lawyer."

Guy opened his mouth to say something for a moment, but stopped himself. After a moment's thought, he spoke. "You know what? You should write your own story. Then they couldn't print these lies. Some of that stuff in the papers was just crazy."

Lee nodded. "Although," he said, chuckling, "some of that was my fault. Reporters will pretty much print whatever you tell 'em."

"I'm serious. You should write your own story. There could be money in it."

His face brightened. "How much?"

"No idea." Molony shook his head. "But some, for sure."

88

Over several afternoons, Lee attempted to get down the main facts of his life, but his powers of recollection were poor, and the effort put a huge strain on him. The doctors became concerned as his condition worsened, and they eventually recommended a blood transfusion. Guy Molony stepped forward as the donor. Soon, a pint and a half of the police chief's vigorous blood circulated around Lee's body.

The transfusion put him back on his feet, and he recovered something of his old self. Reporters swarmed around him once more, camped outside his little house on Chestnut Street. An old soldier of fortune being saved by the chief of police was too juicy a headline for the press to resist. The media attention put him back in the public eye, and he was approached by Doubleday, Page to write his memoirs. When one of the reporters returned to finish an interview, Lee told him about the publisher's interest. "I'm not much of a writer," he explained, "but I like talking, and you can write some. I have boxes of old letters. I can give you the whole story."

The reporter was interested, until Lee demanded a few thousand dollars payment upfront. "These publishers are crooks," he said. "They talk about an advance, but they'll only give me half when the book is turned in and the other half when it hits the shelves."

The reporter sympathized but refused, adding a friendly warning that none of his colleagues would have that kind of money. Lee decided to have another stab at it himself.

As soon as he began, the details flooded back. Moving to the sawmill town when he was just twelve. Slipping notes under Mamie's kitchen door. Kissing in the woods. Even the names of the little schooners from Lake Pontchartrain: the *Cileste*, the *Surprise*, and the *Lillie Simms*. He set down his time working the railroads, his first journey to Honduras, and how he fell into the new game of revolution.

But he was only on his feet for a month. The transfusion had bought him little time, and he cursed himself for not using it better. With his health deteriorating, his temper became shorter and he tired of his memoirs. He summarized the last twenty years of his life—his salad days—in just a few short sentences. Then, after recounting the army's refusal to commission him, he wrote the final lines. *When a man becomes my age, he's only good for fertilizer. So, goodbye.*

That put him in a foul mood, and after a heated argument with Ida, Lee told her he was leaving. She watched him hobble out of the house, sure he would turn back after no more than a block. But he didn't. He had to rest every block or so, and mop his damp brow, but he struggled on, all the way up to the station.

By the time he got to Memphis and to the home of his son Ed, he was at the point of collapse and was hospitalized once more. The doctors again recommended a blood transfusion, a kindly medical student donating her blood this time. While the transfusion was a success, it didn't give Lee quite the same boost as the first, and the hospital wouldn't discharge him. He was feeling low, until a visitor came calling—a woman whose face he hadn't seen for twenty-five years. She approached his bed with some trepidation, her face drawn with worry. "Anything I can do you for you, Lee?"

"How about a mint toddie?" He grinned. "Like you used to do, Mamie."

She clucked. "And you in a hospital bed."

"Aw, you sound just like your mama."

Their reunion was pleasant, but it made him all the more eager to get back to Ida. A third transfusion was required just to give him enough strength to make the journey. By the time he got to New Orleans, he had to be carried from the train. The shame made him break down and cry. When he inquired as to Ida's absence and was told she had been forced to work in a radio store to pay the bills, he cried once more.

89

Only a week had passed in his house on Chestnut Street before the doctors insisted on hospitalizing him once more. Attempting to stem his protests, Ida promised to visit on her way to work each morning and again in the evenings, but still he complained. "How am I supposed to recover with that crap they feed me?"

Ida smiled sweetly. "Well, then I'll just cook all your meals. Even bring them to you." And so she did, every morning, carrying a steaming plate all the way up to the Touro infirmary. When her shift ended, she would stop at a restaurant across the road from the hospital and fetch his dinner. Each day she saw him, he seemed weaker, more fragile. The doctors warned that his condition was irreversible. Lee was too weak for any further transfusions. It was only a matter of time.

He wouldn't permit any of the nurses to feed him, refusing any food that wasn't brought by his wife. But he never gave up, either. He would ramble on to anyone who would listen—usually Ida or Guy Molony—about how he was going to lick this thing, go back down to Guatemala, and make millions in the oil game.

On January 23, Leon Winfield Christmas was

administered last rites, drifting in and out of consciousness during the ceremony. He perked up a little more when two nuns came to his side, offering to console him in his final hours. Lee summoned enough strength to hurl a string of creative curses at them until they scurried from the room.

But when Guy Molony came calling shortly after, he found Lee unable to speak whatsoever. Lee pointed to some oranges on his bedside table, and then toward his mouth. Molony nodded, fighting back tears, and cut one of the oranges into pieces. Lee was unable to open his mouth more than a crack, so Guy squeezed the slices and let the juice trickle over his friend's dry, cracked lips.

A moan came from the next bed, and Lee rolled his eyes, making Guy chuckle.

"That … son of a … bitch," Lee said, wheezing. "Nothing … wrong … with him." Guy made to speak but Lee shook his head. "Tell … him." He paused, gathering his strength. "To shut … the hell … up. I want … to die … in peace."

Guy frowned. "You ain't dying."

"Like … hell." The effort to speak was enough to put Lee to sleep, and after checking that his friend was still breathing, Molony crept from the room.

Ida sat facing Lee's hospital bed and anxiously watched him sleep. The dinner she'd brought lay untouched on his bedside table. One of the nurses said he had been asleep for hours, and that it was best to let him rest comfortably when he could. The hospital staff had been accommodating, letting her stay long after regular visiting times, knowing their patient was in his final hours. But the nurse on duty that night was unfamiliar with the situation. "I'm sorry, visiting hours are over," she said.

"But I haven't fed him yet," said Ida, pointing to Lee's dinner.

The nurse put a hand on Ida's shoulder. "Don't worry, ma'am. I'll feed him."

Their conversation stirred Lee. "Like hell," he said, his voice clearer than it had been for days. He looked at his wife. "Ida, give me something to eat."

The nurse glanced at the wall clock. "It's well after nine."

"I'm dying," growled Lee. "You want to starve me too?"

She pursed her lips. "We have rules…"

He raised himself in the bed. "Damn the rules!" he shouted, his voice carrying all the way down the hospital corridor.

The effort of this final act of defiance was too much for him, and he collapsed into a coma. The nurse called for the doctor, who did everything to try to revive him. But in a few short hours, Lee stopped breathing altogether. As the nurse went to pull the sheet over his face, Ida elbowed her out of the way and threw herself on her husband's lifeless body, smothering his face with kisses, feeling his dead weight. After all the scrapes he'd been in, she had held out the faintest of hopes that he would find some way out of this one. But there was nothing he could do; there was nothing anyone could do. Lee Christmas, his skin as yellow as the bananas he once hauled along the Honduran coast, was dead.

Acknowledgements

A writer is but one of a whole team of people who help usher a new book into the world. My editor, Karin Cox, stopped me from running off in completely the wrong direction and convinced me to rip it up and start again. And she was right. When I eventually returned with a somewhat functioning story, she was instrumental in smoothing the edges and nudging my flabby prose back into line. Kate Gaughran has designed another wonderful cover. And fellow writers Sarah Woodbury, Melissa Furrer Miller, Tony James Slater, and Deanna Chase, provided crucial advice and support at various stages.

A number of books helped me get a handle on the subject and the period: *The Archaeologist Was a Spy: Sylvanus G. Morley and the Office of Naval Intelligence* by Charles H. Harris; *The Banana Men: American Mercenaries & Entrepreneurs in Central America, 1880–1930* by Lester D. Langley and Thomas D. Schoonover; *The Incredible Yanqui: The Career of Lee Christmas* by Hermann B. Deutsch; *Storyville, New Orleans, Being an Authentic, Illustrated Account of the Notorious Red-Light District* by Al Rose; *Victorian America: Transformations of Everyday Life, 1876–1915* by *Thomas J. Schlereth; Gumbo Ya-ya: Folk Tales of Louisiana* ed. by Lyle Saxon, Robert Tallant, and Edward Dreyer; *Beautiful Crescent: A History of New Orleans* by Joan B. Garvey and Mary

Lou Widmer; *The French Quarter: An Informal History of the New Orleans Underworld* by Herbert Asbury. Also, two magazine features were of tremendous assistance: a revealing portrait of Sam Zemurray in *Life* by John Kobler from 1951 and an excellent piece in *The Nation* written by Lucius Sheperd a few years back (who sadly passed away as I was completing this book) entitled *Lee Christmas and Machine-gun Molony*. My sincere thanks also go to the staff at the University of Tennessee library (Elizabeth Dunham in particular) who were kind enough to scan and email a hoard of documents relating to Lee Christmas: letters, photographs, and newspaper clippings that really helped to round out the picture of the man, as well as the myth that grew around him.

Finally, I'd like to thank my friends and family for helping me throughout my writing career, particularly my parents—Benny and Mary Gaughran—for their unwavering support, even when I didn't have much of a career to speak of! I also want to express my gratitude to Vladimír Vostrovský and Iva Vostrovská for making me feel so welcome in their country, and for all the kindness they have shown. And to Ivča: keep on rockin' in the free world.

About the Author

David Gaughran is an Irish writer, living in Prague, who spends most of his time traveling the world, collecting stories. He's also the author of the South American historical adventure *A Storm Hits Valparaiso*, the short stories *If You Go Into The Woods* and *Transfection*, and the popular writers' books *Let's Get Digital: How To Self-Publish, And Why You Should* and *Let's Get Visible: How To Get Noticed And Sell More Books* which are available from all major e-bookstores. *Storm*, *Visible*, and *Digital* are also available in paperback.

If you want to get an automatic email when David's next book is released, sign up at *bit.ly/dgmlist*. Your email address will never be shared and you can unsubscribe at any time. Finally, word-of-mouth is crucial for any author to succeed. If you enjoyed the book, please consider leaving an online review, even if it's only a line or two; it would make all the difference and would be very much appreciated.

Say Hello!

David talks about writing and the book business on his blog *Let's Get Digital*. He would love it if you dropped by to say hello. You can also pop by *South Americana* where he shares curious incidents from the history of the world's most exotic continent. Alternatively, you can follow him on Twitter, get in touch on Facebook, or send him an email.

Publishing blog: *davidgaughran.wordpress.com*
South Americana: *SouthAmericana.com*
Twitter: *twitter.com/DavidGaughran*
Facebook: *facebook.com/DavidGaughranWriter*
Email: *david.gaughran@gmail.com*

Made in the USA
Middletown, DE
02 November 2016